"This book moves [...] paced beat that C[...] have picked up and run with all night."
—Michael Connelly

"...a deadly, ironic conclusion."
—Lansing, MI *State Journal*

"...the best of the four Horne novels..."
—*Mystery News*

"The jazz moments are high energy—
vividly rendered and engrossing..."
—*Philadelphia Inquirer*

"Intelligent and eccentric characters...and
a bang-up solution make this a highly
readable novel."
—*Dallas Morning News*

"Evan's low-key charm and sound technical
knowledge snares crooks and readers."
—*The Poisoned Pen*

"...brisk, satisfying and airtight..."
—*The Plain Dealer*, Cleveland

★

BIRD LIVES!

BILL MOODY

WORLDWIDE.

TORONTO • NEW YORK • LONDON
AMSTERDAM • PARIS • SYDNEY • HAMBURG
STOCKHOLM • ATHENS • TOKYO • MILAN
MADRID • WARSAW • BUDAPEST • AUCKLAND

For Teresa

BIRD LIVES!

A Worldwide Mystery/June 2000

Published by arrangement with Walker Publishing Company, Inc.

ISBN 0-373-26350-3

Acknowledgments

Thanks once again to Captain Tom Mapes, retired, of the Santa Monica Police Department for advice and procedural insights; Michael Seidman and George Gibson for continuing to allow me to write about jazz; and Philip Spitzer for being a friend as well as a great agent.

And of course, the music of Charlie Parker, Miles Davis, Charles Mingus, Tadd Dameron, Art Blakey, Bill Evans and Keith Jarrett. It will always be here.

PROLOGUE

I'M AT RUTH PRICE'S Jazz Bakery in Culver City, California, and this time it's no dream.

Originally the club housed the Helms Bakery, so Ruth kept that much of the name, and some people swear they can still smell the lingering aroma of baking bread.

Minutes before the first set, I stand in the lobby with Ruth, sipping coffee, running over tunes in my mind, wondering if I've got the right bass and drums with me.

Open with something familiar so the audience can get a fix on what you're up to.

I flex the fingers of my right hand, encased in a fingerless black latex glove that keeps the muscles warm, the pain less. But the memory of that night on the Pacific Coast Highway remains constant. The headlights of the truck looming out of the fog, the shattered glass severing the tendons of my right hand, still hover close to the surface in my mind. It's been a long road, strewn with surgery, therapy, practicing, and squeezing a rubber ball thousands of times. But now it's finally paid off.

"How's it feel?" Ruth Price asks, seeing me look at my hand. She still sings occasionally, and her voice has changed only slightly since her days with Shelly Manne. Today she devotes herself to running this hip, alcohol-free showcase for jazz. Ruth was good to give me this shot, and I know better than anyone how lucky I am to be here. It was short notice—a last-minute substitution for Monty Alexander, who missed a plane connection—but when you're trying to make a comeback, you take the dates when they're offered.

I squeeze my fingers again. "Fine, feels really good," I say, hoping my voice doesn't betray the flutter I feel inside. Practicing is one thing; working a gig, keeping things popping for two sets, is another. This is not a jam session or a futile shopping mall gig, like I did in Las Vegas.

Ruth nods and smiles. " 'Bout ten minutes," she says. "Hey, don't worry, there'll be some new fans who've never seen a detective play the piano." She moves off to greet some late arrivals.

The *L.A. Times* ran a brief article about me, but in an effort to punch up the piece, the writer briefly recounted my moonlighting in three murder investigations that had spilled over into the jazz world. No way to avoid it.

I have to go outside for a final cigarette. Smoky jazz clubs, at least in California, are a thing of the past. My bassist, Jeff Lasorda, and drummer, Gene Sherman, are already there, joking, watching the cars arrive and park on the short block between Venice and Washington Boulevards. We've worked together a few times, but for them it's just another gig. For me it's a test.

They both see me at the same time. "Don't worry, man," Gene says, "just don't make any mistakes." Jeff laughs and slaps Gene's upturned palm.

"Yeah," Jeff says, looking at my hand. "Only your glove should be white, man, like Michael Jackson."

"Thanks, guys, that really makes me feel better." I look at my watch and take a last drag. "Let's do it."

Inside, the rows of green plastic chairs facing the stage are about three-quarters full, mostly college types and their dates. Ruth smiles and shoots me the thumbs-up sign from the sound booth one more time as we walk past her into the room marked "Musicians Only," where we wait for the announcement.

"Ladies and gentlemen, welcome to the Jazz Bakery," Ruth says. "We're very pleased tonight to present the Evan Horne Trio. First, Jeff Lasorda on bass."

There's polite applause as Jeff makes his way to the stage and picks up his bass. Gene follows, and then there's just me. "And now, after too long an absence from the jazz scene, we're very happy to welcome back Evan Horne."

I walk out and sit down at the piano, feeling decidedly self-conscious. The applause is more than I expected. No bar, no waitresses, no whine of blenders mixing up Margaritas here. Just concert-hall quiet as I glance up at Jeff and Gene, then turn my eyes to the keyboard.

I steal one glance at the audience and catch Natalie, Danny Cooper, and Ace Buffington sliding into third-row seats. "Traffic," Natalie mimes.

I begin alone, gathering my thoughts, playing rubato on "My Romance." At the end of the chorus, I ease into tempo and glimpse Jeff, his arms curled around the bass, poised to make his entrance. Gene, brushes in hand, prepares to smooth the way.

We lope through two choruses in a laid-back, two-beat tempo. Jeff's buzzing bass lines spill over the bar lines and anticipate my chords. Gene's brush patterns and the occasional splash of cymbals provide color. The keys seem to shimmer before my eyes. I look up again and nod. Jeff bears down and walks into the next chorus as Gene switches to sticks; then we push it and swing all out for two more. This is how it should always be, I think, as I back off and turn it over to Jeff for his solo, then trade eight-bar exchanges with Gene's crisp drums. Finally, I remind the audience of the melody and take it out to a nice hand. There. First one down. The butterflies are gone.

The rest of the set goes just as well. No pain; the glove is working, and so are my chops. Before I close the set, I introduce Jeff and Gene, and add a personal note.

"This has been a long time coming," I say. "I just want to thank everyone for being here." I catch Natalie smiling, Ace beaming. Coop is fiddling with his beeper.

I feel so confident I close with Chick Corea's "Matrix," a tricky tune that nevertheless seems to flow out of my fingers as I slip into the zone. Somebody recognizes the opening notes and shouts out, "All right, Evan!"

When I get to the lobby, Ace and Natalie are waiting. I push through the lingering crowd, and let the approving looks, the snatches of comments, wash over me like a benediction.

Natalie spots me and waves. "Coop had to go," she says when I reach her. "Some kind of emergency. You know cops." She hugs me close. "God, that was so wonderful to see you up there playing again."

Over her shoulder I see Ace grinning, pacing back and forth. "Man oh man oh man, that was something." His voice booms all over the lobby. Several people turn and smile. "Wish I could stay for the next set," Ace says. He has classes tomorrow at UNLV, a flight to catch, and Natalie is taking him to the airport.

"We better go," she says, looking at Ace. She hugs me again and whispers, "See you at home."

I go outside to smoke and calm down. Then, just when I think it couldn't get any better, it does.

"Evan?" I turn to see a short man in slacks, black turtleneck, and cord jacket.

"Paul Westbrook, Quarter Tone Records," he says, pushing the thick glasses up. We shake hands, and he hands me his business card. "I'm glad to see you back playing. I'd like to talk to you about recording."

I look at his card. Quarter Tone is a small, independent label that's done some nice work. "Recording? Sure, I—"

"Give me a call, please," Westbrook says. "Sorry I can't talk now." He hurries to his car and waves as he drives off. I stand holding his card, stunned, wondering if it really happened.

Back onstage, I begin the second set even more relaxed. Everything feels so natural, so right, I wonder if I've ever been away. More importantly, how long can I stay this time?

For now, there's only the music. I'm back.

ONE

"LOOK AT THIS," Natalie says, turning up the sound on the television.

We have the news on, just kicking back after an expensive dinner to celebrate her birthday and my first gig in over a year. The two nights at the Jazz Bakery linger sweetly in my mind.

I glance at the screen in time to see the anchor cut away to a reporter standing in front of a large crowd. She has on a raincoat and holds a microphone in one hand, brushing her hair out of her eyes with the other. She looks flustered, as if they've cut to her before she was ready. She stares at the camera and puts her hand to her ear.

"Yes, I can hear you now, Jim." She glances over her shoulder once, then looks back at the camera. "Well, as you can see, we're at the Santa Monica Civic, where jazz star Ty Rodman just finished performing to a sold-out crowd."

She falters for a moment as the crowd jostles her from behind. Some of them are waving and yelling, just wanting to get on TV. She turns her head again nervously, then back to the camera.

"Santa Monica police are confirming that Rodman is the victim of a stabbing, but we're not sure of the extent of his injuries at this time. I'm trying to get word from the police. As you can see, many of Rodman's fans are still here." She tries to keep her look serious, but a smile slips through as she's jostled again. "Somehow they've heard the news and are staying around although the concert was over some forty minutes ago. That's all we have at the moment. Jim, back to you in the studio."

"Thanks for that report, Trish," Jim says. He shuffles some papers and glances at his coanchor, a perfectly made up blond. "Looks rough out there. Once again, we have unconfirmed reports of a stabbing at Santa Monica Civic involving jazz star Ty Rodman. We'll have more on this before the end of our newscast, right, Marion?"

"That's right, Jim," Marion says. "When we come back, Bob will have the latest weather. Stay with us, right here on Action News."

"Jazz star?" I look at Natalie as she hits the mute button. "Ty Rodman?"

"You know him, don't you?" she asks.

"I know who he is, maybe met him once, but I don't know him."

Ty Rodman and I don't travel in the same circles. He's one of a half-dozen sax players who've fused blues riffs with a rock beat and turned it into a fortune while breathing down Kenny G's neck.

"I wonder what happened," Natalie says.

"I'm sure Action News will tell us. Want a beer?"

"Sure," Natalie says.

I'm halfway to the kitchen when the phone rings.

"Evan? You busy?"

"Coop? No, just celebrating Natalie's birthday. What's up?"

"I need you to come down to Santa Monica Civic."

"Yeah, I just saw it on the news. What happened? Is Rodman okay?"

"He's not okay, he's dead. There's something here I need you to look at."

"Now?"

"Now." There's none of the usual bantering in Coop's

voice. This is his Lieutenant Cooper, homicide detective, tone.

"Why?"

"Just get down here. In a minute," he yells at someone. I hear other voices. "I gotta go," he says to me. "Come to the stage entrance."

Before I can ask more, Coop hangs up. I put down the phone and glance at Natalie watching me. "Rodman's dead. Coop wants me to come down there to see something."

"Dead? Why does he want you?"

"I don't know. I guess I better find out."

I don't like it, but I go, not only because Danny Cooper is a homicide detective, but because he's also my oldest friend.

FROM VENICE, the drive to Santa Monica Civic is short, but at Pico and Ocean Avenue the traffic is backed up and being diverted. A light rain peppers the streets. I creep up to the intersection, manage to convince a traffic cop I'm expected, and pull in near a fleet of police cars. The news has spread quickly. There's crime-scene tape around the side entrance and a sizable crowd of concertgoers pushing forward against the uniformed cops trying to maintain control.

I get through to the front and identify myself to one of the uniforms, who escorts me down a long corridor to Ty Rodman's dressing room. There's a placard on the door, and Rodman's name has a large *X* drawn through it with a black marker pen. Another uniform standing guard knocks and opens the door.

"He's here, Lieutenant." I get a glimpse of the dressing room through the open door. "Go ahead," the guard says.

Coop and his partner, Ivan Dixon, are squatting down

over Ty Rodman's body, which is half covered with a coroner's blanket.

Coop stands up and looks at me. "Thanks for coming. Want a look?" He nods toward Rodman's body. Dixon recovers it with the blanket, but not quickly enough to keep me from seeing the blood, shockingly bright against Rodman's trademark white suit.

"I'll pass," I say, glancing at Dixon. The police photographer is packing up his equipment, and other forensic technicians are slipping on latex gloves, ready to go to work. Another guy briefly points a video camera at me. I wonder about the rest of Rodman's band.

The dressing room is strewn with discarded clothes and beer bottles. Traces of white powder are smeared on the countertop in front of a large mirror bordered with oversize lightbulbs. I'm already staring before Coop speaks.

"That's what I wanted you to see," Coop says, pointing to the mirror. "What the fuck is this?"

The letters still look wet. They've dripped down in places. It could be paint or nail polish, but I know it's blood—two words scrawled across the top of the mirror:

Bird Lives!

I stare at it for a few moments, then look at Coop. He and Ivan Dixon are both watching my reaction.

"Charlie Parker, right?" Dixon says.

"Another one of your jazz people?" Coop asks.

"Yeah, Charlie Parker, saxophonist. They called him Bird."

"Who called him Bird?"

"Everybody. That was his nickname. Charlie Yardbird Parker."

Dixon and I glance at each other. Dixon is a jazz buff himself. He knew but wanted to be sure. Call your friend Evan Horne. He'll know. Thanks, Dixon.

I look at the words on the mirror again. "When Parker died, that started showing up all over Greenwich Village."

"Dare I ask? When was that?" Coop wants to know.

"March 1955."

Coop nods and glances at the writing, then back to me. "So what does this Bird guy have to do with Ty Rodman?"

Good question. The only thing they had in common was that they both played alto saxophone. "I think it's the other way around. What does Rodman have to do with Bird?"

Coop ignores my question. He doesn't like this; he's out of his element. He scowls at the mirror. "Are we talking about a disgruntled jazz fan here?"

My eyes are drawn to a portable CD player sitting on the countertop. "Oh yeah, there's something else. According to the stage manager, this was playing when he came to get Rodman."

Coop presses the play button with a gloved finger. I recognize the tune immediately. It's Bird with trumpeter Red Rodney, recorded some time in the early fifties. One of Bird's own tunes. A blues called "Now's the Time."

Coop lets it play for a few seconds, then stops the CD and looks at me again, sees the expression on my face.

"What?"

I look around. "Where's his horn?"

Coop nods. "Over there, what's left of it."

In one corner, half covered with what is probably one of Rodman's shirts, is the saxophone case. Coop pulls the shirt aside.

Nobody will play this horn again. It still gleams, but this alto saxophone has been smashed against the wall or the floor. Some of the keys are broken off, and there are large dents in the horn. It looks like it's been thrown back in the case.

Somebody yells for Coop, one of the uniforms. He turns

to me. "Look, I'll be here all night, but I need to talk to you in the morning, okay?"

"Coop, I—"

"I need to talk to you." There's an urgency in his voice that goes beyond the usual. "I'll call you."

I don't feel like arguing. "Okay."

Coop sees me look around the dressing room. I glance again at the two words on the mirror. It's hard to breathe in here. I just want to get away.

"What?" Coop says.

"Nothing right now, but..."

"But what?"

"Nothing."

Driving back to Venice, I keep seeing those words on the mirror: *Bird Lives!*

What I haven't told Coop is that today, March 12, is not only Natalie's birthday but also the anniversary of Charlie Parker's death.

FOR THOSE WHO CARE, March 12 is one of those sacred dates in jazz history. Everyone in jazz knows the story. At age thirty-four, Charlie Parker collapsed in the home of the Baroness Pannonica Koenigswarter, a wealthy eccentric who lived in the Stanhope Hotel and drove to jazz clubs in a silver Rolls.

Her apartment had become a haven for jazz musicians like Bird and Thelonious Monk. There were even songs written about her: "Pannonica" by Monk and "Nica's Dream," by Horace Silver. But it was Bird's death that immortalized her forever. The Bird had flown, died while watching some jugglers on the Tommy Dorsey television show.

Once the news got out, the words *Bird Lives!* started showing up all over New York City, on walls, subway stations, fences, and the sides of buildings. Early graffiti. No one could believe it, but it was true. The most important saxophonist in jazz had been silenced.

Articles appeared in newspapers and all the jazz magazines. The legend and mystique grew, and since then, scores of stories and poems have been written about Bird. Like the poet Dylan Thomas, who died under similar circumstances a year earlier, Bird was a self-destructive legend, but what he did for jazz was incalculable.

I knew the general story, but most of this I had learned from Clint Eastwood's movie, which I'd watched with my professor friend Ace Buffington's commentary in my ear. Ace didn't approve of the movie, but this time he could help me.

Natalie is asleep when I get back; an open law book with notes scribbled in the margin lies nearby. I close the book, turn off the TV, and crawl into bed. Natalie mumbles something and wraps herself around me. I can't get the murder scene out of my mind.

What did Ty Rodman have to do with Bird?

NATALIE IS GONE when I wake up, but she's left me a note. "Coop called, wants you to meet him at ten. Call you later," it says. She's marked the note with a string of question marks. I check my watch, grab a glass of juice, and jump in the shower.

When I get to Coop's favorite coffee shop, he's sporting dark stubble and bags under his eyes and working on a second or third cup of coffee in a back booth. His black Metro Team jacket is wrinkled. "Lt. Dan Cooper" is embroidered on the front. His gun pokes out from his belt holster.

"Wow, you look wonderful," I say, sliding into the booth.

"Don't start. I've had about three hours' sleep."

"I can tell." I signal the waitress for some more coffee. "So what's up?"

Coop takes a breath and watches me add cream and sugar to my coffee. "I need a favor from you," he says quietly.

"Sure, how could I refuse the Santa Monica Police? Hey, I didn't tell you, I may be recording soon. Guy approached me the other night at the Bakery." I watch Coop for a moment, waiting for his reaction, but there's none. "Coop? Try to control your enthusiasm." I can hardly get his attention.

"What? Oh, sorry, it's just this Rodman thing last night." He pushes his cup aside. "Tell me about this Bird guy—Charlie Parker was his name?"

"Yeah, I told you, Bird was a nickname. What's going on, Coop?"

"In a minute. The writing on the mirror. What does it mean again?"

I shrug. "I don't know if it means anything. To a lot of people, Parker was an idol. That Bird Lives phrase started cropping up after he died. People didn't want to believe he was gone, I guess. That was a little before my time. Yours too, if you remember."

Coop nods, and waves off the waitress approaching with a pot of coffee. "Do you think there's any connection between him and Ty Rodman?"

"Rodman wasn't even born when Bird died. Musically? No way. Bird was a pioneer in bebop. He and Dizzy and Monk changed the whole jazz scene. Rodman was a commercial success, but I wouldn't call him a major jazz talent, and don't get me started on that. The only thing Ty Rodman and Charlie Parker had in common was that they both played the same instrument."

"What then?"

"The date, March twelfth. That was the day Bird died in 1955."

"Shit," Coop says. He takes out a notebook and pen, flips through some pages, writes something down, then looks up at me again. "What about January fifth or January twenty-first?"

This time I stop the waitress by holding up my cup. She fills it, and to Coop's annoyance, I order some breakfast.

I add cream and sugar and think for a moment. "No, those dates don't ring a bell with me. Why?"

Coop looks around as if he's worried about somebody listening. "This doesn't go anywhere, okay?"

"Sure. What is it?" I've never seen Coop quite like this. Usually nothing flusters him. He takes his job very seriously, but his offbeat sense of humor is his anchor. It's not there now.

Coop flips through his notebook again. "On January fifth, in New York, a guitarist was found dead in his apartment. The neighbors called the police because the music was playing so loud that pounding on the door didn't do any good. The CD player was on repeat, playing"—he checks his notes again—"something called, 'Better Git It in Your Soul.' " He looks up from his notebook and frowns. "What kind of song title is that?"

"Mingus."

"What?"

"Charles Mingus, bassist."

"And?"

I shrug. "He worked with Bird, but he had his own band. Major composer. I don't know when he died. Maybe ten years ago or more. What's this all about?"

Coop ignores my question and presses on. "On January twenty-first, a piano player was found dead in his car.

Thanks to an anonymous nine-one-one call, the tape player was still running. Cassette called *Birth of the Cool*."

"Miles Davis, the trumpeter." I think for a moment. "Maybe the piano player just dug Miles."

Coop closes the notebook and frowns at me. "Maybe, but I need to know for sure. There were no prints on the case or the tape." He leans back in the booth and rubs a hand over his face, through his short-cropped hair.

"What's all this got to do with Ty Rodman?" The waitress brings my breakfast, and I start in on French toast and bacon.

Coop watches me drench the toast with syrup. "How do you do that? You never gain a pound."

"I burn it up playing piano. So what about Rodman?"

"That's what we want to know." He puts his notebook away. "C'mon, hurry up. I can't tell you anymore, but I want you to look around Rodman's dressing room again."

"For what?"

"I won't know until you find it."

ON THE RIDE to Santa Monica Civic, Coop is silent, intent on driving, except for one question. "Can you find out about these dates, the ones I mentioned?"

"Yeah, I guess. I'll call Ace, but why?"

Coop doesn't answer, which means he'll tell me when he's ready. He pulls into the parking lot near the stage door, flashes his badge at a security guard, and we go inside.

There's some banging and voices coming from the stage area, probably a crew setting up for the next show. In Rodman's dressing room the blood stains have dried on the carpet, and the mirror has been cleaned. Coop shuts the door behind him and leans against it. "Take a look around, a careful look."

I stand in the middle of the room. "What am I looking for?"

"I don't know, maybe you'll see something we missed."

I've been in hundreds of dressing rooms, but this is different. It feels creepy being here when less than twenty-four hours ago, Ty Rodman was lying dead on the floor. I spend fifteen minutes going over every square inch of the room, but I don't see anything out of the ordinary. Except for the saxophone case lying open on the countertop, everything of Rodman's is gone, including his smashed horn.

Coop answers my questioning look. "Oh yeah, I'm supposed to pick that up. Couldn't get the horn back in the case."

There's nothing there either. The interior of the hard-fiber case is lined with a blue, velvetlike material that the alto saxophone would normally be nestled in. It looks like Rodman has taken it out to play, but no more notes will come out of his horn.

I turn back to Coop. "Can I touch the case?"

"Yeah, no prints on that."

I unsnap the inside compartment. There's a small package of Rico No. 6 saxophone reeds. I pick it up, but something else catches my eye. It's wedged in the corner. I reach in and pull it out.

"What have you got?" Coop moves closer to see what I have in my hand. It's white, about four inches long. Coop elbows me aside and carefully picks it up by the edge. He holds it up, and we both look at it for a moment.

"Bird feather," I say.

COOP DROPS ME OFF back at the coffee shop to get my car. I get out and lean in the window. Coop is frowning at the feather, now tucked in a plastic bag on the dashboard.

"You know, that might have just been Rodman's good luck charm or something."

Coop gives me a look. "Sure. You don't talk to anybody about this, understand."

I put up my hands in surrender. "Whatever you say."

"I'm serious," Coop says.

"I can tell."

"Good. Check out those dates for me as soon as you can." Then he's gone.

I drive back to my place, stopping only to pick up a newspaper. I scan the story on Rodman's murder and call Ace Buffington in Las Vegas. This is something I want out of the way as soon as possible. I get Ace's voice mail, leave a message.

While I wait for him to call back, I read the story carefully. There's obviously nothing about a feather, since I just found it, but neither the damage to Rodman's horn nor the writing on the mirror is mentioned either. Coop must have seen to that. There's a publicity photo of Rodman, dressed in a white suit, holding his horn in front of him, smiling at the camera, and a sidebar listing his records. Six CDs, all gold.

Ace calls back in half an hour, sputtering and muttering about the UNLV English Department.

"One meeting after another," he says. "They all think literary criticism stopped in 1950, and the chair spends more time in a bar than his office. Now what can I do for you? Are you coming to Las Vegas?"

"Not a chance. You and that town are trouble for me, but you can do me a favor for a change."

"Sure. I bet it's about Ty Rodman's murder."

"How'd you know?"

"It's all over the papers. He was scheduled to do a concert here next month, not that I'd go. Smooth jazz—isn't that what they call it now?—is not my thing.''

"Nor mine. Listen, get out your jazz reference books and see if you can find anything significant about these dates: January fifth and January twenty-first. Oh yeah, and March twelfth.''

"That was yesterday," Ace says.

"Boy, you Ph.D.s don't miss a thing, do you?"

"Okay, smart guy. I'll get right on this and call you back.''

"Thanks, Ace. Just leave a message if I'm not here."

"Evan, you're not getting involved in anything, are you?"

"Not if I can help it.''

TWO

"PAUL WESTBROOK, PLEASE. This is Evan Horne." While I'm put on hold, I study Westbrook's card and hope he was serious about the recording date. This is L.A., I remind myself. Lots of people hand out business cards.

"Evan. Thanks for getting back so soon," Westbrook says. "How'd the second set go the other night?"

"Great. Sorry you couldn't stay around."

"So am I. So, when can we get together?"

"Whenever you say. I'm pretty free." That's the understatement of all time. With the Jazz Bakery gig over, it's time to start hustling. I can't just wait for the phone to ring.

"Okay, well, how about tomorrow? I have another appointment in Santa Monica, so that would be best for me."

"Santa Monica is fine. I live in Venice."

"Bob Burns then, for lunch? Do you know it, on Second and Wilshire?"

"Sure. What time?"

"Let's say twelve-thirty."

"Sounds good. See you then."

I hang up the phone as I hear keys in the door. Natalie bumps it shut with her hip, balancing two bags of groceries in her arms. She sets the bags on the counter. We've still been spending time at each other's place, but lately it's been more at mine than hers unless she's doing some heavy studying.

She sees me punch the air. "Good news?"

"Yes. That was Paul Westbrook from Quarter Tone Records, the guy I told you came by the Bakery the other night. We're meeting tomorrow to talk about a recording date.''

''Oh, Evan, that's wonderful.'' She hugs me tightly to her. ''I'm so happy for you.''

''Well, it's not Blue Note or Verve, but Quarter Tone has a nice list, and I think I'll have some freedom to do what I want.''

''You better, or Mr. Westbrook will have me to deal with.'' She stands back, her hands on her hips. ''I think this calls for a celebration. How about some pasta for dinner? Do we have any wine?''

''In the cupboard above the fridge.'' Getting a record deal out of the blue was a real break. It will help with getting gigs and really put me back on track. It's Coop's timing that isn't good, but what the hell. All I have to do is pass on whatever Ace comes up with to him, and I'm out of it.

''So what did Coop want with you last night? I saw the story on Rodman. That must have been horrible.''

''It wasn't pretty.'' Recalling the scene in Rodman's dressing room sends a shudder through me. ''Whoever killed him left a message on the mirror. Bird Lives! Coop wanted to know what it meant.''

Natalie's smile dissolves into deep and sudden concern. She looks at me for a moment, then turns away and starts ransacking the cupboards. She pulls out a large pot, fills it with water, and puts it on the stove to boil. She crosses her arms in front of her and turns around to face me. I know what's coming.

''Evan, you're not going to get involved in this. Please don't tell me that. You're playing again, you're going to record, you don't need any distractions.''

Of course she's right. Having a homicide detective for a friend sometimes comes in handy, but it has its downside.

"Don't worry, I'm just going to pass on some information to Coop that Ace is looking up for me. That's all." Natalie studies me for a moment. "Really, I don't want to get involved with this at all."

She turns away and sighs. "Yeah," she says, as she rips open a package of pasta. "Where have I heard that before?"

JUST INSIDE the door at Bob Burns Restaurant is a photo of pianist Howlett Smith. Nightly, the notice says. I haven't seen Howlett for a while. I take it as a good omen, the perfect place to sew up a recording contract.

Paul Westbrook is already there, talking on a cell phone as I slide into the booth. He presses the off button and puts the phone in a small leather briefcase. "Sorry. I hate these things," he says, chanting the mantra of Los Angeles. "You never get a minute alone."

The room is busy with the lunchtime crowd from nearby offices, but we get our order in quickly. "I don't know how familiar you are with Quarter Tone," Westbrook says. "The distribution is not what I'd like yet, but we're getting there, and we try to do quality music, which is why I want you on our list." He takes out a catalog and slides it across the table. "That's our current one," he says.

I flip through the catalog quickly, leaning back in the booth. Westbrook sports a shock of dark curly hair and thick glasses that he keeps pushing up on his nose. He's dressed in jeans and a pullover shirt today. He looks nothing like a jazz record producer, but then, who does?

"Well, you're the best offer I've had in a long time. There's some good people here," I say, tapping on the catalog.

Westbrook nods and slices into a chicken breast. "Because we're small and I personally supervise all the sessions, we have quite a lot of freedom. I've got several other businesses that are doing well, so I can afford to indulge my passion for jazz. I assume you would want to work with a trio, right?''

"That would be my choice, maybe the guys I used at the Bakery.''

Westbrook nods again. "This is your date. You pick the guys. Can you be ready in about a month?''

"Sure.'' My answer is quicker than I thought, but so is his offer. Is it really going to be this easy?

"Great. We've got a deal, then.'' Westbrook signals the waitress for more iced tea.

"That's it?''

"That's it.'' Westbrook pushes his plate aside. "Look, Evan, I read the papers. You've had some tough breaks. That injury to your hand must have been rough, a real setback. I've listened to your first album, and I know what I heard the other night. I think you're a major talent, and I want to grab you now, lock this up before somebody else knows you're back. Judging by what I heard at the Bakery, there's no question in my mind that you are back.''

"I really appreciate that, Mr. Westbrook. I—''

"Paul, please.'' He takes out a date book and pen and thumbs through the pages. "Now, let's think about some studio time. Let's say, four weeks from today? That'll give you time to think about things, do some rehearsing.'' He looks up. "I know the guy who books Chadney's in the Valley. Might be able to get you in there for a weekend.''

"Yeah, fine. That would be great.''

"Okay, then.'' He smiles and signals the waitress for the check. "I'll draw up a tentative contract for your approval. The advance will be small, but you'll do okay on the royalties. I'd rather put some money into promotion. You get a list of tunes together and think about a title for the CD.

I'll probably try to talk you into a couple myself, but we'll work it out." He reaches his hand across the table. "Welcome to Quarter Tone Records." He starts to get up. "Oh, one more thing."

"What?"

"I've also read about your—I don't know what to call them—detective exploits. We want to keep focused on this CD, so—"

"Not a problem. Those were accidental involvements."

"Whatever. Great, that's all I wanted to hear."

Westbrook leaves me sitting there for a few minutes, taking it all in, the excitement churning inside me. I feel like I've just won the lottery.

"Will you be having dessert, sir?" the waitress asks.

I look up at her. "What? I think I already did."

I call Coop from the pay phone in the lobby. For some reason he doesn't want me to come to the station.

"I hope you've got something for me," he says. "Meet me down at the Palisades, between Idaho and Montana, in about half an hour."

"Coop."

"Not on the phone."

He hangs up before I can protest.

With some time to kill, I walk over to a record store on the Third Street Promenade and do a quick search of the jazz bins for Quarter Tone Records. I find two trios: one with a young lion I'd seen profiled in *Jazz Times,* now with Blue Note; and one with a veteran who hasn't recorded in a long time. I fit somewhere in the middle of that mix, but I'm pleased to see I'm in such good company.

PALISADES PARK stretches north from Santa Monica Pier on the west side of Ocean Avenue, just past San Vicente, then dips down into Santa Monica Canyon. A narrow strip of grass, asphalt paths, and benches, the park was for a time a homeless camp until the police chased them away.

Today the bright sunshine has brought out strollers, joggers, and women pushing baby carriages. Parts of the bluffs have crumbled away over the years, but the park is still one of the city's best features.

Coop is already waiting for me, pacing around, oblivious to the view of Santa Monica Bay. The muffled roar of traffic rushing by on the Coast Highway below us filters up and blends with the distant sound of the surf.

"Well, I'm about to sign a recording contract," I say.

"Great, that's great," Coop says. "What have you got for me?"

I give Coop a look and pull out the paper I've written down Ace's research on. "Okay. January fifth, the bassist Charlie Mingus died in 1979. January 21, Miles Davis recorded *Birth of the Cool.*"

Coop takes out his notebook. "And Mingus wrote 'Better Git It in Your Soul'?"

"Right."

"Let me guess. 'Boplicity' was one of the songs on *Birth of the Cool.*"

"Right again. Was that the song that was playing?"

Coop doesn't answer. He just slaps the notebook with his hand. "I was afraid of that."

"Afraid of what?" I've never seen Coop quite like this. He still looks like he hasn't recovered from his all-nighter at the Rodman scene. He leans on the rail and stares down at Coast Highway.

"They are connected," he says, almost to himself. He's silent for a minute, then turns to me. "Let me ask you a question. What do you make of this? The other two murders I told you about, in New York, and this one here the other night all occurred on the anniversaries of significant jazz events. I assume Mingus and Miles Davis were significant. Hell, I've even heard of Miles Davis."

I was already ahead of Coop. When Ace had called back, it didn't take much to put together the dates and the music playing at the murder scenes. It was too much of a stretch to think more than one person had done these, or that they weren't trying to make a point.

"I'd say whoever did these murders knows a lot about jazz and is making a statement by their choice of dates. Maybe you're right. Maybe it is a deranged jazz fan."

Coop nods as if he already knew what I was going to say. "Would you be willing to tell that to the authorities?"

I stare at him for a moment. "The authorities? You're the authorities. I just told you."

"Not me," Coop says. "The FBI."

"The FBI?" I walk away a few steps from Coop, then turn back. "Look, man, I checked out these dates for you, but that's all. I'm not getting involved in this one. I'm playing again, I've got a record contract in the works. No, Coop, I can't do it. I don't want to do it."

"I know, I know," Coop says quietly. "I need some help on this to convince the FBI I'm not crazy."

"What are you talking about?"

"Look, Rodman's murder was in my jurisdiction. The New York murders are being investigated there, but I think there's enough of a connection to bring in the FBI, maybe a profiler. I think this is a serial killer."

I stand perfectly still, not wanting to listen to any of this, but Coop continues.

"The way it works is, they have to be invited by local authorities, and that's me. There have been three murders, all musicians, all on dates that have some meaning to jazz, but they're in different cities."

Coop presses on, knowing I want to interrupt him. "My

FBI contacts concede we might be dealing with a serial killer, but they want to be convinced, especially the profiler. Nobody has any idea who or why, but this could help narrow down the field.''

Coop pauses and looks at me. ''I want you to talk to the FBI, back me up on this. Ty Rodman's murder was in my backyard, a block from my office, and I don't know where to begin.''

I sigh, walking away a few steps, but already knowing I'll do what Coop wants. I owe him in many ways. If the FBI works like most federal agencies, they'll think I'm a nut case too and let it go at that. They'll just say, Thanks for your cooperation. Go play music.

''All right. I'll talk to them, but—''

''Thanks,'' Coop says. He checks his watch. ''I gotta go.'' He starts for his car. ''Tomorrow morning, at ten,'' he calls over his shoulder. ''I'll pick you up.''

THE FEDERAL BUILDING is on Wilshire, south of the UCLA campus, and just east of the San Diego Freeway. Coop drives straight up Wilshire and parks in the underground garage. He flashes his badge when we go through the metal detectors and head for the bank of elevators. We ride up to the seventeenth floor in silence. The doors open onto a reception area.

''Wait here,'' Coop says.

''We going to see Eliot Ness?''

Coop stops and glares at me for a moment, then walks over to the receptionist and says something to her. She picks up the phone and speaks into it, and Coop comes back to stand with me where I'm looking down across Wilshire toward Westwood.

''Looking for coeds?''

Before I can answer, a door off the reception area opens,

and a tall, heavily built black man pushes through. He's immaculately dressed in a three-piece dark suit, muted tie, and button-down collar that doesn't seem big enough for his neck.

Coop turns around as the door clicks shut behind him. "Morning, Wendell," Coop says. Wendell looks past Coop to me. "You must be Evan Horne." He holds out a massive hand that my own all but disappears into. Only then does he acknowledge Coop. "Thanks for coming. I'm Wendell Cook. Come on, let's go back."

He opens the door with a card key and leads the way down a corridor past a number of rooms, which eventually opens into a bullpen-like area with rows of desks. Most of the people at the desks are talking on the phone or staring at their computers. A couple look up as we pass.

Another door opens to a small meeting room. Inside, two people are seated at a conference table. They both look up as we walk in, and I immediately sense they're sizing me up. I suddenly realize the risk Coop is taking by bringing in not only a civilian but a jazz musician high school buddy to substantiate his theory.

Cook motions Coop and me to chairs. The other two take their cue from Cook. They both have coffee cups and note-pads in front of them. Cook walks around the table and stands between them. "This is Special Agent Ted Rollins and Andrea Lawrence." We shake hands all around. Like Cook, Rollins is uniform FBI—dark suit, white shirt, and tie. He mumbles hello and drops back in his chair.

Andrea Lawrence is only a little less formal in navy skirt and white blouse. She's not pretty exactly, but the short haircut frames her face and accentuates her eyes. There's a definite appealing quality about her. She stands up and smiles. "Thanks for coming."

"Well, let's begin," Cook says. "Would you like some coffee, Mr. Horne?"

"No thanks, I'm fine."

Cook allows himself a slight smile. "Just like to get this over with as soon as possible, right?"

"Well, frankly, yes." I feel like I'm at an IRS audit.

Cook nods and opens a file in front of him. "I don't know how much you've been told, but this conversation is entirely confidential. Lieutenant Cooper has vouched for you"—Cook slides a form across the table—"but we'd like you to sign this, please."

I scan it quickly. There's a lot of fine print, but I accept that it's what Cook says it is and use his pen to sign.

"Thank you." Cook says. He returns the form to the file folder. "We appreciate your coming in."

I study Cook for a moment. His name rings a bell for some reason, as does his massive build, and then I have it. "Didn't you play pro football sometime back?" Of course. Kansas City Chiefs.

Cook looks down and studies the file, but I catch him smiling slightly at the recognition. "That was years ago."

"All-Pro defensive end," Ted Rollins offers. Andrea Lawrence stifles a laugh.

"Anyway," Cook continues, "Lieutenant Cooper has an interesting theory about the three murders being investigated, and it seems you have some similar views. We'd like to have your thoughts, Mr. Horne."

They all look at me expectantly. I feel like a Ph.D. candidate defending my dissertation. Time to make my adviser look good.

"Sure, as long as you understand this is just my opinion."

"Of course," Cook says. "We're looking for someplace to start, Mr. Horne. Three people have died. All three are what we could consider celebrity musicians. Stalking, threatening, even murdering celebrities is nothing new, as I'm sure you're aware. John Lennon was one example. There was even an attempt on Ringo Starr.''

"Somebody tried to kill Ringo?" That's one I haven't heard about.

Cook smiles patiently. "Neither did Ringo until after the fact. His assailant fired one shot, point-blank range, but the bullet glanced off his earring and passed through his beard. Starr was never even aware of the attack. His attacker became obsessed with locating and stalking, in his words, 'any trace of musical ability in Starr's contribution to the band.'" Cook pauses for a moment and looks up at me.

I can't help but smile as a long-standing joke among jazz musicians comes to mind.

"You find this amusing, Mr. Horne?" Cook asks, frowning at me. I can feel Coop's glare.

"Sorry," I say. "Just thinking about something."

"Perhaps you'd like to share it with us," Cook says. His look is stern now, probably the one he gave opposing quarterbacks.

If he could have reached, Coop would have kicked me under the table. "Kind of sick, but when Lennon died, the joke among jazz musicians was, One down, three to go."

Only Andrea Lawrence smiles.

"What's wrong with the Beatles?" Ted Rollins asks, sitting up straighter in his chair.

"Nothing," I say, glancing at Rollins. "It's a long story."

"I'm sure it is," Cook says. "In any case, as I said, stalking celebrities is not new, but there certainly seems to be a common music thread in these three murders, and Lieutenant Cooper has pointed it out to us. As Lieutenant

Cooper's friend and someone who has some expertise in the field, we'd like to hear your views.''

Now I'm an expert. ''Okay, the murders are all people who play what's known in the trade as fusion, smooth jazz, almost pop music, right? The dates of the murders are significant to jazz history, classic jazz. Ty Rodman, March twelfth, the anniversary of Charlie Parker's death. The other two happened on the day Charles Mingus died and the date of Miles Davis's recording of *Birth of the Cool.* The music playing at all three locations was some jazz standard— 'Now's the Time,' Parker; 'Better Git It in Your Soul,' Mingus; and 'Boplicity,' Miles Davis.''

There, it's out. Cook flicks a glance at Coop. Maybe I'm not supposed to know that much. Well, now the FBI can make what they want of it. I want a cigarette badly, but of course I'm in a federal building.

Cook, Rollins, and Lawrence all exchange glances. ''What are you suggesting, Mr. Horne?'' Cook asks.

I'm sure they know exactly what I'm saying, but they just want to hear it out loud.

''I'm not suggesting anything. I'm just saying that I agree with Lieutenant Cooper. It seems like too much of a coincidence. Whoever is doing this knows a lot about jazz, and they're picking on pop jazz musicians who make a lot of money.''

''Classic jazz musicians don't?'' Rollins asks.

''Not usually, unless they're Miles Davis or Dave Brubeck or Wynton Marsalis.''

''Any ideas on motive?'' Andrea Lawrence asks. She's been making notes on her pad all the time I've been talking. ''That's what's bothering us. Revenge, maybe?''

I shrug and glance at Coop. You're doing fine, his look says. ''I don't know really. I suppose it could be some kind of revenge.''

"Are you trying to tell us that some kook who likes jazz, classic jazz as you call it, is pissed off because Kenny G is making millions?" Rollins shakes his head as if it were absurd. Maybe it is.

"I'm not trying to tell you anything. I'm just giving you my opinion, which is what I thought you wanted." At least I know Rollins's musical taste. "I don't think Kenny G has anything to worry about. He doesn't even call himself a jazz musician, and he plays soprano sax, not alto."

"Why not?" Rollins asks. "What's wrong with—"

Cook cuts him off. "Ted, let's move on. Andie, what do you think?" Cook turns back to me. "Andrea is on loan from our Washington office. She's one of our profilers, Mr. Horne."

Andrea nods. "I think he might be onto something," she says. "What about a, I don't know, an angry, jealous, failed jazz musician? Is that a possibility?"

So far, she's the only one I like. "I suppose that's possible. Or maybe it's an angry, jealous, obsessed fan. Like the one that shot at Ringo."

Rollins throws his pen down. "Oh, come on, I'm not buying it."

"Serial killers are studies in obsession," Andrea says. "I shouldn't have to tell you that, Ted."

"No, you don't," Rollins says. He turns to Cook. "C'mon, Wendell. Aren't we getting a little far-fetched here?"

If they work together, I imagine Rollins and Lawrence clash a lot.

Cook's pensive look lets me know he doesn't agree with Rollins. "Okay, let's get back on track," he says. "Andie, I think you need to work up a profile on this, perhaps with Mr. Horne's help. Lieutenant Cooper says you would be willing to cooperate in that regard, right?"

My turn to glare at Coop. "Look, I don't think I could add anything on this, and I'd prefer not to be involved. I'm pretty busy at the moment."

"It wouldn't take long," Lawrence says.

I sit for a moment, feeling pressured, cornered, not wanting to commit to anything, seething inside at Coop.

"Mr. Horne," Cook says, "so far, three people have died. We have, it seems to me, good cause to expect there might be more. I'm sure if you could play even a very minor role in stopping further murders, you'd want to. Am I right?" Cook lets that sink in and then adds, "And I've been told you were previously involved, helped the police on other cases." He flips through the file, then looks up.

Cook has me there. They've probably already done a profile on me.

"Well, Mr. Horne?"

I look at Coop, but he's busy studying the ceiling. "Yes, of course."

"Fine," Cook says. "We won't inconvenience you any more than necessary. Thanks for coming in. Andrea will work out something that suits your schedule."

Andrea Lawrence nods in agreement and gives me a reassuring smile. Cook closes the file folder and stands up.

"Don't worry, Mr. Horne. We'll make this as painless as possible."

I close my right hand into a fist.

THE ELEVATOR DOORS are barely closed before I start on Coop. "I don't want any part of this, Coop. I told you I would talk to them, I gave my opinion, but you didn't tell me I'd have to help them with a profile."

Coop listens stoically, keeping an eye on the floor lights, but he's smiling. When the doors open he says, "Can't tell me you wouldn't like to spend a little time with Andie

Lawrence. Nice legs, and she fills out that skirt pretty well.'' He walks on toward the Wilshire exit. ''C'mon, I'll buy you lunch in Century City.''

No more is said until we're settled at an outdoor table, picking at a selection of Chinese dishes. The mall is crowded. Shoppers swirl around us, and the sun is so bright I can hardly see Coop's face.

''Okay, I might have overstepped a little there, but there was a reason. When the FBI moves in, it can get touchy. Territory and all that shit. Usually they're cool. Cook is okay, but he wants to make a name for himself, solve a serial murder. They're stepping on my neck, and I want some leverage. I—okay, with your help—came up with this theory, so that means they'll keep me in with the proper courtesy.'' He sucks some soy sauce off a chopstick and drops it in an empty carton.

''This is about territory. You against the feds? I know it didn't register, but yesterday I told you about a recording contract. I've got rehearsals, tunes to think about. Jesus, Coop, give me a break. You're getting me mixed up in a serial killing. I don't want to talk to any FBI profiler, even if she does look like Andie Lawrence.''

Coop grins. ''Thought you'd noticed. Look, all she wants is some info to help her work up the profile. It won't go any farther than that. The FBI doesn't want a civilian in this, any more than I do. You just happen to have some information, some insight that could be helpful, that's all.'' Coop grins at me again. ''Think of it as your civic duty.''

I lean back, feel the sun on my face, and squint at Coop. ''We're even, Coop. This one balances the books.''

''We'll see,'' Coop says.

THREE

NATALIE GLANCES UP from the television when I come in. There's a law book open on her lap, a pencil in her hand. I've just come back from a long walk on the beachfront. I drop on the couch beside her, run both hands through my hair.

"Busted," I say, looking at the television. She has a soap opera on. Two impossibly good-looking actresses hold still for closeups before the show breaks for a commercial.

"Who's Andrea Lawrence?" Natalie asks.

"Not a good way to study, is it? Andrea Lawrence?"

"She left a message for you to call her. Is she from Quarter Tone Records?" Natalie lays the law book aside, stretches, and leans back. She taps the book with her pencil.

"You know, even in jeans and an old sweatshirt, you're still very fetching."

Natalie looks at me just long enough to raise her eyes upward before she turns back to the television. "Every once in a while I wonder if I really want to be a lawyer. This Lawrence babe sounded very formal." There's more than a hint of irritation in Natalie's tone.

I just nod, knowing I'm about to enter dangerous territory here. My mind drifts back to the confidentiality paper I signed, Natalie's strong feelings—and my own—to not get involved. I weigh them all with the honesty Natalie and I have maintained throughout our relationship.

I lean forward, my elbows on my knees, and look at the floor. "Andrea Lawrence is FBI. She's a profiler," I say quietly.

"FBI? A profiler? You mean like that TV show, with the blond? When did you meet her? Evan, what's going on?" Natalie sits up on the edge of the couch.

"Okay, let's talk." I light a cigarette. I'm still trying to quit. I've tried the patch, gum, books, articles, even a tape, but I guess I'm not ready. I explain to Natalie about the FBI meeting, Coop's position, everything I can muster to make a good argument for going this far, but Natalie isn't buying it.

"Evan, this has nothing to do with you. Why do you owe Coop?"

"For a lot of reasons. Most of them you know. Anyway, that's not the point."

Natalie shakes her head. "What is the point, then?"

"Look," I say. "You know better than anyone how long and hard I've worked to get back on track with my playing. No one wants this recording to come off well more than I do. This is just something that's come up. All I'm doing is providing some background information that might help Coop and the FBI with their investigation."

"But why, Evan? Why you?"

I tell her about the dates, the FBI's and Coop's theory about the killings, but that it's mainly because Coop has asked for my help. "Andrea Lawrence just wants me to help her with the profile she's working up. It might help to catch this nut."

"They really think this is some crazed jazz fan on a rampage?"

"They don't know what to think. Anyway, I figure if I cooperate now I can be out of it. They won't bother me again. There won't be any reason to, and I'll feel okay about it." I turn so I can look squarely at her. "I'm going to do it, Natalie."

She is silent for a few moments. I crush out my cigarette

and follow her gaze to the window. The fog is rolling in, dampening the air, the sky is gray, but I'm glad for the reprieve on this place, spared for now from the developers who tried to take over the area. I'd even packed up a bunch of boxes when I thought I was going to have to move, but the zoning permits are on hold.

Natalie turns back to me. "So call Lawrence now, get it over with. I want to hear you tell her this is all you're going to do."

"I'll call later." For some reason I don't want to talk to Lawrence with Natalie around.

"Fine," Natalie says as she stands up. "I'll make it easy for you. I've got a lot of cases to review for an exam Friday."

"Come on, Natalie." I reach for her, but she pulls away. She slams the law book shut and grabs her bag.

"See ya." She kisses me lightly on the cheek and slams the door on her way out.

THE NUMBER Andie Lawrence has left is for her beeper. I punch in my own number and wait less than five minutes for her to call back.

"Evan? Andie Lawrence."

"Hi. Just returning your call."

"Good, thanks for getting back so soon. I'm not causing any problems for you, am I? The woman who took my call wasn't exactly friendly. Was that your wife?"

"No, we're not married." I let it ride at that.

"Okay, well, I'd like to get together as soon as possible. Wendell, Ted, and I all agree we should go ahead with this."

"I'd like to get this over with as soon as possible."

"I understand. How about this evening then?"

"At your office?" I'd had enough of the Federal Building.

"I was thinking of maybe something less formal, where we could talk without being interrupted. The Federal Building can be a little intimidating. I thought we could meet someplace for coffee."

"How about dinner?" I throw it out just to see what happens.

"Okay, great." She sounds surprised. "Let me, the FBI, buy you a meal. I'm sure you'll be more comfortable."

I feel like I'm standing in wet sand, sinking slowly as the tide comes in. "Hey, why not?"

"Let's see. There's a place at the beach with patio seating. If it's not too cold, we could sit outside. You can smoke."

"How did you know?"

"Saw the pack in your pocket."

"I forgot. You're an FBI agent."

Andie laughs. "I hope that's not intimidating."

"I can handle it."

"I'm sure you can. Great. The place is called Sam's, near Santa Monica Pier."

"I know it. About seven then?"

"Fine. Oh, one thing."

"Yes?"

"I'm afraid you'll have to come alone. That's not a problem, is it?"

"If it was, I'd tell you."

SAM'S IS NOT very crowded, and except for Andie Lawrence, the patio is practically deserted. There's one woman alone, engrossed in a book, and a couple a few tables away, talking quietly. The tables are lit with candles in hurricane lamps, and the whole area is glassed in to shield diners from the chilly ocean breeze. I can hear the surf pounding on the beach a couple of hundred yards away. The torches and outdoor heaters do the rest to make the patio comfortable if you like fresh air.

Andie waves from a corner table. She's already ordered a carafe of wine. "I hope this is okay," she says as I join her. "House red. Would you prefer white?"

I sit down and look at her for a moment. "This is starting to feel like an awkward date."

Even in the candlelight I can see her color slightly. She's dressed in a dark turtleneck sweater and black jeans and has on more makeup than at the Federal Building this afternoon.

"I'm sorry. I guess I'm trying too hard. Wendell and Ted Rollins weren't exactly friendly. I just wanted to show you—"

"The FBI isn't all bad?"

She laughs easily. It comes naturally. "Something like that."

"Well, you succeeded. This is a big improvement over the Federal Building, and red is fine." I pour myself a glass and scan the menu. I decide quickly on grilled salmon and light a cigarette after offering her one.

"No, thanks. I quit about a year ago."

"Good for you. I'm trying but I guess not very hard."

"I know. It's tough."

We order and settle back to get acquainted. She tells me she grew up in a San Francisco suburb, was a psych major at Berkeley, went on to a Ph.D. at Columbia, and chose the FBI as a career for the excitement.

I don't see a ring, but I ask anyway. "You married?"

"No, I came close once, but this job isn't good for relationships. Long hours, traveling. Too demanding. Just doesn't work." I catch a flutter of regret in her voice. She made a choice at some point in her life and is now living with it.

"No, I guess not."

"How about you?"

I think for a minute. How about me? Natalie and I have been together for almost two years. It's good, the best relationship I've ever been in. Natalie is smart, sexy, and when she wants to, she can turn heads anywhere. What is it that holds me back from taking the final step?

"Divorced. Natalie Beamer—the woman you talked to on the phone—and I have been together quite a while. She's a law student at Loyola. One more year to go. We'll see what happens then."

Andie nods and sips her wine but doesn't probe further. Our dinner comes, and we make more small talk, but she's leading me in a definite direction. She confesses to being a jazz fan, but her tastes run more to smooth jazz than the heavyweights.

"If you say Kenny G, I'm leaving now."

"No, David Sanborn is as far as I'll go."

I nod. "He can play. I saw him go toe-to-toe with Phil Woods on his television show. Sanborn held his own."

Andie suddenly looks guilty. "I'm afraid I don't know who Phil Woods is."

"Well, I won't hold it against you." We've finished most of the wine, and when the waiter comes back, we both order coffee and get down to business.

"Don't panic, but I'm going to take some notes, okay?"

"Fine."

She takes out a notebook and pen and opens it on the table beside her.

"So tell me how this profiling thing works."

"It's not like on TV. I visit crime scenes, but I don't have visions of the killer or anything like that. It's mostly compiling and studying data on previous crimes, analyzing photos of crime scenes. Lots of time on the computer going through old cases. It's become a science really, and we're getting better at it all the time. The idea is to try and make predictions. It's like the airlines profiling drug smugglers. There's usually a behavior pattern that tips them off."

"So what do you think of Coop's theory?"

She clicks her pen several times before answering. "I think Cooper stumbled on it, but you put it together. You and Cooper are old friends, aren't you?"

"Since high school."

Andie nods. "I read the files on the cases you were involved in—the record scam and extortion with Lonnie Cole—God, who would have thought that—the Wardell Gray murder in Las Vegas. Were you as reluctant to become involved in those? When did you have time to play?"

I light another cigarette and stare out toward the ocean. It's only a dark mass, but I can see the white foam as the waves break on the beach.

"I was out of commission for quite a while." I glance down at my hand. "Had a bad accident." When I look up at her, she's watching me closely. There's some kind of empathy in her expression. "Are you profiling me?"

"I'll tell you later."

"I'm going to hold you to that. I was kind of drawn into those cases. I used to work for Lonnie Cole. He tricked me into helping him, made me the go-between for a ransom. With Wardell Gray, Clifford Brown, I had a lot of time on my hands. I was just doing some research for my friend Ace Buffington at UNLV." I shrug. "I don't know, they just happened."

"And you feel obligated to Cooper."

"Yeah, I guess I do. I was in over my head, and he got me out of a couple of scrapes, including one with the guy

I ran up against last year. It started out just listening to a tape for a record collector. Before I knew it, I was involved with a very disturbed person.''

"Raymond Cross," Andie says. "We didn't get involved, but I remember the case. You got quite a lot of publicity. That was also helping someone, at least at first."

I look back at her. "You know about that too."

"Afraid so. Helped me to get a handle on you, since we're going to be working together."

"Working together? What is your handle on me?"

Andie drops her pen on the table and leans back. "Well, you haven't talked about your family."

"No, I haven't."

She studies me for a moment. "Okay, I won't go there. First impressions? Smart, goal-oriented, maybe somewhat obsessed, as most artists are. You're a talented, dedicated, determined musician who's had some bad breaks, and now apparently on the comeback trail."

"I hadn't thought of it myself in quite that way."

"What do you think has kept you going?"

"I feel like you *are* profiling me now."

She smiles. "I guess I am. Sorry, occupational hazard. Helps me to gauge what you tell me. Anyway, let's get to the purpose of this meeting, shall we?"

"That's fine with me."

She picks up her pen again. "Okay, first tell me about the difference between smooth jazz and classic jazz."

"Smooth jazz is a marketing term, a category. It's used by radio stations and record companies. Some stations only play smooth jazz. It's light, not too demanding for listeners, and is usually a horn with a rockish type rhythm section, lot of electronics. Most musicians, the purists, don't like the term. For genuine fans, jazz means Miles Davis, John

Coltrane, Keith Jarrett, straight-ahead, mainstream, swinging music. And it's usually acoustic.''

"Which you play."

"Right again. With all the electronics in music, they had to come up with a retro term. Now there's acoustic jazz—which has always been around—to distinguish it from synthesizers, drum machines. Chick Corea keeps two groups going—the electric band and the acoustic band.''

"And smooth jazz is more commercial. The artists make a lot more money?''

"Oh, yes."

"Why?"

"The same reason writers like Stephen King and Danielle Steele make more money than John Updike or Saul Bellow. Mass market. They appeal to a lower common denominator.''

Andie scribbles while I talk and underlines a couple of notes. "So your theory is that our killer could be a bitter musician, jealous that these smooth jazz players are making it, and they're not. Have I got that right?''

"That's a possibility, I guess, but I don't think so. If you ask Horace Silver or the Modern Jazz Quartet or Phil Woods, they would tell you, Kenny G, for example, has nothing to do with what they do.'' I think for a moment and light a cigarette. "Maybe it's a fan who is bitter about the fact that someone like you knows David Sanborn and not Phil Woods. Phil has his audience and is doing fine though. More sometimes isn't better.''

"So a fan or a musician would be obsessive?''

"A musician for sure. You've already told me I am. But yeah, fans too.'' I think about the collectors I came across when I was tracking down the Clifford Brown tape. "They'd have very strong feelings about the music. Like I said, the dates of these killings have to mean something.

It's someone who knows a lot about jazz history. They're playing with you, making a statement by leaving clues."

"Like the bird feather?"

"Exactly." I'd thought a lot about the feather. Unless there was a jazz buff with the FBI, the killer was counting on them taking a long time to figure that one out.

Andie nods. "In most cases with serial killers, if that's what we're dealing with, the crime scene tells some kind of story. The killer usually has a signature. Subtle or not, the clues tell us mainly whether he's organized. If he is, he obsesses over details, which usually means he's progressing."

"Was there a feather at the other two scenes?"

"No, and that bothers me."

"Because the feather is some kind of progression?"

"It could be."

"You keep calling this killer a he. What about women serial killers?"

"You think this could be a woman?"

"I don't know. Isn't it a possibility? It must be someone who knew these musicians. It isn't easy to get backstage. A woman, especially a good-looking woman, would have the best chance."

"Groupies, you mean." Andie smiles. "Maybe, but very unlikely. There have been very few female serial killers. Women tend to internalize their feelings. They usually don't act out on them. The classic cases are men with horrible, dysfunctional childhoods, murdering their mothers over and over again. The patterns are awfully convincing."

"How do you know when you're dealing with a serial killer?"

"We don't, really, but the signs are there. Three killings, all musicians, victims are similar type, the same crime scenes, the music playing."

"So how do you go about catching them?"

"We compile as much data as possible, then hope for a break."

"Or a mistake by the killer."

"Exactly. They always trip up some way. Sometimes they want to be stopped. Sometimes they get arrogant, think they're invincible. We just hope that happens before there are too many deaths."

"So does this help, brainstorming like this?"

Andie nods and finishes her coffee. "Very much." She pauses, listens to the surf for a moment. "I love that sound. Wish I lived near the beach."

"Yeah, it's hypnotic."

She looks over her notes again. "Look, here's what I'd like to do. Let me take this information, add it to what I already have, and work up a profile. I'd like you to see it, go over it with me, see what else you could add. Would you be willing to do that?"

One more step, but I've gone this far. I feel myself being drawn in but unable to do anything about it. I'm talking to the FBI. They think I can help them catch a serial killer because of what I know about jazz. What am I supposed to do?

"As long as you understand that's as far as I go. I don't know what else I could do anyway. I've got this recording to think about, rehearsals, gigs, so I have to focus on that."

"Promise," Andie says.

"Okay." The waiter brings the check, and she signs for it. I walk her to her car, a shiny, dark Saturn.

"Well, thanks, Evan. I enjoyed this, and you've been a big help. You've given me a lot to think about."

I look at my watch. Still early, and I don't feel like going home. "Would you like to hear some real jazz?"

Andie is digging in her purse for keys. She hesitates for a moment. "I don't know." She looks at her watch.

"Yeah, you're probably busy."

"No, it's not that. I, yes, I would like that. I can chalk it up to research."

"Good, it's not far from here. Piano player is an old friend of mine."

"Fine, lead the way."

Andie follows me to Bob Burns on Second and Wilshire. There's a scattering of late diners, a handful of people drinking at the piano bar, and Howlett Smith at the keyboard. We manage a table near the piano and order Irish coffees.

Howlett Smith has been around Santa Monica for years. He usually works with a bassist, but tonight he's solo. We listen as he effortlessly roams through a set of standards. On two of them, he sings. His plaintive tone makes more of the lyrics than the songs deserve.

Andie listens for a few minutes and notices Howlett's movements as he sways back and forth. "He's blind, isn't he?" Andie says. She seems to really be enjoying the music.

"Yeah, and he's really good with voices. Watch this."

I go up to the piano. Howlett is noodling between tunes, talking with a couple at the bar. "Hey, Mr. Smith. You know 'Melancholy Baby'?"

He turns toward me, cocks his head to one side. "Evan Horne. How you been, man?" He holds out his hand. I grip his long brown fingers.

"Pretty good, Howlett. How you doin'?"

"Hangin' in, man." He laughs and shakes his hand in mock pain. "I know your hand is better. You got a steel grip now. Next you'll be trying to get my gig." He feels for the microphone. "Sit down here and play one. If you play good enough, I might sing along with you.'' He slides down to the end of the bench. I sit down and shrug at Andie. She's brought her drink up to the bar.

Howlett pulls the mike in close. ''Folks, we got a real treat for you. This here is Evan Horne, an old friend and a great pianist. What you feel like, man?''

I play a couple of chords. ''How about 'I Fall in Love Too Easily'?''

''Cool,'' Howlett says.

I play a short intro. I can feel Howlett swaying on the bench beside me. He comes in with the lyric, then touches my arm, signaling me to play a chorus on my own. Howlett comes back, playing with the melody, and when I go for a substitute chord at the end, he's right with me.

The crowd around the bar has grown, and they show their appreciation. I give Howlett's shoulder a squeeze. ''Thanks, man. I enjoyed that.''

Howlett smiles. ''You make me sound good. You come by anytime, Evan.''

I rejoin Andie, and we go back to our table. ''He's great, isn't he?''

''So are you,'' she says. ''He was smiling all the time you were playing. I can see why you'd rather be doing this than being hounded by the FBI.''

''Good,'' I say. ''I'll probably remind you of that.''

We listen to the rest of Howlett's set, and I catch Andie yawning once. ''Sorry,'' she says, putting a hand over her mouth.

''We'd better go, huh?''

''Yeah, it's been a long day.''

I walk her outside. ''Tell the FBI I said thanks for dinner.''

''Thank you for bringing me here. I really enjoyed it.''

We shake hands. Is it my imagination, or does her hand

linger a second longer than necessary? "I'll be in touch as soon as I have something to show you," she says.

I nod and start for my car, then turn back as I remember something I wanted to ask her earlier. "When these killers deliberately leave clues, what do you think they're saying?"

"Catch me if you can."

I DRIVE HOME thinking about what Andie Lawrence said. My mind should be on recording, the next gig, and new tunes, not serial killers and bird feathers, but there it is.

At home I pour myself a Dewars on the rocks and go through my CD collection. I dig out Keith Jarrett and Bill Evans, looking for inspiration. For comparison, I play my own album, which I've made a cassette of. Lots of room for improvement. I'll have to do better on this one.

I lie on the couch for a long time listening to Keith Jarrett moan and groan his way through a selection of standards that includes a wonderful version of "Just in Time." Wouldn't be Keith without the sound effects.

It's too late to call Natalie, but Cal Hughes will still be up. Teacher, mentor, even friend—I can always count on Cal for the truth. He answers after several rings.

"Cal? It's Evan."

There's no sign of surprise in his voice, even though we haven't talked in months. "I thought you'd call," he says. I hear the sound of a match striking. "There's been another murder. Just saw it on the news."

"What? Who?"

"You haven't heard? Another one of those wannabes who call themselves jazz saxophonists. Smooth jazz. They ought to call it jazz light. It's less filling. What rocket scientist came up with that term? Is there anything more smooth than Miles doing 'Freddie Freeloader'? Christ, this guy can't even play the blues.''

"Cal, who was it?"

"Called himself Cochise or some fucking thing. Long hair, wore a headband. About as Indian as I am. Probably from the Bronx.'' There's a few moments while Cal coughs into the phone.

"It's Native American now, Cal. How are you feeling?'' The last time I talked to Cal, he told me he was dying, but I think he's too mean.

"Yeah, whatever. I'm better, so the doctor tells me. Wants me to quit smoking though. Imagine that. Milton doesn't like me coughing though.''

"Cal, Milton is a dog.''

"He still doesn't like it. If the Humane Society finds out, they'll probably bust me for secondhand smoke.''

"Where was this murder?''

"San Francisco.''

"What else?''

"Nothing. Read the papers tomorrow. I hear your gig went okay at the Jazz Bakery.''

"More than okay. I got a recording date. Quarter Tone Records.''

"Good—small, but they do some nice stuff. What are you going to do?''

"I don't know yet. Any suggestions?''

"Yeah, for starters, stay out of this one.'' He laughs amid another fit of coughing. "It is kind of weird though, somebody knocking off these pop jazz jerks. C'mon by, we'll talk about it. Your album, I mean.''

"See you, Cal.''

"If you're lucky.''

I hang up and turn on the TV, but the local news is already into the weather.

Well, at least this wasn't Coop's problem, but Andie Lawrence, Wendell Cook, and Ted Rollins are probably working overtime.

What was in San Francisco? In the fifties and sixties it was the Jazz Workshop, the Blackhawk, premier West Coast jazz clubs that hosted many live recordings. *Miles— Friday and Saturday Night at the Blackhawk, 1961* was one of the most famous.

I know I have a reissue of *Saturday Night* someplace. I find it in a stack of CDs and put it on. Miles, with Hank Mobley on tenor; Paul Chambers, bass; Jimmy Cobb, drums. Wynton Kelly on piano romping through Monk's "Well You Needn't."

In small print, there are Ralph Gleason's original liner notes about Miles, but almost as much about the club and its owner, Guido Caccienti, an eccentric who wrote the names of coming attractions in soap on the windows of the club—Guido's on-purpose mistakes, calling saxophonist Illinois Jacquet "Indian Jacket;" the one-dollar cover charge; the feature on the club in *Time* magazine; the no-reservations policy even for the *Time* reporters.

A leaky roof, wooden tables, and hard chairs, but acoustics so good the Modern Jazz Quartet could work there without microphones. And Guido left the musicians alone. The only important thing was the music, and now, like so many jazz meccas—Birdland, the Five Spot, Shelly's Manne Hole—the Blackhawk was gone.

I stop reading and listen to Wynton Kelly race through "So What" with Chambers and Cobb bearing down on him, the three of them swinging so hard Miles was probably standing at the bar listening, wondering why he was even there.

Did Cochise's killer know all this? I wonder. And if he did, would it make him mad enough to kill someone?

FOUR

JEFF LASORDA'S HOUSE is at the western end of the San Fernando Valley in Woodland Hills. Even though rush hour is a memory, it's slow going at the San Diego-Ventura Freeway interchange. Every time I come out here I think of one more reason why I live in Venice. Someday I might like to leave L.A. altogether. But where? That's the big question. New York? San Francisco? Europe is always looming somewhere in the back of my mind.

Maybe it's the Dexter Gordon in Paris I'm listening to while an endless line of cars stretches ahead of me. I have KLON, the jazz station from Long Beach, on in the car. As Dexter's big horn fades, there's a brief traffic and news update, another mention of Cochise's murder in San Francisco. Nothing I haven't already read about in the morning papers.

I woke early, went out for coffee, bought *USA Today* and the *L.A. Times,* and stayed with CNN for most of the morning, but the story never changed. There was the requisite photo of Cochise, a mention of his ancestry. Cal was wrong; he *was* Native American, but Cherokee and only a smidgen at that, apparently. His real name was Bobby Ware. The rest was about his hit records, his sellout concerts, and his "jazz influences." Cochise claimed to like Cannonball Adderly and David Sanborn. The possible link to Ty Rodman's murder in Santa Monica was also discussed.

CNN interviewed someone from the FBI, but got mostly denials of any connections between the two murders. Later the other California serial killings—the Hillside Strangler, the Night Stalker—were rehashed, and the talking heads predicted there were surely more to come. But these, I knew, were different. They were not random—someone was targeting specific people—but unless someone played jazz, and a certain kind of jazz at that, they had nothing to fear from this killer. The media smelled a big story here. It wouldn't take long for someone to connect the New York killings with Rodman and Cochise.

I had taken it all in, and given the coverage, I'd been surprised at not hearing from Coop or Andie Lawrence. Thinking better of it made me realize I was not really a part of this investigation. All I'd done was explain a couple of dates for Coop and kick around some ideas with Andie Lawrence over dinner. Andie probably wouldn't even call me back about the profile, and in some strange way I can't explain, that kind of disappointed me. But what stung more was not having heard from Natalie for two days.

There's finally a break in the traffic, and as is so often the case, there's no sign of what caused the delay. Just too many cars. I take the Shoup exit off the Ventura Freeway and head north, looking for Jeff's street. I spot the church he's given me as a landmark, just past Oxnard. I don't have to look for the number. I spot Gene Sherman's station wagon in the driveway and Gene in jeans, T-shirt, and a Dodger baseball cap, unloading his drums. He waves as I pull the Camaro in behind him.

I offer to carry his cymbal bag and leave him to the bass drum and trap case. "You piano players are all heart," he says.

Inside Jeff is sitting at the stripped-down baby grand piano, going over some chord changes. The wild tangle of hair and thick glasses bring to mind a mad scientist. "Hey, man,'' he says. "Got a tune I want you to hear. Might be able to use it."

I set down the cymbal bag and join Jeff at the piano. "What's it called?"

Jeff shrugs. "I don't know. 'Wailing in Woodland Hills'? I'll name it later." He shows me the lead sheet, with the notes of the melody scribbled in pencil. I listen while he plays the changes.

When I called Jeff and Gene, they were as enthusiastic as I'd hoped. The Bakery gig had gone well, and although the three of us had only worked together a few times before, we had meshed quickly. Both agreed with me that we should keep it a trio. Adding a horn would just be one more problem. They were also happy to hear about the possible gig at Chadney's.

"I like it," I say to Jeff. His face contorts and his head tips to the side like he's discovered some new formula as he finishes with a wildly altered chord.

"Hear it?" Jeff says. His hands are spread out over the keyboard. Jeff has written several songs, but what I like best about him is, he always plays in tune. Somebody told me he'd once showed up for a rehearsal wearing a T-shirt that read "Tune Up or Die!" The leader, thinking it was meant for him, didn't see the humor and fired Jeff on the spot.

Jeff and I talk over the changes for a couple of other tunes as Gene gets his drums set up. When I sit down at the piano, I can't believe how good it feels to be rehearsing my own trio, prepping for a recording date.

I give them both a list of tunes I've written out. "Let's try 'When I Fall in Love.' I'll start, then you guys come in the second chorus. Keep it pretty free for a couple more, then we'll push into it on about the fourth chorus."

Jeff and Gene both nod. With musicians like these, I

don't have to give many directions. They're both talented and have been around long enough that I can rely on their judgment.

I slip my glove on and ease into an intro. Jeff adds some color notes, and Gene follows suit with mallets on the cymbal. By the time they both enter, it's so subtle I can't tell when they decided to go to tempo. Exactly the effect I want. My hand feels fine, and Jeff is reading my mind.

Three choruses in, I stop. "Okay, that's great. Now Gene, I don't want to just do eights all the time. Maybe you can take a chorus or two, just see how it feels, and Jeff, just let me know which tunes you want to play on."

"This is going to be cool," Gene says, nodding.

We play around with several tunes for a couple of hours, trying out arrangements, just getting more used to each other. If we can get the Chadney's gig before the date, we'll be pretty tight by recording time.

"Okay, thanks, guys, that's enough for today. I think we have the concept down. If either of you come up with anything you want to do, just let me know." I gather up my music and start to go when Gene stops me.

"You heard about that Cochise dude getting whacked in San Francisco?" he asks.

"Yeah," Jeff says. "Getting dangerous to be a musician." He's running a cloth over the fingerboard of his bass. "I was talking to a friend of mine yesterday, works with this group, Monk's Dream."

"Oh shit," Gene says. "I heard them on the radio. They sound like every other band."

"I don't know the group," I say, "but with a name like that, it can't be all bad."

"They play some straight-ahead stuff, but mostly they're in the smooth bag," Jeff says. "This friend of mine told me the leader is freaked by these murders. Thinking about canceling some gigs, and they have a lot.''

"Tell your friend to stick to bebop," Gene says. "Whoever is doin' these guys is a bebopper. Mark my words.''

"What guys?'' I ask Gene.

"Cochise and Ty Rodman.'' Gene looks up from his packing. "Who else?'' He looks at me strangely, then he and Jeff exchange glances.

"Hey.'' Jeff suddenly looks at me. "You're not in this, are you, Evan?''

I feel both of them watching me closely. Gene has a cymbal stand halfway collapsed. Jeff is standing by the piano.

"Not at all.''

DRIVING BACK to Venice, I'm still wired from the rehearsal. Jeff and Gene are going to be great for the recording, and there seems to be a real musical connection between the three of us. No egos, just a concerted desire to make good music. If we get the Chadney's gig, we could really get locked in.

I let myself in, still allowing the earlier relief at not hearing from Coop or the FBI to stay with me, but it's ended by the answering machine. There are messages from both, and also one from Natalie. "I'll cook you dinner tonight if you like," her voice says with a tone that I hope means forgiveness.

I know she's at school, but I call and leave her a message. "Yes, I like.''

Next I call Coop at police headquarters, but the desk sergeant tells me he's signed out for the day. "I can give you his voice mail if you like.''

"That's okay. I'll catch him at home.''

"He's definitely not at home," the sergeant says.

"That's okay, thanks."

I think I know where Coop is. I call Andie Lawrence's beeper number. Her return call comes almost as soon as I hang up the phone.

"Evan, it's Andie."

"Yeah, got your message—"

"We need to see you right away."

"Look, Andie. About the profile, I don't know if—"

"Wait, hang on a minute," she says.

"Hey, sport, you need to get down here right away."

"Coop? Where are you?"

"Federal Building. I think you recall its location."

"What's going on?"

"You haven't heard?"

"Cochise's murder, you mean? Yeah, I heard, but—"

"Okay, then just get down here. They need your input, and Special Agent Lawrence has a profile for you to look over." Coop puts an extra spin on "Special Agent."

"And what if I don't? What if I have other plans?" FBI or not, I don't like being on call. Next they'll give me my own beeper.

"Change them." Coop's voice is getting more irritated by the word. I think I know why. He's sitting there in front of Andie, maybe Wendell Cook as well, assuring them he'll get me there.

"Okay, okay, but we're going to have to get a few things straight—you, me, the FBI."

"See you then," Coop says and hangs up.

IT'S TOO CLOSE to rush hour to chance the Santa Monica Freeway, so I use surface streets for the drive to Westwood. I pass through the metal detectors, take the elevator to the seventeenth floor again, and I give my name to the receptionist. She picks up the phone, and in a couple of minutes, Andie comes out.

"Thanks for coming," she says. "This way." She's all business today, much more distant than she was at dinner and Bob Burns.

I follow her through the bullpen area to Wendell Cook's office. The scene is a little different today. Coats are off, ties are loosened, and the wastebasket is stuffed with fast food bags and soft drink cans. Everybody has a coffee cup in front of them at a long table, and they're all looking at a large white board covered in multicolored marker pen writing—four columns, one for each victim in a different color, with notes below the names. I don't recognize the first two; the column for Ty Rodman is blue, and Cochise's column is red.

A crime scene photo of each victim is taped to the board. I'd almost put Rodman's face out of my mind, but no more.

"Sit down, Mr. Horne," Wendell Cook says. Coop is sprawled in another chair alongside Cook. He waves a finger at me. The only one missing is Ted Rollins. "Special Agent Rollins is in San Francisco," Cook says as if reading my mind. "We're doing a little brainstorming here. We'd like your input, and then Andie will work with you on the profile. Can I get you some coffee?"

"Yeah, coffee would be good." So would a cigarette, but I don't see any ashtrays.

While Cook is gone, Coop leans in next to me. "Play along, make them happy, and you'll be out of here in time for dinner. They're really buying this jazz theory."

I catch Andie watching me while Coop talks. She looks tired, and I wonder if she's just come back from San Francisco herself. Cook comes back with coffee, a handful of sugar packets, creamers, and a wooden stir stick he sets in front of me before returning to his own seat.

"Okay, Andie, why don't you bring us up to speed."

She walks up to the board, glances at it for a few moments while she gathers her thoughts. "Okay, these are the four victims, and in each column I've listed the similar crime scene elements." She draws lines between the columns, matching up things like music playing at the scene, song titles, instruments, cause of death. In both the Cochise and Ty Rodman columns, bird feathers are listed. No feather under the New York names. I scan the board and take it all in.

"So far we have no witnesses, no prints, and no weapon. Shall I play the tape?" She looks at Cook for approval.

"Sure, go ahead," he says.

"This was playing at the Cochise scene in San Francisco. See if you recognize it," she says to me.

She presses the play button on a small cassette player. The tinny speaker emits an alto saxophone I know in the first five notes of the melody. "That's called 'I Remember Bird,'" It's a recording by Cannonball Adderly, and I tell them that too.

Andie shuts off the tape, and all of them stare at me as if I'd just correctly answered the final Jeopardy question. "Are you sure?" Andie asks. "Do you want to hear it again?"

"No, I have the album, and I've played the tune."

Andie and Cook take a few moments to absorb my quick response. Only Coop is smiling. I know he's dying to say, "I told you so."

It's Cook who speaks first. "Can you give us any input as to why San Francisco?" he asks. "We've got three cities, four victims."

"The first thing that came to mind was a jazz club." I tell them about the Blackhawk, the Miles recording, everything I can remember from the liner notes on the CD. When I finish, they just stare at me again.

"How is it you know so much about all this? I know you're a musician," Cook says, "but—"

"I have the Miles album too," I say. "When I heard about the murder, I started thinking about San Francisco, and it just came to mind. I dug it out and read the liner notes."

Cook nods and stares at the board, watching Andie write in Cannonball's name and the song title. "But you said Miles Davis. This recording was Cannonball," Cook says. "What do you make of that?"

I shrug. "Cannonball played alto, the song fits, and you found white feathers at both scenes. The Blackhawk recording Miles did was a famous one. I don't know for sure, but I think Cannonball might have played the Blackhawk too. I know he recorded at the Jazz Workshop. That was going at the same time as the Blackhawk."

I catch a look of relief from Coop that I don't give away it was me who found the feather. I don't imagine the FBI would have liked me at a crime scene.

"Where was the feather?" I ask Andie.

"In the saxophone case. His horn was heavily damaged too," Andie says.

"Well, there you go." I look at all of them, thinking hard. "Do you need me for anything else?" Nobody seems to know what else to ask me, and I can't think of anything more to tell them. I don't like any of this, and I'm dying for a cigarette.

"No, I guess not," Cook says. He looks from Andie to Coop. "We appreciate your help. Andie wants to run her profile by you, but you can do that in her office. Andie?"

"Yes, we can do that now. Save you another trip," she says.

I hope that means I won't be back. I get up and we start to go, but Cook stops us. "Mr. Horne, would you mind waiting outside for a moment?"

"Sure." I glance at Coop, but his expression reveals nothing. I shut the door behind me and lean against the wall, watching all the activity in the bullpen. I wonder how many cases they're working on at this minute and how much of that effort is being directed to these murders. There must be forty people reading files, talking on the phone, or staring at computer screens. I'd read somewhere that L.A. was the bank robbery capital of America.

Andie comes out in a couple of minutes, with Coop just behind her. "Have fun, you two," he says, and winks at me.

Andie catches it and rolls her eyes. "This way," she says. "Your friend has a vivid imagination."

She takes me down the hall around the corner to her office. It's much smaller than Wendell Cook's and standard government issue. File cabinets, a desk, some bookcases— all government gray—and of course, a computer fill out the room. Her suit jacket is thrown over the back of her chair. She shuts the door, walks across the room over to one of the lever windows, and opens it. From her desk she pulls out a tiny gold-foil ashtray embossed with a fast food logo.

"From the old days," she says, setting it on a corner of her desk. "Go ahead. Bet you need one."

"Aren't we violating federal law?"

She laughs. "It's my office. I'm sure you're allowed some kind of immunity from prosecution, since you're helping us."

"And maybe Wendell could call me Evan."

Andie smiles, but there are worry lines around her eyes. "Wendell plays it by the book. He's usually not so formal, but he's under a lot of pressure on this case."

"So are you, I imagine." I light up and blow the smoke toward the open window.

"Yeah, well, it comes with the territory."

Andie sits down at her desk and taps a couple of keys. The screen changes to blank, and she types in PROFILE: near the top of the screen.

"So what was the secret meeting about?"

"How much to involve you in this investigation—but I'm sure you knew that." She doesn't even look at me. She just calls up a couple of files, scans them quickly, then returns to the screen we started with before I can read anything. Her fingers fly over the keyboard at Oscar Peterson speed. I know as much about computers as I know about country music.

"I guessed. Was Coop in favor? How do you do that so fast?"

"I just work with them all the time. He speaks very highly of you, said you had been invaluable in those other cases."

"Invaluable. My, my."

"He also argued to keep your involvement to a minimum."

"Haven't we already gone beyond that?"

Andie ignores that. "He told us about the recording date you have coming up, but of course I already knew about that."

"Yes, you did." I wonder if she told Wendell Cook about our dinner and jazz night out. I doubt it. Well, I haven't told Natalie either.

I smoke for a moment, watching Andie gather her thoughts. "Look, Evan, whether you knew what you told us about the Blackhawk or it came from the back of an album cover doesn't matter. We wouldn't have any idea how to start on that. It could have taken us forever to find somebody to recognize the song on that tape. That's the same reason Cooper called you to the Rodman crime scene." She glances at me. "Yes, I knew about that. The FBI doesn't have any jazz experts that I know of, and except for you, neither does the Santa Monica Police. Cooper knew you'd know what those words on the mirror meant. Just now, you knew that song instantly. You've saved us a lot of time."

"Is it that important?" I just didn't see how me being able to identify Cannonball Adderly playing a Leonard Feather song fit in.

"It could be. That's the point. We never know when some little bit of information will break a case. We have very little to go on here except for the jazz and the possibility that it might be a musician or a jazz fan doing these murders. Frankly, I have to admit it's looking better all the time. That's what we're going to focus on in the profile."

I take one last drag on my cigarette then stub it out in the ashtray. I suddenly flash on the FBI taking me from murder to murder, playing a horrible game of Name That Tune, a perverted version of the *Downbeat* blindfold test.

"Look," Andie says, breaking in on my thoughts. "Let's run through this and see where we are."

I look at the blank screen. "I thought you were already going to do one, just have me add to it."

Andie nods. "I have. I just want to see how yours matches up with mine, sort of compare notes. Keep in mind, what we're doing here is creating a picture of the artist, sick as that might sound. To understand jazz, for instance, doesn't it help to understand the musician? These crimes are our killer's art."

I think it's more than that. Andie is not telling me everything. I don't know the details about how the murders

were done except for what I've seen on the news. Most of
what the FBI knows is probably off limits to me.

"Okay, let's do it," I say. I pull my chair in closer and
watch Andie type on the screen

UNSUB:JAZZ MUSICIAN/FAN
SERIES OF HOMICIDES
NEW YORK, SANTA MONICA, SAN FRANCISCO
NCAVC/VICAP

"Unsub?"

"Unknown subject," Andie says. "The other two at the
bottom are National Center for the Analysis of Violent
Crime. VICAP is a computer database—Violent Criminal
Apprehension Program."

However reluctant I am to get involved, unconsciously
I've been thinking about this since the night I saw those
two words scrawled on Ty Rodman's dressing room mirror.
What kind of person would do something like that? I'm
intrigued by the process of finding out, but the more I've
thought about it, the more I'm convinced it's not a musician.

"For what it's worth, my guess is it's a fan, someone
steeped in jazz history. A record collector who is thoroughly familiar with important dates, or at least has access
to someone who does."

If it was a musician, bent on some kind of revenge, what
about a musician who hasn't been able to play for almost
three years and was filled with rage that Ty Rodman and
Cochise have been playing, recording, and making a lot of
money? Then I suppose the killer could be a musician, and
I could be describing Ace Buffington and myself. Those
thoughts I don't share with Andie.

Andie stops typing at that point. "I don't think so. Serial

killers almost always work alone. They never involve any-one else, but I see your point.''

I add everything else I can think of while Andie types. She leans back, rubs the back of her neck, and reads it over with what seems a satisfied smile. ''Your profile is pretty on target with mine.'' She continues to stare at the screen, then swivels her chair toward me. ''You asked the other night if it could be a woman?''

''Yeah, I thought it was a possibility. You still don't?''

''I don't know. I'm wavering. All the victims have been men, and what you said about it being someone who knew the victims or could get close to them makes sense. But this has to be more than a groupie. This person is very intelligent, high IQ, very organized, a professional.''

I'd thought about that too. ''What about somebody in the business—publicity, booking agents, record people? A lot of them are women.''

Andie's eyebrows pinch together as she considers it. ''Yes,'' she says, ''I hadn't thought of that, but...'' Her voice trails off as she looks back at the screen. She stares at it for a couple of minutes, totally lost in some world of concentration. She taps on the save key, and we both watch the screen dissolve to the program page again.

She turns her chair toward me. ''Thanks for doing this, Evan. Your input, as Cooper said, is invaluable. I don't know where we would have started on this without you. This one is really different from anything I've seen. If any-thing else comes up, I'll be in touch.''

''That sounds like I'm through.''

''Yeah, I guess it does.

I stand up and start for the door. ''Oh, thanks for the cigarette.''

''You're welcome.''

We look at each other for a moment. "Well," she says, "I can't think of anything else."

"Neither can I."

COOP HAS PULLED his car next to mine in the garage. "That didn't take long," he says. "Get in for a minute."

"Well, they didn't tell me everything, and she's too quick on the computer. I think there was something she didn't want me to see."

Coop nods. "Magic fingers. This is the FBI sport, need-to-know basis, eyes only, and all that Elliot Ness stuff. They don't tell me everything either. The more media coverage this gets, the more weirdo phone calls. There's always somebody out there ready to confess. In these cases, certain details are always left out. It's a way to separate the kooks from the real killer. They're worried about leaks."

"You mean someone is going to call the FBI and say he did it?"

"Hey, it happens."

"Well, I'm the last one to want any of this leaked. That's all I need."

Coop pauses for a moment. He doesn't look at me, but he says, "You're right, I owe you or we're even, however you want it. I appreciate you keeping certain things to yourself." Only then does he turn to me. "That is good news on the recording date. Going to do any Garth Brooks songs?"

"Don't make me gag." I light a cigarette.

"This is a nonsmoking car, sport."

"Yeah, right. Does your captain know about your cigars? Thanks, Coop. I hope that's all I have to worry about for a long time."

"They'll call you back in, you know, if they need something else. It's out of my hands now. Besides," Coop says, "you and the lovely Miss Lawrence seem to get along just fine."

I give Coop a look. "Why don't you ask her out?"

Coop starts his car. "She already told me she doesn't date cops. Besides, that's your specialty."

FIVE

WHEN I OPEN the door, I smell what I hope is the aroma of sausage and peppers. Natalie is at the stove, stirring a large pot with one hand. With the other, she brushes back wisps of her fine blond hair. She's in sweats, no makeup, and she's never looked more beautiful to me.

"Hi," she says. "Want to open the wine?"

Just like that, she's back. She puts the lid on the pot while I open something called Bob's Really Good Red. There's a caricature drawing on the label, a guy with a white beard and glasses. "Where did you get this?" I ask, looking at the bottle. I pour two glasses and hand her one.

"Friend of mine brought a couple of bottles back from San Francisco. She thought the picture looked like our contract law professor." She holds up her glass. "Here's to Bob."

We take a sip. "Not bad, huh?" she says. She looks back at the stove. "We've got some time. That has to simmer for a while," she says, nodding at the stove. "I wasn't sure when you'd be back. How did the rehearsal go?"

I sit down at the table and light a cigarette. "Great—this is going to work out well. We ran over a few tunes, just talked about the concept for the recording."

Natalie stirs the pot once more, then joins me. "Any more calls from the FBI babe?"

"Special Agent Lawrence, you mean? Yeah, they had me come in again, help with the profile they're putting together." I tell her about the meeting and our discussion. Natalie's face grows more serious as she listens.

"You really think you're helping?"

"They do, but I don't think there's anything else I can tell them."

"I saw the story about Cochise. I imagine there are some musicians out there who are getting nervous. Do they have any idea who it might be?"

I shake my head. "Not really, although there's a possibility it might be a woman."

"A woman? Why a woman?"

I give her a brief rundown of what I'd told Andie Lawrence. She drains her glass and pours more wine. "Sounds like you spent a lot of time with this Andie Lawrence." She holds up her hand in front of her. "I'm sorry, I'm sounding like a jealous bitch, aren't I?"

"Coop and Wendell Cook were there too. Cook is the boss." Natalie looks like she's only half listening, trying to appear cheerful. "C'mon, Natalie, what am I supposed to do? Four people have been killed; they have little or nothing to go on. They're grasping, and I just happen to be a convenient straw."

"I know, I know," Natalie says. "I'm just—"

"What?"

"Afraid you'll get in this too deep and won't be able to get out."

"No, I think I'm done. There's nothing else I can tell them."

Natalie sets her glass down and comes over to sit on my lap. She puts her arms around me. I feel her warm breath on my neck. "I'm sorry," she says. Her look turns mock serious. "But I know this Lawrence is a babe, or you would have told me she's forty and frumpy."

"You're right. She looks like Pamela Anderson Lee's twin."

Natalie playfully slaps me on the shoulder. "Stop it.

Look, we'll have a nice dinner, finish this wine, and then later…''

"Yes?"

"I'll show you—" The phone rings. "Damn," Natalie says. "Hold that thought. I'll get it."

She walks over to the phone and picks it up. She's looking at me, still smiling, as she talks. "Hello. Yes, he's here. Just a minute." She holds the phone out to her side and looks away. Her smile has changed to a glare. "Andie Lawrence." I take the phone from her, and she goes into the bedroom.

"Yeah, Andie. What's up?" I catch myself talking louder than necessary.

"I'm sorry to call you. Hope I'm not interrupting anything."

"No, just about to have dinner." I watch Natalie come back, but she won't meet my eyes as she stomps back to the kitchen. She takes the lid off the pot and stirs viciously.

"Lucky you," Andie says. "I'm still working. Well, I won't keep you. I'm working on the profile, and I just thought of something else."

"What?"

"I've been trying to make a connection between the four victims beyond the fact that they're all successful jazz musicians."

"Yeah?"

"Well, I think I've found something. Two of them, Ty Rodman and Cochise, Bobby Ware, went to Berkeley. It was in the bios I got from their record companies. But Berkeley is not necessarily known as a music school. I just thought it was strange."

"It's not UC Berkeley, it's the school in Boston. B-e-r-k-l-e-e. People confuse the two all the time. Berklee in Boston is a jazz school. I went there myself."

Now I recall seeing notes about both Cochise and Rodman in the alumni update section. I still get the magazine.

"You went to Berklee too?" Andie asks. "You didn't know Rodman or Ware then, did you?"

"No, they were long after me, and I never graduated. So what does it mean, that they both went to Berklee?"

"Well, I don't know if it means anything. It's just another thread really. Anyway, thanks for clearing that up. I'll check the Boston school tomorrow. Sorry to interrupt your dinner and please apologize to—it's Natalie, isn't it?"

"Yeah, I will. Good night."

"Bye, Evan."

When I hang up, Natalie is standing there, her coat on, her bag in her hand.

"Natalie—"

She nods toward the stove. "That's almost ready. You just have to cook the rice. I'm sorry, Evan, I can't do this."

"Do what?"

She doesn't answer. She looks at me once more, goes out, and quietly shuts the door behind her. I stand for a moment, wanting to go after her, but there's nothing I can say that will change her mind, at least not now.

I'm too hungry to let the dinner go. I put water on to boil and turn on some music—an early Art Blakey and the Jazz Messengers. Listening to it, I wonder how jazz has come to Cochise, Ty Rodman, Kenny G, and a slew of other groups with one-word names I don't even know about. Smooth jazz, acid jazz, sampling, much of it from old Blue Note artists. What would Bird have thought of a limpid sax over a monotonous synthesized rock beat?

Blakey and his messengers roar through "Night in Tunisia." The crackling solos by Lee Morgan and Wayne Shorter, pushed and prodded by Blakey's drums, seem to be the best answer.

I have another glass of wine, but the rice doesn't come out right. I don't seem so hungry with Natalie gone. I pace around the apartment. I'm too restless to just stay home, so I call Cal Hughes.

"You busy, Cal?"

"Yeah, Chick Corea wants me to sub for him in his Electric Band."

"I need to talk. Can I come over?"

"Sure, bring something with you. Maybe you can take Milton for a walk."

I stop at a liquor store on Sunset and wind my way up into the Hollywood Hills to Cal's tiny bungalow. "Door's open," he calls from inside. He's in his usual chair, Milton at his side, with the perennial stack of books on a nearby table.

"What are you reading?"

"The Concrete Blonde." He holds it up. "It's a detective novel." He lights a cigarette and eyes the paper bag. "That for me? You do the honors."

I dig out a couple of glasses and some ice and pour us both hefty drinks. Cal does actually look better, but he still has the cough. Each spasm shakes his body and forces him forward in the chair. Milton looks up at him disapprovingly with sad basset eyes.

"I knew a woman like that in Chicago once," he says, putting the book down to take the drink. "Tits hard as a rock. Early silicone. They didn't have it together yet. You still with the wannabe lawyer?"

"I don't know. We're not getting along so well these days." I tell Cal about Andie Lawrence, the FBI, and my meetings with them. He listens quietly, not commenting until I've told him everything.

"The FBI. Fucking Bureau of Intimidation. Thought you were going to stay out of it?"

"I was. I'm not in it, really."

"No, you meet this FBI broad for dinner and help their task force with a serial killer profile. That's really staying out of it. What's this Andie Lawrence like?"

"She's nice." Cal holds my gaze for a moment. "Okay, she's good-looking too."

Cal snorts. "I thought so." He rattles his glass. "Encore?"

I fix him another drink. "What am I supposed to do?"

"Nothing, I guess. Four people have died." He shrugs. "If you can help them catch this guy, I guess you have to, but watch yourself with the FBI."

"I think it's a woman."

"Really."

I tell Cal my female theory.

"Well, you might be right. What about the record deal?"

"It's on; had one rehearsal already. The other guys are good, we're just picking tunes."

"Do some familiar ones, standards, but there's also a lot of good tunes nobody does anymore, obscure ones. It works for Keith Jarrett." Cal shakes his head. "Guy's a fucking genius."

We talk music some more, then both of us notice Milton's inquiring look. "Can you take him for a spin around the block before you go?"

"Sure. C'mon, Milton." The big basset hound lumbers to the door and allows me to snap on his leash. I take him around the block, letting him explore at his own pace. I wonder if Natalie has changed her mind or called, and I suddenly want to get Milton back, go home.

Back inside, Cal has the TV on. "Look at this," he says.

It's no longer the lead story. Too much time has passed. But just before the weather, the Cochise and Ty Rodman murders are rehashed.

"And in a local note," the anchor says, "FBI task force leader Wendell Cook reports the bureau is being assisted in their inquiries by a local musician."

They cut to Cook coming out of the Federal Building with Andie Lawrence and Ted Rollins trailing behind him. He almost looks surprised to see the reporters.

"Yes, this musician knew one of the victims, Bobby Ware, at the Berklee College of Music in Boston. We have no other leads at this time," Cook continues, "but he is being very helpful. That's all I can say at this time."

They cut back to the studio then. "Action News has learned that the musician referred to has assisted the police several other times in the past three years. Next—"

Cal hits the mute button and looks at me. "Oh-oh, you've just been sandbagged, buddy."

I'M SITTING IN MY CAR, waiting for Andie Lawrence in the Federal Building parking garage at eight o'clock, sipping 7-Eleven coffee from a paper cup, smoking my third cigarette. I have on the same clothes from last night, and my eyes feel gritty as I scan the cars arriving.

I ended up crashing at Cal's after the newscast and several more scotches. I imagine my machine is full of messages from Jeff, Gene, Paul Westbrook, Coop, Natalie, and maybe even Andie, who is the only one I want to talk to at the moment.

At ten after eight, she pulls into the garage and parks in the reserved parking area almost directly across from me. I get out and walk to her car. She takes a box out of the backseat and kicks the door shut with her foot.

"Andie."

She turns, startled, sees me, and bows her head slightly. I'd hoped she hadn't been in on the leak. It's hard to believe she isn't. She knows why I'm here. She straightens up, sits the box on the hood of her car. "I tried to call you last night."

"Yeah, I'll bet." I angrily flip my cigarette away. "What were you thinking about?"

"Evan, look, it wasn't me."

"No? It was you I had the Berklee conversation with. I told you I didn't know Bobby Ware."

"I think you need to come upstairs and talk to Wendell," she says.

"Oh, I'm definitely looking forward to that."

Andie locks her car, and we go inside. I let her wrestle the box on her own, and I'm too angry to speak until we're in the elevator.

"Is Rollins here too?" I ask.

Andie nods. "He should be."

We get off the elevator, and I follow her back through the bull pen to Wendell Cook's office. It's all getting just a bit too familiar.

Cook looks like he knows we're coming. He's standing in the doorway of his office. Over his shoulder, I can see Ted Rollins and Coop already inside.

"Good morning, Mr. Horne," Cook says. "We'd—"

"Don't bother with the formalities, Wendell. And by the way, it's Evan. We need to talk." I brush past him and sit down at the long table opposite Rollins and Coop. At the door, Cook takes the box from Andie and sets it on the floor. They both come in and join the rest of us. "Can somebody please tell me why it was necessary to tell the television folks a local musician was helping you? Don't you realize anyone that's read the papers, seen the news, the past couple of years can figure out it was me?"

Nothing but silence. I look from face to face, but not one seems to be able to look at me. Andie stares ahead into space. Rollins fidgets with a pen, and Wendell Cook sits quietly, his hands folded in front of him.

Finally, Coop looks at Wendell Cook. "Well, are you going to tell him?"

I take out my cigarettes and light one, an insignificant act of defiance, but Cook says nothing. He just pushes a paper coffee cup toward me. I tap an ash in the cold coffee.

"I'm afraid they've already figured it out," he says. He gets up and brings back a newspaper from his desk. It's folded over to page three. Cook slides it across to me and taps on the sidebar of yet another story on the murders. My name is in the second paragraph: "...Special Agent Ted Rollins revealed to this reporter that the musician named by Task Force Director Wendell Cook as assisting the FBI with its inquiries is pianist Evan Horne. Horne assisted police in several investigations over the past three years. He recently played an engagement at the Jazz Bakery with his trio."

There's more. The story briefly summarizes the Lonnie Cole case, the Las Vegas murders of Wardell Gray and record collector Ken Perkins. He doesn't bother to mention that Gray's death was in 1955. I turn back to the front page. It's below the fold, but the headline reads: LOCAL MUSICIAN HELPS FBI IN JAZZ LAND MURDERS.

I take a long, last drag on my cigarette and drown it in the coffee cup. "Evan," Cook begins. "I know—"

"What the fuck were you thinking about?" I lean toward Rollins. I sense Coop give me a warning look, but I ignore it. "Who authorized this?"

"Nobody authorized it," Cook says. "It was a mistake."

Rollins shrugs and glances at Cook. "There was a *Times* reporter," he says. "I thought it was off the record."

"Bullshit. You wanted to see your name in the paper," I shoot back.

"That's not true," Rollins says. He's glaring at me now.

"All right," Cook says. "That's enough. What's done is done."

"Oh, let me write that down. I'll tell that to Paul Westbrook when he cancels my recording date. Jesus Christ."

Cook gives me a few moments to calm down. "I understand that you're upset, Evan, but we had no choice. This was a Bureau decision."

"I thought you said it was a mistake."

"Releasing your name was. Letting the media know a musician was assisting us was not."

"What? I don't understand." And then suddenly, I do. "You're hoping the killer will contact me. That's it, isn't it?" Nobody says anything for a moment. Except for Coop, they all steal a glance at me. Coop's eyes meet mine, letting me know he had nothing to do with this.

Cook sighs before he answers. "We have four murders, all seemingly related. Your input has convinced us it's either a musician, someone related to a musician, or a fan. We have no other leads, no direction to go."

"And you figure this UNSUB—that's what you call him, isn't it, Andie?—will be smart enough to figure out, even without my name, that I'm the local musician. Then what?" I can't resist the dig at Andie.

"We're not sure exactly," Cook says. "I don't think it's enough to stop him, but it might give us some time, cause him, or her, to rethink things. We just don't know."

I shake my head. "In the meantime, I'm supposed to do what? Just go on with life as normal?"

"We're going to issue a denial that you're the musician. In fact, Ted has already taken care of that."

Rollins just sits there looking arrogant. "You know what, Rollins," I say, "you didn't have to give them my name. If this killer is as smart as you all think he is, he wouldn't need my name.''

Rollins looks up. "Just for the record, Horne, I was against you being in on this from the get-go. I still am. The last thing we need is some cockamamie musician—''

"All right, Ted, that's enough,'' Cook says.

I'm already headed for the door. I want out. Coop gets up. "I'll walk you out.''

I give Andie one last look, and Coop and I ride down to the garage.

We stop at my car. I light a cigarette and lean against the door, my mind still on the newspaper story.

"Well,'' Coop says, "here's another fine mess I've got you into.'' He taps his finger on my chest. "You know I had nothing to do with leaking you to the media. I was madder than you when I heard. That's why they were all so quiet up there.'' He looks away at some cars pulling into the garage. "Andie didn't either, in case you're wondering.''

"I wasn't.''

"Well, you were a little rough on her. She nearly ate Rollins alive.''

"Rollins is—''

"An FBI prick. Hey, what else do you call someone who likes Kenny G?''

"Musically challenged?'' I know what Coop's doing, and I laugh in spite of myself. "Look, Coop. I didn't mind helping them, but I don't need this kind of publicity. The guy at Quarter Tone asked me about this stuff when we talked.''

"I know,'' Coop says. "It'll probably blow over. Just hang in there. Get some sleep.'' He starts toward his car. "I'll stay in touch.''

I'M TOO KEYED UP to go home. I drive up the Coast Highway to Malibu and park in a deserted lot at Zuma Beach. I sit there for over an hour, listening to the surf, running everything over in my mind, finally realizing there's nothing I can do. Cook was right. It's done. Even if there's a denial, nobody will believe it.

When I get home, my answering machine light is blinking crazily. I don't even check the messages. Unplugging the phone, I just take off my clothes and fall into bed. When I wake up, it's almost dark. I stand in the shower long enough to wake up and then put on some coffee. I plug in the phone and face the answering machine.

The messages are predictable. Coop, Andie, Natalie, and Jeff Lasorda, who hums the *Dragnet* theme and then says, "Call me, guy."

Paul Westbrook simply wants me to call him immediately, probably to cancel the recording date. There are also two calls from someone who identifies himself as a reporter. That's one I won't answer.

I decide to call Natalie first, but before I can dial, the phone rings. Without thinking, I pick it up.

"Hello." Nothing. "Hello. Anybody there?" I'm just about to hang up when I hear music, a saxophone. I listen for a moment. "Who is this?"

"Oh, you know who it is." The voice is low, at once smoky and clear. "This is a test, Evan. Who's that playing?"

"John Coltrane."

"Which album?"

"*Soultrane.*"

"Right again. And the tune?"

" 'Good Bait.' "

"This is going to be so much fun, Evan."

"How do you know my name? Who is this?"

"I need you, Evan. You're going to help me."

"Help you do what? If this is some kind of joke—"

"Just shut up and listen." I strain my ears, but there's nothing but Coltrane's unmistakable tenor saxophone sound and some breathing.

"Sorry, Evan. I got angry for a moment, like I did with Ty Rodman. He wouldn't listen either."

I turn around, stare out the window at the darkness. My legs are suddenly rubbery. "What do you know about Ty Rodman?"

"I know he's dead." The voice is calm, dispassionate.

"So does anyone who reads the newspaper or watches television. Don't call—"

"You found the feather, didn't you, Evan?"

"What feather? What are you talking about?"

"The one in Rodman's horn case. I know it was you. Just like the one in Cochise's case. Beautiful and pure and white."

I slide down the counter, find myself sitting on the floor, and wonder how I got there.

"What do you want?" The sound of my own voice is shaky, stuck in my throat.

"Don't worry, Evan. You have nothing to fear. We'll talk again." There's a few more seconds of Coltrane, then nothing.

I sit on the floor for several minutes, my head against the counter, the phone still in my hand. My pulse is racing. I feel cold. When I finally get up, my hand is shaking as I light a cigarette. I think for a moment, then dial Andie Lawrence's number.

"Special Agent Lawrence."

"Andie, it's Evan."

"I'm so glad you called. I—"

"Just listen to me, Andie." I take a breath. "Andie, I just got a call from the killer."

"What? Oh, my God! How do you know it was him?"

"She knew about the feathers. You hear me, Andie. She knew about the feathers."

"She?"

"Yes, the killer is a woman."

SIX

I JUMP WHEN the phone rings again. It penetrates the silence, the sound magnified, the space between rings agonizingly long. Nothing but the hum of the refrigerator to compete with it. Mesmerized, as if it's a poisonous snake coiled to strike me, I wait tensely for the third ring. The machine picks up, and I hear my own voice.

"Hi, this is Evan Horne. Who are you? Leave a message and let me know."

"Evan, please pick up, it's Andie Lawrence." Her voice sounds desperate, pleading. "Evan?"

I close my eyes, realize I've been holding my breath. I feel my shoulders relax as I exhale deeply and reach for the phone. "Yes, Andie."

"Evan, thank God. When you hung up, I thought something happened. I—"

"I just couldn't talk anymore. Something did happen, Andie."

"Evan, are you all right? You sound, I don't know, distant."

I know what she's hearing. I can't seem to make my voice go beyond a monotone. "I'm here, Andie. I, I don't know what to do."

"All right, Evan. Listen to me. You've got to snap out of it. You must have a tape recorder, a small cassette player?"

"Yes, have to find it."

"Good, get it out and keep it near the phone. Keep it

near the phone. Do you understand? If she calls back, you can at least record half of the conversation.''

"Yeah, okay.'' I feel like I've been under water, but now I'm slowly swimming toward the ray of light on the surface. "I think I have one of those attachments to record the caller. I used it for interviews when I was writing.''

"Good. That's it, focus, Evan.'' Andie says. "Find it if you can, and hook it up. We'll bring some equipment. I've patched through a call to Cooper. He's on the way.''

Even now I can hear a siren wailing in the distance. "Okay. Andie?''

"Yes.''

"What's going to happen now?''

"Just hang in there, Evan. We'll talk about it when I get there. We're on the way.''

I put the phone down. The siren is louder now, probably only a couple of blocks away. I open the door and look out. It's twilight. A gray haze filters back from the beach. Lights glimmer softly in windows across the street.

Leaving the door ajar for Coop, I turn on some lights, then sit down on the couch and light a cigarette. My head is starting to clear when I hear Coop's car screech to a stop, his footsteps quicken up the steps, then stop.

He pushes the door open with his foot, comes in with his gun drawn, his body in a crouch. "Evan?''

"I'm here, Coop.''

He sees me on the couch, straightens up, and holsters his gun. He glances around quickly, then sits down next to me.

"Jesus, I saw the door.... Andie called me. I was on the way home.'' He studies my face. "Shook you up, huh?'' he says. "You okay?''

I look at him and know he sees I'm not.

"You got some booze in this place?'' He goes to the kitchen and starts opening cabinet doors. "Scotch, right?''

He doesn't wait for me to answer. He brings the bottle of Dewars and a glass and pours a healthy shot. "Drink up, sport."

I gulp half of it, feel it burn going down, then settle warmly in my stomach. "Andie said to hook up my cassette player to the phone. I forgot. It's in that drawer under the TV."

Coop digs in the drawer. Throwing aside cassettes and speaker wires, he comes up with it. "This it?"

"Yeah, I think the recording wire is still in it."

"Right," Coop says. He goes to the phone, plugs in the recorder, and attaches one end of the wire with the suction cup to the receiver. "There's a tape in this. You need it?"

"No, go ahead." I listen to the whir as he rewinds the tape, picks up the receiver and listens for a dial tone, then hangs it up.

He sits down with me again, puts his hand on my shoulder. "Listen to me, man. This place is going to be swarming with FBI and police any minute, and you've got to be ready."

"What do you mean?" He's leaning toward me. His eyes flick to the sound of more sirens.

"The FBI likes overkill. They don't know what to expect. They've probably told the cops to surround the house. I'll handle that, but Andie, maybe Wendell, are going to be here any minute asking you a lot of questions, so get it together. They're going to want to know your first impressions, anything you can remember about the voice. This is vital. You with me?"

"Yeah, I'm okay, but I need some ice in this, or I'm going to be drunk by the time they get here."

"Coming up." Coop takes my glass and goes back to the kitchen. I can hear him in the fridge, dumping ice cubes in the sink, then he's back. "Here you go," he says.

I take another short drink, lean back against the couch, and close my eyes.

"I'm fucked, Coop. You know that, don't you?" When he doesn't answer, I open my eyes and look at him.

He looks away. I know he doesn't want to answer. "We'll see."

There's loud knocking on the door. When Coop opens it, I can see at least four dark uniforms. Venice Police. Coop turns back once to glance at me, then steps outside. He knows one of them. He shows them his badge, gives them some instructions I can't make out, and they go back out to the street. I watch it all like it's a movie unfolding in front of me.

Coop leaves the door open and comes back to me. "They're going to secure the street, take care of traffic. You okay?"

"Yeah, I'll be all right."

We sit in silence for a few minutes. I can feel Coop's edginess. He's like a rottweiler on a choke chain that smells trouble. I close my eyes again, rerun the call in my mind, know I'll never forget the voice.

A few minutes later, Andie comes in, followed by two other guys in jeans and warm-up jackets. I've never seen them before. They're both carrying cardboard boxes. One also has a small plastic toolbox. Coop nods Andie toward me. "I'm going to check outside," he says.

Andie looks at me. "Where's your phone, Evan?"

"It's—"

"Over here," one of the guys says.

Andie nods at them. "Do it."

I watch one of them take out a tape recorder, wires. They're fast and efficient. One opens the tool kit, starts unscrewing the phone receiver. His buddy hooks up the tape recorder after disconnecting mine and pushing it aside on the countertop.

Andie watches them work. In just a few minutes they have everything set up. One of them checks for a dial tone. "We're in business," he says.

"Okay," Andie says. "I'll show him how to work it. Thanks, guys." They don't even look at me as they leave.

Andie sits down on the couch, eyes the drink in front of me. "Are you okay? We need to talk."

"Yeah, I'm fine." I'm not, really. I still hear that voice in my head. *You're going to help me, Evan.* What did she mean?

Andie takes out a pad and pen. "Okay, tell me everything that happened."

I take a deep breath. "Okay, I had just finished playing back my messages when the phone rang. I wasn't even thinking. I just picked it up, thought it might be Natalie."

"And what did you hear first?"

"Nothing at first, just silence, then music."

"What was it? Did you recognize it?"

"Coltrane, John Coltrane, saxophone, an old recording. The album is called *Soultrane,* the song was 'Good Bait.' "

Andie writes it all down, checks the spelling with me. "Did you hear anything else? Background noise, anything like that?"

I think for a moment, take a drag on my cigarette, and exhale. "A blowing sound, just like that." I watch as Andie writes on her pad. *Maybe a smoker.*

"Good, that's good," she says. "Anything else?"

"No, I don't think so. Just the music, the blowing sound, and the voice."

"Okay, describe the voice. You're sure it was a woman."

"Yeah, I'm sure, it was…smoky, low, not a real high pitch."

"It couldn't have been someone using something to disguise the voice? Any kind of echo you could detect?"

"No, I don't think so."

"Okay, tell me exactly what she said, what you said, as best as you can remember."

Andie transcribes the conversation, then has me read it over.

"Yeah, that's it. Then she hung up after a few more seconds of music."

"Still Coltrane?"

"Yeah, that was playing all the time in the background."

Andie reads over her notes, then underlines three sentences: *This is going to be so much fun. I need you, Evan. You're going to help me.* "Any idea what she meant by that?"

"None."

"It wasn't anybody you recognized, was it?"

I shake my head slowly.

"Okay, and this is important. You're sure she was the one who mentioned the bird feathers?"

"Absolutely." I put out my cigarette. "It's the killer, isn't it?"

Andie pauses a beat, taps her pad. "No one else knows about the feathers."

I look up then and see Natalie standing in front of us, Coop just behind her. I didn't even notice them come in.

"Evan, what happened? What's going on?" Natalie is in a white warm-up suit, some kind of crinkly material. She's made up, and her hair is brushed back off her face. She looks ready to go out.

Andie stands up and holds out her hand. "I'm Special

Agent Lawrence. You must be Natalie. I believe we talked on the phone.''

I watch them size each other up. Natalie takes Andie's hand briefly. "Hi," she says, then looks back at me. "Evan?"

"I'm sorry, Natalie," Andie says. "I'll be through here in a few minutes." She nods at Coop, who takes Natalie by the elbow and starts to walk her out. Natalie turns, looking back over her shoulder. "Evan, are you all right?"

I nod and look to Andie.

"Sorry," Andie says. She smiles slightly. "I just want to keep him focused here." She turns back to me, then looks at her pad again. "Now anything else at all you can remember, no matter how small."

I light another cigarette and think. "No, nothing. Wasn't that enough?"

Andie nods her head, raises her eyebrows. "Yeah, it was plenty."

"She's going to call me again, isn't she?"

Andie holds my gaze for a moment before answering. "Yes, but not tonight, probably not for a couple of days, which is good, gives us some time."

"How do you know?"

"This was an exploratory call, just to let you know she's out there, knows who you are, but there will be more. You can count on it."

"What do I do then?"

"We'll talk about it tomorrow." Andie looks toward the phone. "C'mon," she says.

She shows me which buttons to press to activate the recorder. It looks brand-new, very high-tech. "This will record all incoming calls. We'll try, of course, but I don't think there's a chance in hell of tracing her. Every call you get, you push this record button first. We want her voice on tape.''

She reaches into one of the boxes and takes out a cellular phone wrapped in plastic. It also looks brand-new, and not much bigger than a pack of cigarettes. She hits the talk button, listens for a moment, keys in some other numbers, and finally presses Off.

''You keep this with you at all times, okay? Even if you leave the house to just go buy cigarettes or a newspaper. If you're not home, your number will be forwarded to the cell phone. I'm the only one who will have the cell phone number, so we can talk without being on your home line.'' She thinks for a moment. ''Maybe Cooper too, if you want.''

I nod. ''What about Natalie?''

''No,'' she says, ''I don't think so. I've programmed my direct line in the cell phone. It's hooked to my beeper.'' She hands me the cell phone. I look at it for a moment, dreading what's on the other end. I've never even had call forwarding. Now I've got a cell phone, caller ID, and a direct line to the FBI.

''One more thing,'' Andie says. ''We'll have someone on the street, unmarked car, at least till we know what's going on, okay?''

''Andie?''

''Yes.''

''What do you think she meant?''

''You've got to be ready. She wants you to do something.''

I SIT FOR A long time on the couch with Natalie, just holding her. The TV is on low, but neither of us are really watching it. The cell phone lies on the coffee table in front of us. When it rings, we both jump. ''Jesus,'' I say.

I pick it up, look at Natalie, and press the talk button. Natalie sits on the edge of the couch, her hand to her mouth. "Hello."

"Relax, sport, it's just me checking in."

I sigh and sag back on the couch. "Coop. You scared the shit out of me."

"Just checking the line. Andie gave me the number. I'm only a beeper away, remember that. Get some sleep if you can. You've got a long day tomorrow."

"Thanks, Coop. See you."

"Bye."

I turn off the phone. Natalie flops back, runs her hands through her hair. "God, this is nerve-racking."

"Tell me about it."

Natalie picks up the phone and suddenly giggles. "I'm sorry, I was just thinking."

"What?"

"Now you've got a cell phone, for jazz emergencies."

I laugh with her. "Yeah," I say, "come quick, I need some blues changes on the double."

It's not much, but it breaks the tension momentarily. When we settle down, we look at each other for a moment. "It's going to be okay, Evan."

"I wish I could believe that."

"You have Coop and the FBI, Special Agent Lawrence." She shakes her finger at me. "You better watch it, buddy. She's definitely not forty and frumpy, but it looks like she knows what's she's doing."

"Let's hope so."

I SLEEP BADLY, of course, tossing and turning most of the night. Twice I wake up and listen for the phone. For a while I just sit on the edge of the bed and watch Natalie sleep, thinking maybe she shouldn't be here. That will be a battle.

Former cop or not, Andie Lawrence will want to keep Natalie at a distance. Those lines have already been drawn.

I lie back down, squeeze my eyes shut, and feel nothing till Natalie is shaking me. "Evan, it's almost eight. You have to be at the Federal Building at nine."

I feel like I haven't slept at all. After coffee and a long, hot shower, I walk Natalie to her car nearly half a block away. Just down the street, I catch a glimpse of a man sitting in a dark sedan. He looks up as we pass, gives me a brief wave.

"Who's that?" Natalie asks.

"I don't know. Efrem Zimbalist Junior, my babysitter? I'll call you later, probably from a pay phone."

Natalie looks surprised. "Why?"

"I don't know if they want me to tie up my phone. I'll find out."

Natalie gets in her car and starts the engine. She looks up at me. "It's going to get complicated, isn't it?"

"It already is."

I GET TO THE Federal Building just after nine. Andie is pacing around the lobby, talking with a security guard, looking at her watch. She cuts him off in midsentence when she sees me walking toward her.

"Bad night?" she asks.

"Do I look that bad?" I just threw on jeans and a pullover shirt.

She smiles. "No, not at all."

"Well, I've had better."

She nods. "We're all set up. We want to go over the call again, see if we can come up with anything else, something you might have missed."

"I don't think so, but whatever you think."

"Listen," Andie says. "I know this has gone farther than

we thought, but before we go upstairs, I just wanted you to know, I had nothing to do with the press leak. It was Ted. I'm not excusing him, but he got sandbagged by the reporter.''

I look out the doors to Wilshire Boulevard. Traffic is heavy, and a small group of demonstrators, mostly men, are walking back and forth, carrying handheld placards, handing out flyers to passing pedestrians. One of the signs reads, GULF WAR VETS NEED BENEFITS TOO!

''Well, it doesn't really matter now, does it. I didn't mean to jump on you, but I was really pissed.''

Andie follows my gaze. ''That goes on all the time. Somebody is always protesting something.'' She turns back to me. ''It does matter. You had every right to be angry. I want you to feel you can trust me.''

''I guess I have no choice, do I?''

''Okay. I'll settle for that now.''

We start toward the elevators, but Andie stops. ''Where's your phone?''

''Shit, I left it in the car.''

Andie glares at me for a moment. ''Get it.''

I run back down to the garage and grab the phone. It's still sitting on the seat. I jog back to the lobby, thinking maybe I subconsciously just don't want it with me.

I hold it up to show Andie. ''Here,'' she says, holding out her hand. ''You don't need the call forwarding on while we're here.'' She shows me how to program the phone. ''Turn it back on when you leave here, though.''

I give her a mock salute. She shepherds me through security, and we go up to the seventeenth floor. This time it's not Wendell's office but a different room that's set up with several agents managing recording equipment, some small tables, and the whiteboard.

Wendell Cook is talking with one of the agents, and Ted

Rollins is looking over some computer printouts. They both turn to us when Andie and I come in.

Cook comes over and is almost consoling as he shakes my hand. "Don't worry, Evan, we're really on this, and with your help we hope to wrap it up very quickly."

"Thanks, I feel better already."

"I know," Cook says, picking up my sarcasm. "But we do know what we're doing. If it turns out the caller is the killer, we have a great advantage in this one."

"What?"

"You," Cook says. "I think Andie will agree. Granted, this is not the usual scenario, there are some different twists, but we've also never had someone with the inside knowledge you have."

I look at Andie. "He's right, Evan. The more you help, the quicker we can reach a solution. You know things it wouldn't even occur to us to ask, so jump in when something comes up, no matter how small. This is a two-way street. We'll be as forthcoming as possible."

I can translate that on my own. The FBI will decide what and if I need to know.

"Okay," Cook says. "Let's get started. The first thing we want to do is go over the transcript of the call."

We gather around the table, and Andie passes out copies. When I get mine, I look at it, surprised to see my own words in print. "Look this over," Andie says. "If there's anything that doesn't look right, tell us."

It's like the first reading of a play. I scan through it slowly, the sound of the voice ringing in my head as the words come into focus. Andie or someone has typed it up in script format. All the lines are numbered.

1 E.H.:   Hello? Hello? Anybody there? (music playing, John Coltrane, "Good Bait." Composer: Tadd Dameron)

2 E.H.:	Who is this?
3 Voice:	Oh, you know who it is. This is a test, Evan. Who's that playing?
4 E.H.:	John Coltrane.

My eyes go back to the first line. "How did you know Tadd Dameron wrote 'Good Bait'?" I ask Andie.

"I bought the CD last night on the way home."

"Okay, okay, enough with the music," Rollins says. "Why didn't you just hang up?"

I glance up at Rollins. We've somehow come to an unspoken though probably temporary truce. "I don't know. Doesn't everybody do this? I thought maybe there was a bad connection—sometimes people are distracted for a few seconds when you answer the phone. Then I heard the music."

"What did you think then?" Cook wants to know.

"I thought maybe I was going to hear some musician's voice, someone playing music in the background when they called."

Cook nods, satisfied with my answer. We all turn back to the pages of transcript. I read it all the way through. "Yeah, I think that's it."

"And you're sure that was the sequence about the bird feathers? You didn't maybe get smart and see if she knew about them, ask her, I mean?" Rollins asks.

Andie jumps in quickly. "Oh, for Christ's sake, Ted. Back off."

"Okay, okay," Rollins says. "I thought we were going to check everything."

"No, Ted," I say evenly. "This is the sequence."

"Okay," Andie says. "We're looking for voice inflection, speech patterns, and you're the only one who knows about that. Does anything else come to mind? What about when she says, 'Shut up and listen.' What happened there?''

"Yeah," I say. "She really sounded angry there. Her voice went up in pitch, and then there was a few seconds' silence. When she came back, her voice was back to the original pitch. Like she'd taken the time to get control of herself."

Andie, Cook, and Rollins all exchange glances. Cook may be in charge, but he's clearly deferring to Andie.

"Can you characterize her voice in the rest of the conversation?" Andie looks up, shrugs, searching her mind for words "Was it sincere, flip, emotional, anything like that?"

I lean back in my chair and think for a moment. "I have the impression she was smiling, amused, kind of a dreamlike quality, like she'd had a couple of drinks or was smoking grass."

"You'd know about that, wouldn't you?" Rollins puts in.

Somehow I manage to ignore him. "Except for the shut up part. Then at the end, when she said I was going to help her, it was, I guess you could say, earnest, determined."

"Good," Andie says. "That helps a lot." She makes some notes on her copy. "Now, for the big question. Any idea at all what she meant by that?"

I don't have to think about that one. "None. I don't have a clue."

"And it wasn't any voice you recognized. You're sure of that."

"Yes, absolutely."

We start over then, going through every word until I feel like a wrung-out sponge

Andie looks at me and then her watch. "Let's take a break. Come on, I'll buy you a cup of coffee."

On the way out, one of the technicians stops her and

hands her a slip of paper. "You had two calls," she says, catching me off guard. "Jeff Lasorda and Paul West-brook."

I take the slip of paper from her. "How do you know that?"

"We accessed your answering machine," she says, as if it's routine.

"I need to answer these," I say. "Jeff is my bass player, and Westbrook is the CD producer. What do I tell them? They're probably calling about the news stories, and West-brook probably wants to cancel the date."

Andie thinks for a moment. "Yes, answer them. Tell them—"

"What?"

"Nothing about what we're doing, just that the press exaggerated your involvement, something like that."

"That might work with Jeff, but Westbrook is about to invest some money in me. He's going to want to know if this is going to interfere with the record."

"Tell him not to worry. He's a businessman. Tell him you were assisting the FBI in a very minor way." Andie looks at me directly then. "We can help there, you know, intervene if necessary. I don't want you to lose the record-ing date."

"Hold off on that," I say. "I don't want the FBI leaning on the guy I'm going to record for. Let me see what he says first."

"Okay, you handle it," Andie says. "Use the phone in my office. I'll bring us some coffee."

I call Jeff first, and it seems to work on him. I assure him the record is still on, we'll rehearse again this week, and well, you know, the press.

"Hey, man," Jeff says. "That's cool. You can call the album *Misterioso*."

"Think Monk already took that one, Jeff."

"Yeah, I know. We'll think of something. Listen, if you need a place, you know, to get away from things, you can always crash here."

"Thanks, Jeff. I appreciate it. I'll be in touch."

Paul Westbrook isn't so easy when I call him.

"Listen, Evan, I don't believe everything I read or see on TV either, but the FBI?"

"It's all been blown out of proportion, Paul. They just wanted some information about the musicians who were killed. Did I know them, what kind of music did they play, that kind of thing."

"How were they killed? Stabbings, I think the papers said."

"I don't know any more than you," I say. "You know how the FBI is."

Westbrook relents, but he doesn't sound totally convinced. "I just want you to be able to concentrate on the music without distractions." He laughs. "Hell, it's not the publicity. That might even help with marketing, you know?"

I wonder what Westbrook would say if he knew I'd had a phone call from the killer herself.

"Believe me, Paul, I want the same thing," I say. Andie comes in, carrying two cups of coffee. She sits them on her desk and hauls out the ashtray. She goes to the window and opens it, but I know she's listening. "I'll keep you up to date, but there's nothing to worry about."

"Okay, Evan. Thanks for getting back to me."

I hang up the phone and look at Andie.

"Is he okay with things?" she asks.

"Yeah, I think so. At least for now." I take a sip of coffee and light a cigarette. "There's someone else I want to ask you about."

"Natalie, right? She's a very attractive woman."

"That's what she says about you. Calls you the FBI babe." Andie colors slightly.

She grins and nods her head. "Well, that's a first. Coming from Natalie, I'll take it as a compliment."

"I'm just wondering…if this, the calls, continue, I don't want her in any danger. We kind of halfway live together. She stays at my place a lot unless she's really studying."

"Yeah, law school is tough. She was a cop for a while too, right?"

"Santa Monica Police. She's known Coop for a long time. He introduced us."

Andie taps her fingers on the desk. "Okay, you can give her the cell phone number, but if you need to"—she hesitates, looking for the right phrase—"spend time with her, do it in public." She stops, flustered. "That didn't come out right, did it? I don't think she should stay with you until we see where we are. In the meantime, Wendell wants me to handle working with you when and if we get another call."

"Natalie is going to love that."

"I don't think she'd like Ted much either."

"Trust me, she'd like Ted a lot better, but I wouldn't."

We go back to the other room and spend another two hours going over the transcript until there doesn't seem to be one more ounce of meaning that can be extracted. By two-thirty I've had enough, and from the looks of them, so has everyone else.

"I guess that's it for today," Cook says.

Rollins throws his pen down. "I don't know, I think this is just somebody fucking with us."

"Wrong, Ted," Andie says. "What about the bird feathers? Nobody knew about that except us and the killer."

"Horne knew." He throws it out like a challenge, and I'm just tired and irritated enough to take him up on it.

Andie starts to say something more, but I hold up my hand. "Rollins, the FBI must have been desperate when they hired you. Are you so stupid that you think I'd make up this call, get myself into all this, just so I could see the inside of the Federal Building? Don't you think I hear every word of that conversation in my mind forever?"

Rollins just sits there, looking at me. Andie and Cook are silent for a moment, and I catch the technicians across the room stopping to listen. Finally, Cook breaks through the hum of the air-conditioning.

"Well, like I said, I guess that's all for today."

"Thanks, Evan. This has been a big help," Andie says.

I go back downstairs and through the lobby doors. The demonstrators are gone, but some of the flyers have been dropped on the sidewalk. I head for my car, digging for my keys, anxious to call Natalie. When I insert the key, my hand freezes. It's already unlocked.

I open the door and see a piece of paper on the driver's seat. It's one of the flyers. I glance at it briefly and start to throw it away. But it's the writing at the bottom of the page that suddenly grips my attention. The printing is done with a red felt-tip pen in a white space on the flyer.

I take out my cell phone and use it for the first time. Andie picks up immediately. "Evan?"

"Andie, you better come down to the parking garage. There's something you need to see."

"On the way."

I light a cigarette and lean against my car. Wendell Cook was wrong.

That's not all for today.

SEVEN

On Coltrane's Soultrane
Jazz is always great Good Bait
Tadd's Long Gone—Delight

"WHAT THE HELL is that?" Ted Rollins asks, squinting over Andie's shoulder at the flyer. She's holding it carefully by one corner.

"Do you know what haiku is?" Andie ignores Rollins and nods her head like she's counting silently. She's talking to me.

"Isn't it some kind of Japanese poetry?"

"Did you touch it?" Rollins asks me. He looks like he wants to draw his gun.

I roll my eyes. "No, Ted, it just flew into my hands by magic."

"Come on," Andie says. "Let's get this upstairs."

"Do you need me?" Andie stops, turns around, and looks at me like I'm crazy. "Just checking," I say and follow her and Rollins back inside.

We wait in her office for a fingerprint report, but she's already copied the poem onto a notepad. My ashtray is still out, so I smoke while Andie is on the phone to the UCLA English department.

While she's put on hold, she tells me, "I've known this guy for quite a while. I want to check something." She looks away and grabs a pencil. "Dr. Collier? It's Andie Lawrence. I'm fine. Glad to hear it. Listen, I've got a quick question for you. What's the format for a haiku?"

I watch Andie as she listens, takes some notes, underlines the number *17*. "Got it. Thanks so much," she says. "No, I'm not studying poetry." She laughs. "You too. Bye."

She hangs up the phone and counts the syllables in the poem again, marking each with her pencil. She looks at it for a moment, then drops the pencil on the desk and swivels toward me.

"It is haiku," she says. "Seventeen syllables and usually broken down into three-line patterns of five, seven, and five for each line. That's exactly what we've got here." She taps the pad again.

"Well, so what? You look worried."

"I am. We're dealing with someone extremely bright here."

"Why, because she can write a three-line poem about jazz? I don't get it."

Andie shakes her head. "No, it's not only that. Haiku form is taught in a lot of English classes. Haikus are usually about nature, but she's able to use the pattern, incorporate dialogue from her phone call with you. Clever and very smart." She taps the pad again, continues to look at the poem. "I recognize everything from the call. Coltrane, Soultrane, but what about the last line? Tadd's long gone—Delight. Tadd is for Tadd Dameron, who wrote 'Good Bait,' but what about the long gone and the last word, delight?"

"You're right, she is clever," I say. "Tadd Dameron is dead—long gone—and 'Tadd's Delight' is—"

"Also one of his compositions?" Andie looks up from the pad.

"Exactly." I stand by the window, looking out at the San Diego Freeway, choked with traffic, a narrow layer of yellow smog on the horizon. For once I wish I was out there, with nothing to worry about but getting home.

"What about the title 'Good Bait'? Does it have any significance? I mean, did Dameron have something in mind?" Andie asks.

"Hard to tell. Sometimes a composer has someone or something—a word, a phrase—in mind with a title, but a lot of tunes are named after they're recorded."

I remember seeing a documentary film about Charlie Parker. A very earnest interviewer asked him about the titles of several tracks he had recorded. Bird just smiled patiently and said, "I have no idea. Those tunes were named after I left the studio."

I crush out my cigarette and sit down again. "So what do you think she's doing?" I ask Andie.

"There's the obvious connotation of good bait."

"Well, she's on the same page as the FBI. Wendell's plan worked just fine. I'm the bait, right?"

"Maybe," Andie concedes. "She's showing off, for one thing. She wants us to know how smart and clever she is, how much she knows about jazz. The poem itself is to confirm the call, let you know she's still around and knows where you are."

"Great," I say, "my car is not even safe in the FBI garage."

Before Andie can answer, there's a knock on the door. "Come in," Andie calls.

A man in a short-sleeved shirt and tie and a brush cut opens the door and holds up a plastic bag with the flyer inside. "Zero, couple of smudges is all," he says.

Andie nods her head. "Thanks," she says. He hands her the bag, glances at me, and goes out. "I didn't expect any," she says to me, "but at least we've got another little piece of information. It adds up quickly."

"Are you getting a picture of her now?"

"Yeah, she's not only clever, she's a bit arrogant, and I

don't like that. She's enjoying this. She wants someone to
acknowledge her cleverness. That's going to be you, Evan.
You're the link.''

"Me?"

"When she calls again, you're going to have to keep her
talking."

I LEAVE ANDIE still pondering the poem at the Federal
Building and drive aimlessly down Wilshire Boulevard toward the beach.

By the time I reach Lincoln, I realize I'm famished and
thirsty. I pull into a drive-through for a couple of tacos and
the largest Coke they have. At Third Street, I stop for a
paper at a corner news rack, then ease down the California
Incline to the Pacific Coast Highway and start looking for
a beach parking lot.

I find an almost deserted lot and park close to the beach.
Pulling up at the edge of the sand, I roll down the window
and wolf down the empty calories, watching the surf roll
in and the huge clouds on the horizon, feeling the glare of
the sun, and breathing in the sea air.

Having grown up here, I've always found the beach to
be a special place for me to clear my head, get a perspective
on things. I try to focus on songs and arrangements for the
CD, but it's no use. The voice, the call, and now, the poem,
keep breaking in on any thoughts about music. I get out of
the car—this time I remember the cell phone and make sure
the call forwarding is on—dump the remains of my lunch
in a trash can, sit on the concrete wall, and get a cigarette
going. A few strollers pass by, nod, but it's mostly noisy
seagulls I have for company.

Four people have been killed, stabbed to death by some
crazy who's now decided to talk about it and send me a
poem. How did I get so lucky? Is she still in L.A.? Two

of the murders were in New York; one in L.A., one in San Francisco. And now she wants me to help her do something. What? What could I possibly do for her?

I grab the *Times* out of the car. There's a long story about the murders, complete with photos of the victims and their backgrounds. Most of it is a rehash of earlier stories, but the quotes from other musicians—pop jazz artists with big recording contracts—indicate that everyone is taking things very seriously. Some dates have been canceled, security at all concerts has been doubled. I don't even recognize some of the names, but I'm not alone.

There are quotes from some mainstream musicians, obviously putting on reporters. "Cochise?" saxophonist Phil Woods says. "He plays jazz? I thought he was an Indian." Dark, but it's the only funny thing about the article. Nowhere is there any mention of my name, but there's no mention of the denial that Wendell Cook promised either.

I search the paper and find it finally on page twenty-two, in a small paragraph that essentially says that the previously reported story that named pianist Evan Horne is assisting the FBI has not been confirmed. Cook has tried to minimize the damage, but I'd still like to spend a few minutes alone with Ted Rollins. I can't figure out why he's so hostile toward me. I'll probably never know, but it's hard to believe it's just a personality conflict. Disgusted, I drop the paper in a trash can.

Despite Andie's okay, I hike across the parking lot to call Natalie from a pay phone near the public restrooms. I get her machine and tell her I'll call later. We will have to talk. I agree with Andie that Natalie should be kept out of it, but it's going to be difficult; there's so much I can't tell her.

I stroll back to my car, one last look at the ocean, but the cell phone, sticking out of my back pocket, takes me by surprise. I spin around when it rings. I reach for the phone, get back in the car, roll up the window, and make sure I press the right button.

"Evan Horne."

Andie said maybe a couple of days for the next call, but she was wrong. The music is already playing this time. Pianist Bill Evans, one of the Village Vanguard-Sunday afternoon sessions. Scott Lafaro, bass; Paul Motian, drums.

"You like this one, don't you?" the voice says. It's the same smoky, low pitch.

Think, what does Andie want me to do? Is the call being recorded? I'd already turned off the call forwarding. How did she get this number? Keep her talking.

"Yeah, I do. What can I do for you?"

"Oh, you can do a lot for me, Evan. You were naughty going to the FBI. Don't you trust me?"

I try to keep my voice even. "They came to me. I don't even know your name. How can I trust you?"

She pauses, while Scott Lafaro's bass resonates in my ear. Even on the phone the notes are clear. I dig out a pad and pen from the glove box and write down, *Good sound system.*

"Does that mean you want to talk?"

"Do I have a choice?"

"No, Evan, you don't. Remember that." She pauses to let that sink in. "You can call me Gillian. Do you like that?"

"Sure, it's fine. Gillian. Okay, Gillian, I'm going to be honest with you. The FBI is monitoring my calls, you must know that."

"Do you think I'm stupid?" There it is again. Rise in pitch, short outburst of anger, then several seconds' silence. Bill Evans has it again now, his fingers flying over the keyboard as he exchanges eight-bar breaks with drummer Motian. "You're on a cell phone, Evan. So am I."

"Okay, okay, I'm not trying to make you angry. I'm just trying to be up front about how things stand. It's out of my control."

"That's where you're wrong, Evan. It's completely in your hands."

I hear a metallic sound, then the blowing noise as she exhales. I write: *Zippo type lighter.* "What is?"

"Whether I keep still or not."

"Keep still?" I grip the phone tighter, glance in the rear-view mirror. A car is pulling up about a hundred yards behind me. I twist around in the seat, but it's only a man with his dog.

"Leave the jazz pretenders alone. Some of them are probably getting worried now." There's a lilt, almost a smile, in her voice now.

"Keep still? That's your euphemism for not killing?" I blurt it out without thinking. There's a moment of silence when I think she's going to hang up.

"I'm sorry, it's just—"

"Forget it." She says it quickly, like she doesn't want to talk about it anymore. "Euphemism. I like that. This is going to be interesting. Let's set some ground rules here, Evan, shall we?"

"I don't know what you're talking about."

"First, FBI or not, here's our bargain. As long as you keep talking to me, I'll be still. Second, forget about your friends at the FBI tracing the calls. Even if they do, I'll be gone before they get here, so tell them not to bother. If I decide not to be still, it will be your fault, Evan. Do you understand me?"

I slide down in the seat of the Camaro, look at the surf,

feel the sun burning through the windshield. "Yes, I understand," I say quietly.

Her tone changes now. "Good, then we understand each other."

"I'm sorry, I could never conceive doing what you've done."

"Think about it, Evan. They didn't deserve to live, don't you realize that? Calling themselves jazz musicians, calling what they play jazz. They're defiling the memory of Bird and Dizzy and Miles, playing that shit, that electronic, wimpy, worthless shit, and calling it jazz."

She runs out of breath then, takes another drag of her cigarette, and exhales. I squeeze my eyes shut. Is this any crazier than the guy who took a shot at Ringo Starr? I wait a second more, thinking, stalling. "Is that what this is about?"

"No, it's only part of it. The other part you're going to help me with."

"How? I don't know how I could help you."

"You will. It's about my brother; that's what you're going to help me with."

"You have a brother? Does he know what you've done?"

"My brother knows nothing, Evan. He's dead." Her voice is bitter.

"I'm, I'm sorry, I—"

"I don't want your sympathy. Just listen." She spits out the words, then calms down again. "My brother killed himself, so the police say. And he might have, after what was done to him. But I have to be sure. You know about being sure, don't you, Evan?"

"I don't understand."

"Last year. You had to be sure about Clifford Brown, and before that, Wardell Gray. I know all about you, Evan.

You couldn't let go. You're a seeker of the truth, and you're good at it. Do you know why?''

"Why?"

"Because you don't give up, and when it has to do with the music, you can't conceive giving up. That's why you fit into my plans perfectly.''

I take a deep breath, wipe the droplets of sweat from my forehead. "What plans?''

"Did you like my poem?'' She exhales again, and I imagine her smiling. Andie was right. She's showing off. Where is she? Driving around someplace in L.A.? I strain to hear some traffic noise over the music.

"That's enough for today. You'll find out soon enough. Tell that FBI bitch Lawrence you're going to keep talking to me. You're turned on by her, aren't you, Evan? Is it because she carries a gun?''

I don't answer. I don't know how.

"Remember our bargain, Evan. As long as you keep your end, nobody has anything to worry about. Break it…''

I pause a moment, thinking as her voice trails off. She knows she doesn't have to finish the sentence. There's so much more I want to know, but she seems just on the edge, like she can go either way.

"I'll keep talking to you, but you know they're going to catch you eventually.''

"Perhaps. I don't really care. I'll call again, Evan. You're going to get something that will explain everything.''

"What? How will I get it?''

"Let me worry about that, Evan. You've got rehearsing to do, for your CD.''

She turns up the music then, lets it play for a few seconds more. I shut my eyes, picturing the scene at the Vanguard. Bill Evans, head bent over the keyboard, hair in his eyes, the audience listening intently. Then the music stops, and Gillian is gone.

I press the off button, take a deep breath. Sweat pours off me. I can feel my pulse racing. I struggle out of the car, gulp air, and walk around, trying to clear my head. The sun is still warm, the surf still pounds, but everything has changed. When the phone rings again, I want to throw it out on the sand.

"Evan, it's Andie. That was her, right?"

"You mean you don't know? Didn't you trace it, record it?"

"No. She's on a cell phone, moving. We got the time. It's complicated. We don't know yet."

I sit down on the wall, not believing what Andie is telling me.

"Evan? You did good, though. You kept her talking. We've got to talk about this one, right away. Did she tell you her name?"

"Gillian. Her name is Gillian. She wants me to do something for her brother."

Even through the phone I can hear Andie sigh. "At least we have a name. She's no longer UNSUB. Gillian, such a pretty name."

"WELL, THIS IS a new way to hire a detective," Ted Rollins says. "Kill four people, then threaten to kill more if he doesn't deliver."

"Ted," Andie says. "Come on."

"We don't know for sure that's what she means," Wendell Cook puts in.

"I think we do." Coop has been sitting quietly, listening to the four of them analyze what I've told them about the call, trapped in this room at the Federal Building that I'm growing to hate. I feel like I live here.

Coop is right, and I know it. Gillian will dictate the play, and I'll have to keep talking to her, do whatever she wants as long as I can. Right now, I want to talk to Andie, but not in front of the others.

"Why can't you trace the call? Why wasn't it recorded?" I ask. "We must have talked for ten minutes."

"Seven minutes, forty-seven seconds," Rollins says, looking at a slip of paper. "That's how long your phone was engaged."

I lean my elbows on the table, my head in my hands, and watch them look at me as if they've just discovered I'm there.

"It's much harder with cell phones, Evan," Andie says. "We have to zero in on a moving tone. She could be switching phones. Anything is possible." She pauses and looks at the others, but the explanation is really for me. "With call forwarding, the incoming call to your place goes back to the phone-company switching center first, so there was no recording. We didn't figure on that."

Andie shrugs and turns back to me. "She bypassed your home phone and called you directly on the cell."

I look up at Andie. Her face is pinched into a frown. "How did she get my cell phone number? I thought nobody but you and Coop had it." I glance quickly at Ted Rollins.

"Cloning cell phones is amateur stuff," he says. "All you need is a scanner. In L.A. it's as easy as buying a gun."

"She knew you'd have a tape set up at my house, so she bypassed that, called me direct on the cell phone, right? So the phone is cloned."

Andie shrugs. "Probably."

"Great." I get up and walk around. "She knows everything about me—the other cases I was involved in, the recording—and you're telling me there's nothing you can do, I have to go along with whatever she says?"

"What you tell us she said. You're not going along with anything," Rollins says, "except what we tell you to do."

I feel Coop stiffen. He knows I'm about to go across the table at Rollins.

"No, you listen to me, Rollins. Until I came along, you didn't have squat. You don't know anything about the music. Gillian, or whatever her name is, has decided I'm the go-between, and now you're telling me the FBI can't do anything, not even trace or record the call. I'm not going to risk anyone else's life."

"We're hoping at some point she'll call you at home," Andie says weakly.

"So I'm just supposed to hang around the house waiting?"

Wendell Cook gets to his feet. "All right, all right, this isn't getting us anywhere." He glares at Rollins. "Ted, please, just shut up."

Rollins glowers at Cook. He looks away, but he and Cook will have words later. I'd bet on it.

"What about the music?" Andie asks. "You said it was Bill Evans at the Village Vanguard in New York. Any significance there, about New York, I mean?"

I shake my head. "No, that was for me. I'm sure of it. She knows or guessed, Evans, that album would be one of my favorites. She knows I play piano."

"Jesus, what else does she know?" Coop asks.

"I don't know," Andie says. "We're going to have to wait for her to tell us." She looks at the notes she's been making. "Let's not forget we got some information. Her name is Gillian, she has a brother, she's a smoker, and she probably drives a newer car."

"How do you know that?" I ask.

"What you said about the music, the sound quality."

"Right," Cook says. "We can assume it's a newer car,

with a CD player.'' He's been pacing around the room.
Now he wheels toward me. ''Whatever it is, Evan, whatever she wants you to do, we're going to help you. Whatever it takes. All our resources will be at your disposal. We
don't want any more killing.'' He looks at everyone, making sure they all understand. ''Evan,'' he says, ''believe it
or not, I like this even less than you do, but we have no
other choice. You're the only link we have.''

''Any suggestions?''

''Yeah,'' Coop says. ''Stay home.''

EIGHT

AT JEFF LASORDA'S HOUSE in the Valley, we run through four tunes for the CD. For the moment at least, I'm almost able to put everything else out of my mind and concentrate on the music. But Gillian's voice, echoing in my head, fights for my attention.

I feel the trio coming together, as if Jeff, Gene, and I have worked together more than a handful of times. Nothing replaces steady gigs to sort out the kinks, fine-tune that mental telepathy that happens in working groups, and we don't have that luxury; but something else is happening with us. I'm just lucky that Jeff and Gene are the two right people.

The rehearsal is punctuated with smiles and comments as we surprise each other at times, trusting that side trips, excursions beyond the confines of the tune, will lead back home.

I'm reminded of pianist-singer Mose Allison's philosophy about working with bassists and drummers he doesn't know. "After the head, guys, I'm going out there. You can come with me or just wait here till I come back." Jeff and Gene like to explore as much as I do. They come with me. I don't want to overdo rehearsing; I want the music to sound fresh when we get to the studio.

It's been three days since the call from Gillian, the poem, and just as long since I've heard from Natalie. She isn't returning my calls. I put it down to her heavy study schedule, but I know it's more than that. In a way, I'm relieved. I don't have to tell her about things or talk her out of wanting to be with me while this sparring with Gillian continues. But the other side is that I miss her, want her with me.

Gillian's silence has been strange, uncharacteristic, according to Andie Lawrence. I haven't received anything, and the waiting is getting harder and harder, but at least it's allowing me to plan for the CD.

"What about a Miles tune?" I ask the guys. Taking Cal's advice, we've just finished running through a couple of old, obscure standards.

"Cool," Gene says. "Something up, though. We've already got enough ballads, don't we?"

I look to Jeff. He stands with his arm cradled around his bass, lost in thought. "Got something in mind?" he asks.

"Yeah, I was thinking of 'Solar,' " I say. It's always been one of my favorites and not too heavily recorded.

"Yeah," Gene says. He hums the first few bars, taps out some time on the cymbal.

"Jeff?"

Jeff nods approvingly. "Yeah, that could work."

"All right, let's try it, see what happens." I begin in tempo with the first four bars, just a single note line with my right hand. When I hit the fifth measure and go for a two-handed, altered chord, Jeff is right with me, and Gene splashes in with cymbals.

While I play it out, Jeff and Gene roam freely behind me, intimating the rhythm, but by the first solo chorus it's burning, and I know it's a good choice for the CD. I don't look up for six choruses, then nod to Gene. He plays two that are nothing like a conventional drum solo while Jeff and I get into a question-and-answer thing behind him that fits perfectly with Gene's musings.

When we take it out, everyone is smiling. "Yeah, that's the one," Gene says. He stands up and stretches his arms over his head.

Jeff agrees. "Yeah, Evan, that was smoking."

I sit at the piano, smile, feel the rush course through me. Good moments count, whether they're in a rehearsal or on a gig. I flex my fingers, look at the black glove, and feel fine.

"Listen, guys, Paul Westbrook said he might come by and listen a little bit. Let's take a break." I glance at my watch. "He should be here any minute."

"Oh-oh," Gene says. "We're being scouted. I'm going to run down to the 7-Eleven. You guys want anything?"

"Not for me," Jeff says. I pass too, and Gene goes out to his car. I look at my cell phone, which has been sitting on top of the piano. "When did you start carrying one of those?" Jeff asks.

I'm a beat slow with the answer, and Jeff catches it. "Just trying it out," I say. "I got a special trial deal."

Jeff doesn't say anything, and heads for the kitchen. I take the phone, go outside for a smoke, and call Andie Lawrence. She answers on the first ring.

"Evan?"

"Yeah, it's me. Just checking in." We both know it's more than that. I still haven't had a chance to talk to her alone.

"Gillian's profile is filling out, but there's still so much we don't know."

"There's a lot I don't know, Andie," I say. "Can we get together, somewhere besides your office?"

"Sure," Andie says. "I think I know what you want."

"All right. My place? I'm rehearsing now, but we'll be through in a couple of hours."

"Okay, I can do that." She pauses, then says, "What about Natalie?"

"Don't worry about it. She won't be there."

"Okay, see you then."

Just as I press the off button, Paul Westbrook pulls into the driveway. He gets out and comes over smiling.

"Good news, Evan. The Chadney's gig came through, next Friday and Saturday."

We shake hands. "That's great, Paul. Great. The rehearsal is going well. I'm glad you could stop by."

He shrugs. "Afraid I can't stay. Something else has come up, but I wanted to tell you about Chadney's." He turns around as Gene drives up and parks his station wagon alongside Westbrook's Lexus.

"Gene Sherman, my drummer," I say, as Gene gets out of the car carrying a sandwich and a couple of bottles of beer.

"Oh, yes, I remember, from the Bakery."

They shake hands while Gene balances the beer bottles under his arm and holds the sandwich with one hand. We go inside and find Jeff noodling at the piano. I introduce Jeff and Westbrook.

"I've got a few minutes," Westbrook says, glancing at his watch. "Want to give me a sample?"

"Sure. Guys?"

Gene sits at his drums, his mouth stuffed with a bite of sandwich. Jeff picks up his bass, and we launch into one of the tunes we'd rehearsed earlier while Westbrook pulls up a chair.

I feel his eyes on me. I'm conscious of the glove, but the wrist is still warm, and when I comp for Jeff's solo, Westbrook comes over and says in my ear, "Sounds good, Evan."

I nod and keep playing as he taps me on the shoulder and goes out. We finish the tune, and I give the guys the thumbs-up.

"Chadney's Friday night," I say.

ON THE DRIVE BACK to Venice I replay the rehearsal in my mind and look ahead to the date at Chadney's, allowing myself to feel some sense of normality, as if I were just driving back from a rehearsal, bitching to myself at the traffic on the 405. Then, just near Sunset, a cluster of brightening taillights in front of me, my phone rings.

"Hello." I'm thinking it's Andie putting off our meeting, but it's Miles Davis from *Kind of Blue* and Gillian. I jerk the wheel, look over my shoulder, and cut off two cars as I pull over into the emergency lane and stop. Horns honk at me, but the blues "Freddie Freeloader" has my ear.

"Did you think I'd forgotten you, Evan?" Gillian says.

I glance at the traffic lanes to my left and glimpse a pretty blond passing in a BMW convertible, a phone to her ear, her hair blowing in the wind, a broad smile on her face.

"No, I knew you'd call."

"I can't talk long, Evan. I'm busy today. Just wanted to let you know you'll be receiving something later."

"What? How?" I press the phone to my ear, try to pick up any background sounds that will tell me something about where she is, but there's nothing but the music.

Gillian laughs. "Don't you like surprises, Evan?"

I get a few bars of Miles's mournful trumpet solo, then Gillian is gone.

I sit for a few minutes watching traffic go by. I throw the phone on the seat beside me and pound the steering wheel. Why now? I keep asking myself. Why now?

I jump when there's a tap on my window. I look up to see a motorcycle cop in helmet and mirrored sunglasses, gloves in his hand. I hadn't even seen him pull up. I roll down the window and look at him. He leans in, one hand on top of the Camaro.

"You okay?"

"What? Oh, yeah. Just got a call." I point to the cell phone. "Thought it would be better to pull over."

"Must have been bad news," he says. "Saw you pounding on the wheel." He looks over his shoulder at the traffic, then back to me, studying my face, deciding I'm no threat to southern California traffic "Well, let's move it along. This is the breakdown lane."

"Oh, sure, sorry." I start the car. The officer walks back to his motorcycle but waits till I pull out into traffic. I watch him in the mirror as he follows me till I exit at Washington Boulevard, and wonder what he'd say if I told him I was assisting the FBI.

I pull into my parking space, turn off the engine, and sit for a moment listening to traffic noise, the distant surf. Gillian has already been in my car once, so I start looking there, but my car has only been at Jeff's today, so it's a halfhearted attempt. I check the mailbox, look under the mat, but there's nothing. Inside, I throw my keys and cell phone on the counter. No phone messages either. The green light glows steadily.

I stand in front of the refrigerator for a couple of minutes, trying to decide if I'm hungry. There's not much choice, so I settle on some leftover tuna and make myself a sandwich. I open a beer and eat half the sandwich before Andie shows up.

She comes in carrying a file folder. Today she's in a short, pleated skirt, white blouse, and a light jacket.

"Gillian just called me," I say. "Andie, I was in the car. The call forwarding was turned off."

Andie nods and sits down on the couch, smooths her skirt over her legs. She seems distracted, resigned, troubled abut something. "She's got your number. Like we said, it's easy to clone a cell phone."

"She sure does."

We look at each other and almost laugh, realizing what we've just said. I remember the blond who passed me on the freeway. Gillian could have been that woman or anybody in any of those cars.

"She said I'd be getting something today."

"What?"

"I don't know. We only talked a minute or so." I sit down opposite Andie and take a swig of my beer. "I hate this, Andie. I can't handle it."

"I know, but you have to, Evan." She holds up the file folder. "Look, Wendell doesn't know I've done this, but I want you to see what we're dealing with, why you have to handle it. This isn't the official report, but I've summarized things."

I get a cigarette going and open the file. There are three printout pages clipped inside. I read through it quickly, a queasiness rising inside me. The background of the four murder victims, the autopsy reports, the profile of Gillian, none of it seems real. I glance up at Andie, see her watching me.

I look back at the file. "What's this about semen samples?" There are two: one for Cochise and one for Ty Rodman.

"I think you're right about Gillian. Both of them had sex before they were killed. We have to allow that it might have been with Gillian. I think she is somebody who could get close; maybe she even knew them."

I take a drag on my cigarette, put it out, and think that over. Jesus, like a black widow. For all four victims, the cause of death is listed as the same: stabbing, not slashed or cut up but clean, concise wounds.

"She knows what she's doing," Andie says. "The entry wounds were precise in all cases. That suggests some medical knowledge. I wanted you to know how she works, what you're up against.''

I look at the file again. Hearing that someone has been stabbed is one thing. It's in the paper, on the news, every day. But seeing it in black and white, having seen Rodman's body, even briefly, is something else again, especially when I've talked to the person responsible.

Did she look into their surprised eyes? Did she smile? Did she say something to them? What were the last words they heard?

I walk over to the window and look out toward the beach. The glare of the late-afternoon sun slashes through the glass like a spotlight. Dust particles swirl in the air.

I'm turning back to Andie when there's a loud knock on the door. I flinch, but Andie simply stands up and looks at me. "Natalie?"

"No, she has her own key." I go to the door and look through the peephole. There's a man in a uniform and cap, chewing gum, looking toward the beach. I open the door.

"Evan Horne?"

"Yeah."

He nods, pops his gum. "Sign right here, please." He hands me a clipboard and a pen. I sign, trade him the clipboard for a flat, cardboard FedEx envelope. "Have a nice day," he says, touching the bill of his cap with his fingers.

I shut the door and hold up the envelope for Andie.

"Here, let me," she says. She rips back the perforated strip on the envelope, then stops. "If Wendell ever asks, you got this and called me."

I look at her for a moment. She meets my eyes, and I realize our relationship just changed.

She presses the two end edges toward each other so the envelope bows and looks inside. "Wait a minute," she says. She puts the envelope down and digs in her purse, pulling things out, laying them on the coffee table.

Most women carry a wallet, keys, tissue packs, lipstick in their purse. Andie carries all those things plus a gun and a small dispenser of latex gloves. "There probably won't be any prints," she says, handing me a pair, "but just in case."

The gloves are tricky to get on. They're tight, and the elastic pops as I struggle to stretch them over my fingers. For a moment I flash on the Simpson trial, O. J. in court, giving his best performance for the jury. Andie has hers on in seconds, and she helps me pull the top of the glove over my wrist.

She opens the envelope again and lays the contents, one typed sheet of paper, on the coffee table. She looks inside again and pulls out something else—another white feather. She glances at me and lays it aside. The note is addressed to me. At the top is another poem.

All Blues and All Hues
Freddie Was a Freeloader
So What?

Andie leans in for a closer look. "Who's Freddie?"

"Miles Davis. That's what she was playing when she called today. Those are all Miles tunes—'All Blues,' 'Freddie Freeloader,' and 'So What?'"

"And the 'all hues'?"

"Somebody wrote lyrics to 'All Blues,'—the singer, Mark Murphy, I think."

"Was Freddie a musician?"

"No, I don't think so. There are lyrics to 'Freddie' too. Jon Hendricks recorded it a few years ago. The lyrics are

on the liner notes. I think Freddie was some kind of leg-
endary bartender in Philadelphia.''

"Have you got the CD?'' Andie asks.

"Yeah, it's around here somewhere.''

"Okay, I want to hear the music and see those lyrics
later.''

I nod, and we look at the text of the note.

Evan,
My brother died. His name was Greg Sims. He played
saxophone. The police say it was suicide. I don't believe it. You find the truth; I'll be still. Remember our
bargain. Don't fail me.
Gillian

Andie and I both stare at the page for several minutes,
not speaking. I don't know what Andie is thinking, but I
can't shake the cloud of disbelief and apprehension that
begins to envelop me.

"What am I supposed to do with that?'' I lean back on
the couch and shut my eyes.

"This is interesting,'' Andie says.

"Interesting? Jesus, it's scary.''

"No, look. This is a woman who writes haiku—she's
three syllables short on this one, by the way—and carefully
selects music to play when she calls you. Now she writes
like this, these short sentences.''

I look at Andie, then pick up the page and stare at it. "I
don't get it. So what?''

"She's not only typed on paper that probably can be
found anywhere, she's also disguising her writing style.
Have you ever heard of Greg Sims?''

"No, never.''

Andie takes out her cell phone and picks up the FedEx

envelope. She calls, identifies herself as FBI, and asks for a trace on the delivery, then gives them her number and hangs up.

"This will be a dead end too, but I've got to follow through." She reads the page again and looks at me. "Anything else you can think of?"

"No." I strip off my gloves and go into the kitchen, get a bottle of water out of the refrigerator. "Want some?" I ask Andie, holding up the bottle.

"Sure, thanks."

I bring back two bottles. We both take a long drink while looking at the page again.

"What does she expect me to do with this?"

Andie puts her bottle down. "There's going to be more. Another delivery, a call. She'll give you more details. This is just to let you know what it's about."

"And to let me know she knows where I live."

Andie nods. "I'm not worried about that. She knows we would have your place under surveillance, and anyway she wants your help. I've called that off already. She doesn't want to harm you."

Unless I don't do what she wants. "Well, that certainly makes me feel better."

Andie kicks off her shoes and looks at me. "Do you mind?"

I shrug. "Make yourself at home."

She leans back and rubs her forehead, pushes her hair back. "God, I'm so tired," she says. She closes her eyes, crosses her arms across her body. "I'll get this back to the office and run the usual tests."

"But you won't find anything, will you?"

Her eyes blink open. She sees me watching her but doesn't move. "Probably not, but it's one more piece of the puzzle."

She closes her eyes again. A blur of emotions and thoughts race through me as I watch her. This is Andie's job, it has a fascination for her; but it's objective, another case that will go into the computer to be drawn on later.

Thrown together by necessity, we've somehow connected in a way I don't yet understand, something beyond Gillian, the urgency of stopping her. Does Gillian know that too? But it's on hold, and it's in my power to let it go or stop it. And of course there's Natalie, who knows what I've gone through to get back to the piano and wants to protect me from something she doesn't understand.

"What about that CD? You want to hear it now?"

Andie opens her eyes again and sits up. She finishes off her water and clasps her hands on her knees, notices the gloves, and peels them off. "Yeah. Sorry, I almost went out for a minute there."

"Okay, a brief jazz lesson." I find the Miles *Kind of Blue* CD and the Jon Hendricks one of *Freddie Freeloader,* recorded forty years later. "You want to hear where the lyrics came from first?"

"Sure," Andie says.

I put the Miles on. "This is what Gillian played on the phone today." I let it go all the way through Wynton Kelly's solo and half of Miles before I switch discs. "Okay, there are two more solos—Cannonball Adderly and John Coltrane. What Hendricks did was write lyrics not only to the melody line but to the solos as well, and he had some help. Bobby McFerrin, George Benson, and Al Jarreau."

"I know them," Andie says, "but not Jon Hendricks."

"Yeah, well they've all gone pretty commercial, but they did this date for Jon, I'd bet on it. Try to keep the Miles CD in mind while you listen to this, and follow along with the lyrics." I hand her the CD jewel case.

She unfolds the notes. "Okay, I got it."

I put the Hendricks CD on and play the title track. I'd forgotten how good this is. The voices blend well on the head, and then Bobby McFerrin sings the Wynton Kelly solo; Al Jarreau for Miles. Hendricks has captured all the nuance of the original solos in such a way that the story of Freddie Freeloader is told from four points of view, and the voices are a perfect match. No wonder it almost won a Grammy.

I watch Andie listen and read along with the printed lyrics. She looks up when Jarreau finishes and George Benson is suddenly Cannonball Adderly. "That's amazing," Andie says. "I don't understand how Hendricks could do that, how they can all sing that fast."

"Well, you have the idea." I get up to stop the CD, but she holds up her hand.

"No, wait. I want to hear all of it."

We both listen as George Benson tackles Hendricks's lyrics to the more intricate lines of Cannonball. We're halfway through Jon Hendricks, somehow managing to perfectly catch Coltrane's sound, when we hear a key in the door.

Natalie comes in, carrying a small plastic supermarket bag. She sees me first. "Hi, I—" She stiffens and takes in Andie, her shoes on the floor, then glances at the CD player, listens for a moment. "Well, this is cozy."

Andie drops the liner notes on the coffee table and stands up. "Hello, Natalie. We're just going over some things on the case."

"Yeah, right," Natalie says.

"Natalie, I—" I don't finish. For a few moments the three of us stand in silence. The tension hangs over the room like smoke.

"Hey, it's okay," Natalie says, but her voice is shaky. "I don't want to interrupt anything." She absently sets the bag on the floor, gives me one probing look, then turns and goes back out, pulling the door shut behind her.

I glance at Andie. She says, "Okay." Her head is bowed.

I follow Natalie out and catch up with her at her car. She's fumbling with the keys, trying to get the door unlocked.

"Natalie, come on." I turn her around, holding her by the shoulders. She looks up at me. Her eyes glisten. She looks away, swallows, then looks back at me.

"I don't know what's going on, Evan. You haven't told me anything."

"Every time I try, you either shut down or run away. Let's talk about it. There's a good reason I'm trying to keep you out of this."

"Yeah," Natalie says. "One of them is sitting in your apartment in a short skirt, her shoes off, listening to music. Is that official FBI procedure?"

"Look, let me see how much I can tell you. Let me check with—"

"No," Natalie says. "I don't want you to check with anybody. I can't stand around and watch you throw away this second chance you have. I won't do it." She takes a few breaths. "This is hard for me to say, but you know what, Evan? I think you like this. Working with the police, solving old crimes. Maybe you got into it by accident, but I think you like it. And now it's the FBI. You've hit the big leagues."

"I like this?" I shake my head, feeling like I'm going to snap. Gillian, the FBI, Natalie, juggling rehearsals, it's all too much. "Jesus, Natalie, people are getting killed. What am I supposed to do?" I hear my voice bounce off the building. An old woman clutching her purse stops, stares at me, then hurries on. I drop my voice till it's almost a whisper.

"You think I like being used by the FBI?" I look away and shake my head, feeling the anger and frustration still churning inside me, but it's as if a curtain has dropped over Natalie's face.

"I think you don't even know it." She puts her head back and sighs. "I don't know, maybe you have to, but right now, I...I don't think we should see each other for a while, at least until this is over." She gets in the car, rolls down the window, and starts the engine. "Anyway, you've got Special Agent Lawrence to keep you company."

She pulls the door shut, guns the engine, and races off, leaving me standing in the street. I watch for a few moments until her car disappears around the corner. When I go back inside, Andie is standing by the kitchen counter. Her shoes are on, her bag is on her shoulder, and she's just hanging up her cell phone.

"That was FedEx," she says. "Paid in cash. No way to trace the sender." She watches me for a moment when I don't react. "I've gotten you in trouble with Natalie, haven't I?"

"Don't worry about it. We're just going through some changes."

"I feel responsible."

"Don't. It wasn't anything you did." I look at her and manage a slight, unconvincing smile.

Andie picks up the grocery bag Natalie left and sets it on the counter. She looks inside. "Looks like she was going to cook dinner." She looks at me questioningly. "Be a shame to waste this."

"Andie, I don't think—"

"Give me a couple of hours. I have to do something." She takes out a pen and pad from her bag. She writes quickly and tears a sheet off the pad. "This is my address," she says, handing it to me.

I take it from her. "I don't know."

"Hey, if you don't come, I'll understand. I would like to take the two CDs if I can. I want to hear them both again and take another look at those lyrics. Maybe there's something there."

"Sure." I get the Hendricks CD out of the player, put it back in its case, and hand it and the Miles CD to her.

She stuffs them in her bag. "See you later, I hope."

She goes out, and I stand at the counter for a few minutes, clenching and clenching my fingers, listening to the silence. My hand is perfect. Now it's my mind that's going.

I lie down for a while, but my eyes are wide open. I try deep breathing, stretching, tensing all my muscles for several seconds, then letting go. It works for about twenty minutes. I glance at the clock on the night table and give up. I shower and shave and change into jeans, a denim shirt, and loafers.

I look at the slip of paper with Andie's address on the counter. I stand for a moment, thinking, then put it in my pocket and head for the door. My hand is on the knob when the phone stops me. I try to convince myself it's Andie, canceling, or Natalie, changing her mind, wanting to talk. Coop, just checking in. Maybe even a wrong number, or somebody wanting to sell me insurance. But I know it's none of those.

I press the record button and pick up on the third ring. I hear Thelonius Monk, a record he did with Gerry Mulligan—"Undecided."

"It's Gillian, lover, complicated as Monk."

NINE

ANDIE'S PLACE is near Westwood, not far from her office at the Federal Building. It's a large complex with carports, a pool in the center, and a bank of mailboxes next to the manager's office. I park in a visitor spot in front and walk back past the pool to Andie's second-floor apartment.

When I knock, she opens the door quickly, as if she'd been standing there, watching for me. She has on a faded Berkeley sweatshirt that's endured many washings, black jeans, and sandals. Her hair looks damp, and the smells of shampoo and scented soap compete for dominance.

"Did you bring the tape?"

I have the cassette in my hand as I walk in, and I hand it to her. She shuts the door behind me and goes right to a bookshelf on one wall that holds a small stereo system and a large collection of paperback and hardcover books. There's a couple of framed posters on the wall, some plants, a love seat, and two chairs facing a television on a stand and shelves below it, crammed with videotapes. Under one window is a rolltop desk. The cover is up, and a banker's light burns on top. I can see a laptop computer and an assortment of file folders and papers scattered beside it.

"Help yourself," she says. "There's beer, wine in the refrigerator." I get a beer and sit in one of the chairs as she turns on the tape. She adjusts the volume, and we hear Gillian's voice with Thelonius Monk and Gerry Mulligan's baritone sax softly under it.

"It's Gillian, lover," the voice says, "complicated as Monk."

Andie grabs a pen and a yellow legal pad from her desk and sits on the love seat. She sets the pad on a small glass coffee table and listens, her pen poised over the pad.

"I got your delivery." I hear my own voice. It sounds strange, like another person's.

"Good," Gillian says. "Now you're ready to go to work."

"What do you mean?"

"You remember our bargain. You keep talking to me; I keep still. Now we're going to expand that."

"How?"

"You're going to investigate my brother's death. Greg Sims is his real name, in case you're wondering. Like Zoot, he was a tenor player."

I watch as Andie writes *Zoot Sims* on her pad.

"I don't know what it is you want me to do. I thought you said it was a suicide?"

"I told you that's what the police said." Her voice rises in pitch. That languid quality is gone briefly. There's a pause of a few seconds, then, "I want to know for sure."

"Where and when did he die?"

"In San Francisco. Almost a year ago." Her voice is monotone now, just reciting facts.

Andie writes again on the pad and looks up at me.

"You can start there," Gillian says. "Let's see just how good you are."

"Hey, I'm not a professional detective. How am I supposed to do this?"

I take a drink of my beer and listen to the note of panic in my voice. I can hear that blowing sound as she exhales on her cigarette. "You did just fine with Wardell and Clifford Brown, and you put Lonnie Cole in prison. I'm sure the FBI will help you." She pauses then. "Lawrence wants to help you, Evan."

Andie looks up from the pad, holds my gaze for a moment.

"I was lucky, that's all. Why don't you just hire a real detective?"

"Because I want you, Evan. You understand the music. You'll know what really happened to Greg and why."

"That's all I get? His name and the city?"

"There'll be much more."

"How? Another delivery?"

"Exactly, but different the next time."

"Different how?"

"Don't worry, you'll know. Greg was a serious musician. He studied long and hard until he couldn't stand it anymore."

"Couldn't stand what? Why don't you just tell me?" I hear myself sigh, the frustration in my voice. "If you really want me to do this, I need to know more about your brother."

I get up and walk to the sliding glass door that opens onto a small balcony. I go out, leave the door open, and light a cigarette. I can still hear the tape.

"I told you there'll be more. I want to keep it interesting for you, Evan. Sharpen your investigative skills." She laughs softly. She's playing again now, enjoying the control. "We might even meet, but don't look for me."

"Gillian, I can't do this."

There's a pause on the tape, then Gillian again. "You have to, Evan. People's lives depend on it."

The music comes up, Gerry Mulligan negotiating Monk's "Straight No Chaser," with Monk behind him, comping like he's playing with the palms of his hands, then an abrupt silence. Andie gets up and shuts off the tape.

I put my cigarette out in the beer bottle and come back

inside. Andie is leaning back, staring at the pad, covered now with her notes.

"I just don't believe this," Andie says finally. "She's so...so brazen, so sure of herself. So sure of you."

"That's what worries me," I say. I drop down in one of the chairs. "I have to do this, don't I?"

"Yes," Andie says. "She's very serious, over the edge. What a voice."

"What do you mean?"

"Well, she's in effect telling you that if you don't keep talking to her, don't investigate her brother's death to her satisfaction, she's going to kill again. But her voice is so smooth, even dreamy at times. Is it possible she was a singer? It's like she's talking to her lover."

I feel a shudder go through my body. "That's a scary thought."

"Yes, it is," Andie says. She gets up and takes the tape out of the machine and puts it on her desk. "Well, at least we've got her on tape now. I'll listen to this again and get it enhanced, see if we can pick up any other background noise that will help us find her."

"I don't think she was in a car this time."

"No, I don't either. It was too clear, no traffic sounds, but we'll see what the lab technicians say when they hear it."

Andie stands, thinking a moment, her hands on her hips. She's returned the pad and pen to her desk and now bends over to circle something she's written.

"Okay," she says. She straightens up. "Let's eat. I've got lasagna and a salad, if that's all right with you." She studies me for a moment, cocks her head to one side. "Would you have come even without the tape, if Gillian hadn't called?"

I pause for a moment before answering, but there's really

no need to. "I was on the way out the door when she called."

ALL THROUGH DINNER, Andie keeps the pad with her notes on the table, referring to it between bites of lasagna, sips of wine. She probes for details, with Miles Davis playing low on the CD player.

"Tell me about Zoot Sims."

"It would be easier to show you. Very opposite from Coltrane, not that hard, harsh sound. Zoot was out of the Lester Young, Stan Getz bag. Very melodic, smooth sound. Another good one to add to your collection."

Andie nods and makes a few more notes. "You want some coffee?"

"Sure." I help her clear the table, then go out on the balcony for a cigarette while she gets the coffee going. I can hear somebody splashing around in the pool, and just over the building tops I can see the lights of Westwood glowing in the sky.

Andie joins me, balancing two mugs of coffee and cream and sugar on a tray. "Don't know how you take it," she says, "so I brought everything." She drags two plastic chairs from the corner. "We can sit out here if you like."

"Fine." I fix my coffee and sit down. Andie holds her cup close to her face, sips hers, and stares out over the rim of the cup.

"Does this job ever get to you?" I ask her.

"Sure," she says. "All the time, but this one is different. I've never gotten personally involved before." She glances at me and then quickly adds, "I mean, the way this one has evolved. It's usually just bureau people or local police, and—"

"What?"

"Nothing. I was just going to say, survivors of the victims."

I feel her studying me for a moment. When I look at her, she holds my gaze. "I really am sorry about that thing this afternoon, with Natalie, I mean. She'll come around, won't she?" Andie looks away. "I'm sorry. If this is uncomfortable, we don't have to talk about it."

"No, it's okay. It wasn't your fault. I don't know. Natalie can be pretty stubborn." I drink off my coffee and light another cigarette. "She thinks I like this."

Andie looks surprised. "Being a go-between for a killer and the FBI?"

"Not just that, but working with the police, tracking down things."

"Do you?"

I shrug. Good question. "I wouldn't have chosen to get into this, but I know I can't walk away from things, just let them go. When I was looking into Wardell Gray's death or chasing down a tape I thought was Clifford Brown, I don't know, those things were in the past, but it didn't matter that they happened so long ago. I just had to know. This is different. It's happening right now.

"I've got an old friend, a former teacher, Cal Hughes, who says I'm exactly the one to be doing this because I'm so connected with the music. He said Wardell Gray and Clifford Brown were reaching out to me." I laugh. "Of course, Cal is a tad eccentric, and he'd had quite a bit to drink."

"And now it's Bird and Miles and Coltrane," Andie says. "And Zoot Sims."

"Yeah, but it's not the same. I don't have much choice now. If Gillian can be believed, if I walked away now, I could be responsible for more deaths."

"Oh, I'm sure she can be believed. When I listen to that

tape again, I'll find out more. I'm betting on some real disorder we can pinpoint.''

"Real disorder? Well, that's a given, isn't it? Anybody who's killed four people because of the music they play definitely has something more than a disorder.''

"Of course. I mean something we can put a name to. From the transcript of the first call and listening to her voice, I'm thinking big mood swings. Manic depressive, maybe.''

"How will that help, knowing that?''

"It will give us a better idea of what we're dealing with. I'd be willing to bet that she's undergone some kind of treatment. When we run down her brother's background, we might make a connection.''

We both sit quietly for a while, each lost in our own thoughts. It's nearly eleven when I glance at my watch. "I'd better go,'' I say.

Andie nods. "Yeah, long day for me tomorrow with all this to go through.''

"And I've got a gig tomorrow night. Going to stop by? Chadney's, in the Valley.''

"I'll see, but I don't want to—''

"Don't worry. I don't think Natalie will be there.''

Andie's eyes flicker and darken. "She should be.''

NATALIE ISN'T THERE when I arrive at Chadney's, but a lot of people are. Paul Westbrook has seen to that. Somehow he's arranged for some radio spots on the jazz station KLON, and Chadney's has been featuring jazz for quite a while. Several people look up from their drinks when I sit down at the piano and try it out. It's been recently tuned, and the keyboard action is good. Jeff's bass is lying on the floor beside the piano, and Gene's drums are crammed into a corner opposite the piano. I spot them both at the bar and sit for a moment, absorbing the good feeling that washes over me.

My own trio again, a good piano, and nearly a full house, at least for the first set. I look over my shoulder and see a couple right at my elbow. Close quarters here. There are several small tables just behind me. I look through the music I've brought along, some of the new tunes we might try later in the evening, but the first set is going to be familiar territory.

I've spent the day alone, not hearing from anyone. Practiced a couple of hours, thought about the gig, and walked on the beach later. No calls, no messages, just some welcome time alone. I made one call to Natalie to remind her about the gig, but there was no response.

Andie, Ted Rollins, and Wendell Cook, I assumed, had spent the day running down Greg Sims and going over the tape of Gillian's call. The only thing that could make this night better would be for them to tell me they'd caught Gillian and I had nothing further to worry about. Meanwhile, it was time to play.

Jeff and Gene wander over, drinks in hand. "Hey, guys, you ready to do it?"

Gene sits down at his drums, moving the stool slightly so he can see me clearly, Jeff picks up his bass and runs a towel over the fingerboard, and we tune up. Jeff nods, and Gene looks at me expectantly.

" 'Solar'?" I say. I slip on my glove, flex my fingers. There's no announcement or introduction here. For many, the jazz is background, something to go with drinks and conversation. I take off over the hum of the audience and feel it dim immediately.

I hit the third chorus, shift slightly on the piano bench, and lean back from the keyboard. I can sense the eyes of the people at the table behind me as I build gradually, pushed on by Jeff's gorgeous bass lines, Gene's sparkling cymbal work. Eventually, the audience becomes white noise. All I hear are the bass and drums and my own lines, rolling off my fingers through four choruses.

I look up, catch Gene's eye, and he explodes into his solo. Jeff listens, head down, his arm around the bass. As Gene comes into the final eight bars, Jeff and I exchange glances. I raise my eyebrows and Gene, instead of a loud crash, simply taps the edge of a cymbal so that it rings through the first note of Jeff's solo.

I comp behind him, dropping in the chord changes lightly, and scan the room, unconsciously looking for someone who might be Gillian, then discarding the idea just as quickly. Surely she wouldn't chance showing up here. I do catch a glimpse of Coop and Andie, half hidden behind a waitress taking their order. I hadn't even seen them come in. If any more of the FBI contingent are here, I don't see them.

Jeff starts walking on the last eight, and we take it out. "Yeah," says Gene. Jeff adjusts his amp slightly, and I start alone, out of tempo, on a Tadd Dameron ballad, "If You Could See Me Now." I've worked out some new chord changes for this, and Jeff studies the keyboard as I play the intro, then decides on the spot to play a chorus solo. I nod my head forward to begin the next chorus, and Jeff comes in with me, one long, aching note that perfectly sets the mood for this haunting tune. Gene scrapes the handle end of his wire brush across the cymbal, then begins to circle the brushes on the snare.

I fall into the song then, plunging its depths, occasionally surprising myself with turns and twists for two choruses, then leave it to Jeff to sum things up. When we finish on the chord Jeff showed me at the rehearsal, he smiles at me. I feel the familiar rush. There's one moment of complete silence, as if the audience doesn't want to interfere, then a burst of applause, and I know we've got them.

For the rest of the set I mix it up with standards, a bossa nova version of "Old Folks," and one Monk tune, and finish off with Miles's "All Blues." The melancholy waltz fits the trio as well as the glove on my right hand.

I stand up and walk around the piano to the microphone. "Thank you very much," I say to the audience. "You've been listening to Gene Sherman on drums and Jeff Lasorda on bass. I'm Evan Horne. We'll be back very shortly."

I turn and look at the guys. "Let's go on the road," Gene says, standing up at his drums. He's pumped.

"Yeah, Evan," says Jeff. "Jesus, what are we going to do next set?"

"We'll try a couple of these," I say, tapping the music on top of the piano.

I make my way through the maze of tables to Coop and Andie. They're deep in conversation when I come up. Coop kicks out a chair for me, and I join them.

"That was wonderful," Andie says. She's wearing a black turtleneck sweater and white pants and has on more makeup than I've seen before. She touches my shoulder, a gesture not lost on Coop.

"You on duty?" I ask him, glancing at the tall glass of Coke in front of him on the table. He's in jeans, T-shirt, and his Metro Team jacket.

"Yeah, can't stay, sport. Got some warrants to serve."

"Well, thanks for coming by." I don't have to look for Natalie. She'd be with Coop if she was here.

I look at Andie. "Anything?"

"Yes, there is, but we can talk about it later. I don't want to spoil the mood."

I catch Coop leaning back in his chair, watching me, a nasty little smile playing on his face. When I glare back, he gets busy checking his watch. "Walk me out, sport. Want to talk to you about something."

"Sure." I look at Andie. "Back in a minute."

Coop and I shoulder our way through the crowd. There are more people in the foyer waiting to get in. Outside, valet parking is busy. I follow Coop to his car. I know what this is about, but I let Coop get to it. He unlocks his car and I light a cigarette.

"Natalie called me today," he says. "She thinks you're putting the moves on the lovely Miss Lawrence. Anything to that? Or maybe it's the other way around."

"Come on, Coop. I tried to explain to Natalie, but she doesn't want to know. She came by yesterday when Andie and I were talking."

"I heard." Coop watches for my reaction. When I give him nothing but a long stare, he shrugs, spreads his hands. "Okay, it's none of my business, but she's pretty upset."

"What am I supposed to do? I can't not work with Andie, and I can't tell Natalie what's going on. Remember the agreement Cook had me sign? Why isn't she here tonight?"

"You'll have to ask her," Coop says. He opens the door. "Meanwhile, you've got to take Special Agent Lawrence home."

"What?"

Coop grins. "Yeah, she came with me, but I've been called away on an emergency, catch some bad guys. See ya." He pulls away and leaves me staring after his car. I'm getting tired of people doing this to me.

I hurry back inside and run into Andie on the way out. "You're not sticking around?"

"I wish I could," she says. "Something's come up on Greg Sims. Call me tomorrow, okay?"

I stare at her for a moment, silently cursing Coop.

"Evan? Are you all right?"

"Yeah, fine. Talk to you tomorrow."

Jeff and Gene are already waiting for me. I shuffle through the music on the piano. "Want to try one of these?" I ask them. I find the one I'm looking for and hand the bass part to Jeff. He looks it over. "In two for the first part," I say to Gene. "Then go for it."

I look through the stack again for my part, finally find it. "Here we go," I say, then sit down as if I've been pushed. Across the bottom on the lead sheet, in the same red pen that was on the flyer, are the words, *Don't let me down, Evan*. Under the sheet is a manila envelope that I don't recognize.

"What's the matter?" Jeff asks.

I stare at the envelope, wheel around behind me, but the table is empty.

"What? Oh, nothing." I push the envelope aside.

"Never mind," I say to Jeff and Gene. "Let's play 'All of Me.'"

They look at each other and shrug. It's going to be a long set.

I GOT THROUGH the next set somehow, but it was different. My concentration was gone, and I was playing on automatic pilot. The changes to hundreds of tunes were under my fingers, but the heart was gone. It was nothing anybody in the audience would notice, but Jeff and Gene knew. Often you come off the bandstand and hear people say, "You guys sounded great." And you know it's a lie.

Jeff and Gene were quiet as we packed up for the night. I'd let them down as much as myself, and now, standing in front of Andie's door at two-thirty in the morning, I wonder what I'm doing here.

I knock twice, hear some kind of noise inside, and then

a shadow crosses the peephole as she looks out. There's a clicking of locks, and the door opens.

"Evan. What is it?" Her hair is disheveled, and a short robe barely covers her legs.

"Can I come in?"

She looks over her shoulder and gathers her robe to her. "Yeah, sure, come in." She steps aside to let me pass and shuts the door. I look at her and wish I were here for some other reason. She sees the envelope in my hand. "Gillian?"

"Yeah, she was there tonight at Chadney's." I hand the envelope to Andie. "Here, read this."

She takes it from me, sits down on the love seat, and turns on a lamp. I unlock the balcony door and go outside. I light a cigarette and lean on the railing. There's no sound from the pool, no lights on anywhere except for the complex's outdoor lights. Once I glance back at Andie. She's totally unaware of me, lost in concentrating on the envelope's contents, which detail the police reports on Greg Sims's suicide. At least, that's the official line.

Andie has her legs crossed as she squints at the pages. I turn back to the pool, thinking I've got to get out of here. When she finishes, she comes outside. She's changed into a long cloth robe, belted it around her.

"Where was this?" she asks.

"On the piano, mixed in with some music. I found it when I came back from the break. Gillian was right there in the club, for God's sake."

Andie is silent for a moment. "She has almost more here than we do. I pulled the file from the San Francisco police."

"Well, it was her brother, but how did she get all this?"

"God, who knows? I was going to tell you then. That's when I said I didn't want to destroy the mood. How did the rest of the night go?"

''Not good. I sort of lost my edge.''

''I don't know how you can concentrate at all.'' She pauses, thinks of something else, but looks like she's trying to decide something. ''Why did you look at me so strangely when I left Chadney's?''

I wait for a moment to answer, just shrug. ''Coop, fooling around. He told me he'd brought you and I'd have to give you a ride home.''

Irritation flickers across her face for a moment. ''And you didn't want to?''

''It's not that, it's just—''

''No, you don't have to say anything.''

I nod. There isn't anything to say.

TEN

THE PHONE wakes me up. I stumble to the kitchen before the third ring, press the record button, and steel myself for Gillian.

"Evan, it's Andie Lawrence. We need you down here as soon as you can make it."

"Yeah, okay. Has something happened?"

"We want to brief you and discuss some plans."

"All right. About an hour?"

"Fine, we'll be waiting. Lieutenant Cooper will pick you up."

I'm relieved that it wasn't Gillian, but wonder at the formality in Andie's voice. Cook or Rollins were probably standing nearby while she made the call. I look at my watch, surprised at how long I've slept.

I chug a glass of orange juice, and by the time I'm showered and dressed, Coop is banging on my door. "Let's go, sport," he says when I let him in. His car is double-parked in the street, the motor running.

I follow him to the car, get in, and light my first cigarette of the day. At this rate I could quit if I delayed the first one an hour every day.

"Thought you'd already be there." I watch Coop drive, looking straight ahead, both hands on the wheel, one of his little cigars clamped between his teeth. He stays north on Main until Pico Boulevard, then turns right, up the hill past Santa Monica High School.

There's a chain-link fence surrounding the campus and a security guard on the gate these days. When Coop and I

were at Samohi, playing football and chasing girls, it was
an open campus. Different times, different people. Everything changes.

"Andie called me this morning and filled me in," Coop
says. He turns north on Lincoln and heads for the 10 Freeway. "We're checking with the valet parking guys at Chadney's, see if anyone remembers a woman alone in a new
car."

"Well, will that really narrow it down? Do you know
how many women go to Chadney's alone? The Valley is a
little out of your jurisdiction too, isn't it?"

Coop shrugs as we hit the on ramp to the Santa Monica
Freeway. "Wendell Cook has fixed it so I'm temporarily
attached to the FBI's unit, mainly because the Rodman
murder was in Santa Monica and you and I are friends."
He glances over at me. "Give me more latitude, as we say
in the law enforcement game."

"Yeah, friend. That was cute last night, the bit about me
having to take Andie home."

Coop smiles. "Yeah, it was, wasn't it." He moves to the
right lane as we near the San Diego interchange.

"Don't encourage Andie," I say. "I'm having enough
trouble with Natalie."

"In case you haven't noticed, Andie doesn't need any
encouragement. But enough about your love life." I feel
him glance at me. "How are you holding up?"

"Oh fine, I always like dealing with serial killers, having
them at my gigs, calling me, writing me poems."

Coop ignores my sarcasm. "I got you into this, so I'm
going to be around, but you're going to be on your own a
lot. That's how Wendell wants to play it. They're buying
into the whole thing, and they're going to have you at least
go through the motions investigating the death of this fruitcake's brother."

We ease onto the 405 and immediately slow in the heavy traffic. "Just enough to keep her under control while they try to track her down. Is that the plan? I hear her voice in my head all the time, Coop. It's spooky."

"Exactly," Coop says. "First time I've heard the word 'still' used as a definition for not killing." He shakes his head and pulls into the exit lane for Wilshire.

"Can they find her?"

"There's a chance," Coop says. "She's getting pretty daring. Maybe she'll slip, give away too much. Sooner or later they always do."

"You don't sound too confident."

"I'm not," Coop says. "If anybody takes her down, it's going to be because of you." Coop turns east on Wilshire, then into the underground parking garage. He pulls into a space and turns off the engine. Neither of us speak for a moment as we delay the inevitable elevator ride up to the seventeenth floor.

I light another cigarette and stare straight ahead. "I don't know if I can do this, Coop. I just don't know if I can handle it."

"I think you can. Andie thinks you can. Wendell Cook thinks you can. You're going to have a lot of help."

I get out of the car, and Coop follows. On the FBI floor, Coop speaks to the receptionist behind the glass window, and seconds later, Andie comes out . She's wearing a dark pants suit today and low-heeled shoes.

She flicks an irritated glance at Coop, which he ignores, barely looks at me, then motions us to follow her without speaking to either of us. Is she feeling ticked at me because I didn't follow up the chance I had last night? It wouldn't have taken much for me to cross the line.

In the conference room, Wendell Cook and Ted Rollins are already there, seated at the big table. They have files

and papers spread over the surface. Both have their ties
loosened, their sleeves rolled up.

"Hi, Evan, Coop," Cook says. "Have a seat. You guys
want some coffee?"

"Definitely," I say. Coop nods yes too.

"Ted." Rollins looks at me for a beat, then goes out.

"We've got a lot to go through, so let's get to it." Cook,
a silver pen in his hands, leans back in his chair and studies
me. The buttons on his shirt look like they're going to pop
off as he takes a deep breath.

"We've come to some decisions, Evan, decisions that
none of us are happy about. I'm sure you won't like them
either, but we really have no choice on this. I don't know
how much Lieutenant Cooper has filled you in—probably
more than he should—but we're going to accept Gillian's
demands as genuine. We've gone over the tape, the letter,
all the other calls, and Andie has filled out the profile con-
siderably. We have a copy for you and the police reports
on her brother's death. It more than matches what she sent
you."

"Did you think it wouldn't?"

"There was always the chance," Ted Rollins says. He
comes in carrying two Styrofoam cups and sets them on
the table in front of Coop and me. He sets mine down hard,
so that some of the coffee spills out on the table. "Sorry,"
he says and starts to say more, but he stops with a warning
glance from Wendell Cook

"We first want to bring you up to date on what we think
we know about Gillian. Andie? I want to stress the word
think."

Andie picks up some computer printouts. "Yes, keep in
mind, Evan, a lot of this is speculation," she says. Her
voice still has a formal tone that I don't understand. "Anyway, this is what we've come up with. Gillian is thirty-five

to forty years old, drives a late-model automobile, maybe a sports car. She likes expensive things and has the income to buy them, which indicates some kind of well-paying professional job. After analyzing the tape, the speech patterns, her actions, we think she may have been treated for some mental disorder at one time—bipolar mood swings, manic depressive is a possibility—and she is probably on some form of medication, lithium, Prozac."

I begin to understand Andie's aloofness, her formality. Most of this she's already told me, but she doesn't want Cook or Rollins to know we've seen each other outside the office. Is this to get my trust, or is the whole thing a setup, calculated to ensure my cooperation?

"Gillian is a smoker and has extensive knowledge of jazz. Her brother died last year of an apparent suicide, jumped from the Golden Gate Bridge." She pauses and looks up at me. "His body has not yet been recovered."

"Then how—"

"A friend who was with him at the time, positively identified him, according to the San Francisco Police."

"That's somebody you should talk to, isn't it?" I look to Wendell Cook.

"We're coming to that," he says.

Andie continues. "We think Gillian may have some kind of music-related job, or at least did have. She's computer literate and has some knowledge of police procedures regarding phone taps and traces and forensic evidence."

"She must have," I say. "You guys haven't been able to locate her."

"This isn't TV, Horne," Ted Rollins says.

"He knows that, Rollins," Coop puts in. He and Rollins lock eyes for a moment.

"Other than that," Andie continues, "we don't have

anything else. Of course we'll be constantly updating this as more information comes in.''

Wendell Cook leans forward on the table. "Thanks, Andie.''

"So where do I come in?"

"I'm assigning Andie to you on this. We've decided that's the best way to work things. We have to assume Gillian will be watching your progress.''

I glance at Andie, but she's looking down at her papers. There's no surprise in her expression, so she's known all along.

"You and Andie will go to San Francisco, talk with the local police and our office there—Andie will pave the way on that front—and do anything else you can think of, even if you make it up, that will convince Gillian you're making an effort.''

"Make it up?"

"I don't know," Cook says. He spreads his hands. "Talk with some musicians, visit some jazz clubs. We'll leave that to you.''

I don't like the whole idea, but Cook is right. Gillian will no doubt be keeping tabs on me, but I suspect she won't like it that Andie is tagging along.

"Wouldn't it be better if I did this alone?"

"Absolutely out of the question," Cook says quickly. "This is an FBI operation. It's totally against policy to have you involved at all, but we're certainly not going to have you out on your own. Special Agent Lawrence will be in touch with us at all times," he adds formally.

Cook's change of tone is striking. Whenever it's something official, Andie becomes Special Agent Lawrence. Maybe that's policy too.

"There's one other thing," Cook says. He opens a file folder in front of him. "I'm going to insist on this.''

"What's that?"

"You have been in an ongoing relationship with one Natalie Beamer for over two years. We know she's a former police officer and now a student at Loyola Law School. We do not want you to divulge anything to her, and we'd prefer that you not see her until this situation is resolved."

I shift in my chair and stare back hard at Cook. "Or what?"

Cook's eyes don't waver either. "You don't want to go there, Evan." He closes the file and softens a bit. "Look, it's for her safety as well. I'm sure you don't want to put Miss Beamer in any jeopardy."

I don't have to think about that answer. "No, of course I don't."

"Evan, we understand this is very hard on you, but it's for the best, believe me."

I nod. Cook is right, of course, but I hate it that it's gone this far, an FBI file on Natalie. "When do we go to San Francisco? I have some—"

"You and Special Agent Lawrence are booked on a noon flight. You should probably pack for a couple of days. Lieutenant Cooper will be taking you both to the airport."

They could have just sent me a memo. It's all been decided.

"What about my life?"

"I'm afraid," Cook says, "you're going to have to put it on hold for a while."

SOMETIME DURING the ride to LAX, something inside me changes. While Coop and Andie make small talk in the front seat, I sit in back, thinking about Wendell Cook's parting words. I want Gillian's voice out of my head. I want to be free of the FBI, and I want my life back. I decide to do whatever it takes. Coop, I know, is right. I'll have help, but if Gillian is caught, it will be because of me.

We pull into the maze at LAX, and Coop drops us off at the curb. "Watch yourself in the clinches," he says, when Andie is out of earshot.

I slap the top of the car. "Don't worry about me."

"I'm not," Coop says, and he's gone.

Andie and I take a United shuttle to San Francisco. Just a quick up-and-down flight, time for a bag of peanuts and a Coke. A young agent from the San Francisco office meets us at the gate and escorts us outside. He's in the proverbial dark suit, white shirt, and tie and shined shoes. He shakes hands with me briefly, but it's clear he doesn't know what I'm doing there, and he's not asking. Must be FBI policy and he's following it to the letter.

"Phil Rogers," he says, and then acts like I'm not there.

He and Andie walk away a few steps. I light a cigarette and watch as he hands over car keys and a manila envelope she tucks under her arm. They talk for a couple of minutes, then Rogers gets in another car idling at the curb with his partner at the wheel. He gives me his best FBI look, then drives off with his partner.

"Okay," Andie says. "We're all set. We throw our bags in the trunk and head for the city."

Where to start? I'd thought about it a lot. Cochise's murder took place in San Francisco, maybe Gillian's nod to the great clubs of the sixties—the Jazz Workshop, Blackhawk, Basin St. West—so that would be one area to cover, but what did that have to do with her brother? A saxophone player, she'd said. Greg Sims. Zoot would be too obvious— I knew that much about Gillian now—so I'm betting Greg was out of the Charlie Parker or John Coltrane bag, and that's triggered a possibility.

"We're going to church," I say to Andie. She's driving

with one hand, her other elbow resting on the door sill, her hand on her head as we ease onto Nineteenth Avenue and the spires of downtown San Francisco come into view.

Andie gives me a look and smiles. "Yeah, right," she says. Except for the brief conversation with Rogers, the minute we boarded our flight at LAX, the formality dropped again. I suspect her manner at the Federal Building had more to do with Wendell Cook and Ted Rollins than me. For whatever reason, I'm relieved to see her friendly again.

I roll down the window, light a cigarette, and turn slightly in my seat, my arm on its back, so I can see her better. "I'm serious. It's just a hunch, but there is a John Coltrane Church here. Might be someplace to start."

"You're kidding?" She glances at me quickly. "You're putting me on, right?"

"Not at all. I think it's in the Fillmore district." Andie looks at me again, sees I'm not kidding, and nods at the manila envelope on the floor.

"See where we're staying," she says.

I open the envelope and look inside. "Travelodge at Fisherman's Wharf. Do they think we're tourists?"

"No, I think we've got a deal with the Travelodge, is all," Andie says.

Traffic is light as we turn on Lombard and negotiate the steep inclines. We catch a glimpse of the bay as we crest the summit of one of the hills that make driving in San Francisco an adventure. We pull into the entrance at the Travelodge, and Andie gets out to register us. She comes back in a few minutes, waving two keys, gets back in the car, and pulls around back. "We've got adjoining rooms," she says as casually as possible. I just nod and wonder what the night is going to bring.

She parks, and we go upstairs. We glance at one another

as we stand poised, keys in the locks. "I want to freshen
up," Andie says. "Then let's get some lunch."

"Fine," I say and go into my room. It's standard chain-
hotel stuff, right down to the prints hung over the double
bed. I drop my bag and grab the yellow pages to look for
the Coltrane Church. I flip through the listings: Churches,
Evangelical, Friends, Interdenominational, Jehovah's Witnesses. No jazz churches; only a couple under Saint John,
but they have nothing to do with Coltrane.

I shut the phone book and go to the window. Below me
is Fisherman's Wharf, and in the distance, Alcatraz and the
Bay. To the left, the Golden Gate Bridge, still half shrouded
in fog.

I try information, but they have no listing. Maybe I was
wrong. Maybe it no longer exists. Finally I try the *San
Francisco Chronicle* and ask to speak to the jazz writer or
reviewer. I get transferred around several times and finally
talk to a reporter.

"You want Kevin Drake," he says. "He won't be in for
a while. Can I help you?"

"I'm trying to run down a number for—I know this will
sound funny—the John Coltrane Church. Is there still such
a place?"

"Oh, yeah," the reporter says. "Think Kevin did a piece
on it a few months back. Hang on. Let me look through
Kevin's files." I wait for a couple of minutes and then he
comes back.

"Yeah, here it is." He gives me the number and address.

"Hey, I really appreciate it. Thanks."

"Not a problem. Going to get your spirit revived?"

"We'll see."

I GET A local street map from the front desk and meet Andie
at the car. She's changed into a sweater, jeans, and running

shoes. "Just in case we do some walking."

"Good idea."

"Where are we headed?"

"It's on Divisdero, the three hundred block."

When we make the turn, I check the street sign. "It's about thirty blocks," I say.

We go up and down several steep hills while I watch the street numbers. We finally come into to a commercial district of car washes, gas stations, and storefront shops and restaurants.

"There," I say, pointing to my right. Andie nods and starts looking for a parking place. We end up around the corner and walk back to Divisdero.

There's a large green sign with gold lettering over the doorway:

SAINT JOHN COLTRANE
AFRICAN ORTHODOX CHURCH

A big black-and-white photo of Trane is in the window, but the curtains are drawn, and the wrought iron gate is closed and locked. I peer in the window. Through a space in the curtains, I can see another photo of Trane somewhere in the back. In the other window is an old Hammond organ.

"Pretty cool, huh?" I say, stepping back from the doorway to look at the sign again.

"Look here," Andie says. She's reading a hand-lettered sign taped to the inside of the other window.

Sunday: John Coltrane Liturgy 11:45 A.M.
We Serve Vegetarian Meals 1-3 P.M.
Wednesday Service 6 P.M.

"Right day, wrong time," Andie says.

I look at my watch. We've got time to kill. "I don't feel like vegetarian anyway. Let's get something to eat and come back."

We look around. Traffic is steady, and people are walking around, shopping, hanging out. Near the corner, I spot a café. "Let's try that."

"I'm game," Andie says.

Inside there's a few people lingering over coffee, reading the newspaper. A tall, slender guy in jeans, a Grateful Dead T-shirt, a ponytail, and several earrings lounges behind the counter. We order sandwiches and coffee and wait for our food at a window table.

"What do you think we're going to find here?" Andie asks.

"Maybe nothing. It's a long shot, but if Greg Sims ever came here, maybe somebody can tell us something. Maybe somebody knew him. I can't imagine a tenor player not visiting the John Coltrane Church. But most important, I'd bet Gillian knows about the church, and she would expect me to check it out. It's worth a try, isn't it?"

"I suppose," Andie says. She smiles at the skinny guy when he brings our order. He ignores her and smiles at me.

"Evan, I had no idea," Andie says. She stifles a laugh until he's out of earshot.

"Neither did I. Hey, this is San Francisco."

We finish lunch and then wander around the neighborhood—working class, whites, blacks, and Asians, judging from the street traffic—checking out some of the shops. By twenty to six I want to go back to the church.

"If there's a service at six, they'll probably be open now."

We cross the street and go back to the corner, but the gate is still locked and no sign of life inside. A guy in dirty jeans, long hair, and a full beard leans against the building, drinking a beer. He looks at us, gives us the once-over, decides we don't belong, and goes back to his beer.

Andie rings the bell, but there's no answer. By ten after six there's still nothing happening.

"What do you think?" Andie asks. "Maybe the service was canceled."

"Let's give it a few more minutes. We've come this far."

"They will come," the guy in the beard says in a most reverent tone.

Andie rolls her eyes, and I light another cigarette and watch the traffic slip by.

A few minutes later, a large black woman comes around the corner. She's wearing a black T-shirt, black pants, and a brightly colored scarf tied around a magnificent set of dreadlocks. Her smile is open and warm.

"Hello, I'm sorry I'm late," she says, as if we had an appointment. She unlocks the gate, and we follow her inside.

"Let me talk," I whisper to Andie. The bearded guy dumps his beer bottle in a trash can and tags along behind us.

Inside there's an old desk with stacks of postcards showing behind some glass doors. The church itself is small; only a few pews face the altar. But it's a church nevertheless. There are photos of Coltrane everywhere and huge, brightly colored wall coverings of Coltrane holding a saxophone. On the left wall is a full set of drums, a beat-up upright piano, and a large poster, again of Trane. I lean in close for a look at the inscription beneath it.

*My goal is to live the truly religious life and express
it in my music. My music is the spiritual expression of
what I am; my faith, my knowledge, my being.*
                                        —John Coltrane

The black woman is busy turning on lights and switching
on a cassette player. The room is suddenly filled with Coltrane's soprano saxophone playing "My Favorite Things."
McCoy Tyner, piano, Jimmy Garrison, bass, and Elvin
Jones, drums, storm behind him. Elvin is like a hurricane.

I catch the bearded guy gazing at the altar, his eyes
glazed. "The spirit of jazz is here," he says.

"Cool," I say, leaving him and Andie to wander around.
I catch the black woman's eye. She comes over again with
a big smile.

"Hello, I'm Sister Deborah," she says. "Very nice to
meet you. I don't believe I've seen you here before." She
has a soft, lilting, musical voice to go with the smile. I take
her outstretched hand.

"No, first time. Just visiting."

She smiles again. "Welcome then. Sorry I was late. One
of the other sisters was unable to come. I'm afraid there
won't be a service." She holds her head back and looks at
me closely, but in a totally nonthreatening manner.
"You're a musician, aren't you?"

"Yes, not saxophone though. Piano."

She smiles again, nods her head. "I thought so. Your
spirit is very strong. You must come back on Sunday and
sit in. We have a choir and a house band. All the music is
Brother John's."

"Thank you," I say. "I don't know if we'll be here that
long."

"Well, at least sign our guest book. And your lady as
well." She indicates Andie. She takes me back to the front,

pulls out a red book from the desk, and opens it to a page already filled with names and addresses. She hands me a stubby yellow pencil. "What is your lady's name?"

"Andie," I say. "Short for Andrea." I take the pencil and scan the open page.

"Ah, a beautiful name," Sister Deborah says.

I glance up from the guest book. "Would you mind if I looked through this, see if any friends of mine have been here?"

"Certainly," she says. "We're all brothers and sisters here. I'll just see to your Andrea."

I watch her walk over to Andie and point out some photos of Trane in action. I quickly flip through the guest book, looking for dates. Twenty or thirty pages back I spot "Greg Sims" in neat block printing.

"Hey," I call to Andie, "look here." She and Sister Deborah join me at the desk.

"Greg was here, remember him?" I put my finger on Sims's name and address. Andie looks, then glances at me.

"A friend of yours?" Sister Deborah asks.

"He used to live up here. I haven't seen him for years. Do you happen to remember him? Greg Sims."

For the first time Sister Deborah frowns. "I'm afraid not," she says. "We have so many visitors."

"He's dead."

The three of us turn to the bearded man who's come up behind us.

"Suicide."

Sister Deborah closes her eyes for a moment in some kind of silent prayer. "I'm so sorry," she says to me. "You didn't know."

I don't answer and just nod. "Did you know him?" I ask the bearded man. He's wearing a long shirt. It hangs outside, almost reaching his knees. His eyes still have a glazed look.

"No, but Greg was a follower. He was here often and played a few times." He pauses and looks at Sister Deborah. "He was very troubled. I could hear it in his playing. He yearned for something."

Sister Deborah, watching the man more closely, grew somber. "His soul has ascended to a higher level," she says.

The man wanders off to gaze at a photo of Coltrane at the Village Vanguard.

"That's Robert," Sister Deborah says. "He's troubled too." She gives me a knowing look, then glances in Robert's direction for a moment. She turns back to me and smiles again. "Please come again," she says. "You'll have to excuse me now. I have some work to do."

"Thank you, Sister," I say. "Thank you very much. We'll try to come Sunday."

She retreats to a back room. "My Favorite Things" has become "Ascension" on the cassette player.

Andie and I leave Robert to his musings and start back to the car.

"Unbelievable," Andie says, shaking her head. "The John Coltrane Church."

I nod. "Now that's one I could get into."

ELEVEN

SPRAWLED ON THE BED, the entertainment section of the Chronicle open beside me, I dial Natalie's number and wait for her or her machine to answer. For San Francisco, the jazz pickings are surprisingly slim, but one catches my eye: Moose's in North Beach. Good food and good jazz, the ad says. Pianist Dave McKenna.

On the fourth ring, Natalie's machine picks up. "Hi, no one is available right now. Please leave a message after the beep."

I start to hang up, but then decide to let her know where I am. "Hi there. I'm in San Francisco, and—"

There's another tone, then she picks up. "Evan? What are you doing in San Francisco?"

"Getting religious. I just visited the John Coltrane Church."

"What? Let's back up a minute." There's no hostility in her voice, just curiosity.

"It's a long story. I just wanted to say hi, see how you're doing."

"I'm doing fine." There's a pause, as if she's deciding whether to ask me more. "Let me guess. You're there with the FBI babe, and you're getting in deeper."

"C'mon, Natalie, it's not like that."

"What is it like, Evan?" We both let several moments of silence hum through the lines.

"I can't get into it now." More silence.

"Fine, well, you said hi. I haven't changed my mind, Evan."

"I know. Can we talk when I get back?"

"That depends on you. Good-bye, Evan."

I listen to the dial tone for a minute, then hang up the phone. Are Natalie and I over? On one hand I understand and appreciate her concern. But part of me is disappointed that she hasn't trusted me enough to stick it out. Who's wrong here? I fall back on the bed, staring at the ceiling, but there are no answers there.

I get up and pace around the room, then look at the paper again. I glance at the adjoining door to Andie's room for a moment, then go over and knock.

She unlocks and opens it. The television is on, tuned to CNN. The screen of a laptop computer glows on the night-stand beside her bed.

"What's up?" she says. Her shoes are off, and her hair is tousled, like she's been running her fingers through it. She holds the door with one hand, kind of leaning on it and looking at me with a hint of curiosity, a smile just short of a smirk, like I'm an old boyfriend she hasn't seen in weeks.

"How about some dinner and jazz?" I throw it out as casually as I can.

"Something to do with Greg Sims?"

"No, I don't think so. A piano player. Just thought it might be fun, kill some time. We have to eat, right?"

She looks over her shoulder toward the computer. "Well, I have some work to do. I was just going to order in something."

I shrug and smile. "Yeah, fine. It was just a thought." I start to turn away. Rejected by two women in as many minutes.

"No, wait," she says, "maybe it would be. Fun, I mean." She leaves her hand on the door, straightens up and looks at me as if to gauge my reaction, and decides it's genuine. "Give me a half-hour, okay?"

"Sure, no problem."

"Who is this piano player? Anybody I should know?"

"Dave McKenna. You don't know him, but you should."

MOOSE'S IS NEAR North Beach, on Washington Square, a big, brightly lit, bustling place with large plate glass windows facing the square. Judging from the crowd out front, it's a good thing I called ahead.

We leave the car with valet parking and fight our way through to the reservations desk. A harried young woman is telling several couples it'll be at least an hour wait. I give her my name. She checks her list, draws a line through several names, tells me it will be about fifteen minutes, and invites us to wait at the bar along one side of the large room.

The dining room is divided by pillars and a huge grand piano. In the back, we can see a crew of chefs in tall hats, flame-broiling, stir-frying, yelling at each other. The noise level is such that I have to almost shout at the bartender to get our drinks. It's three deep at the bar, and every table in the dining room is full.

"How is he going to play in all this?" Andie says, looking around. A heavyset man jostles her for position at the bar, and some of her drink trickles over the glass. She glares at his back.

"Show him your badge," I say. "You'll see."

We get to our table just moments before Dave McKenna slides onto the piano bench. We both order the grilled salmon special and salads, and decide on the house chardonnay.

"Watch this," I say to Andie. McKenna glances around

the room, seemingly oblivious to the crowd noise. In a dark
suit and tie, his steel-gray hair combed straight back, he
might be mistaken for an account executive who wandered
in, had a couple of drinks, and decided to try out the piano.

It takes only a couple of minutes, not more than half a
chorus of "I May Be Wrong," for everyone to turn toward
the piano and stop in mid-conversation.

For most of the next hour, waiters lean in close so orders
can be whispered, and even the bar noise drops a few
notches as McKenna moves from one song, one style, to
another without stopping. He ends the set with a rousing
stride piano rendition of a Fats Waller tune, then stands up
for a quick bow while the audience cheers and applauds.
McKenna, who seems slightly embarrassed by the display,
ducks out the front door.

"Now that's what you call command of the instrument,"
I say to Andie. "A history of jazz piano in fifty-five
minutes."

"I just can't believe it," Andie says, shaking her head.
"He never stopped. I knew half those tunes, but I've never
heard them played like that."

I get up from the table. "I just want to say hello and
have a smoke. Be right back."

"Do you know him?" Andie asks.

"Met him once in Boston, but I doubt if he remembers.
Why don't you order us some coffee?"

I go outside, spot Dave standing off to the side, away
from the crowd at valet parking. When I approach him, he
does remember.

"Oh, yeah," he says, "you were conducting for Lonnie
Cole. I heard he was in prison. Tough way to lose a gig."

Fortunately, he doesn't remember I helped put Cole
there. To my surprise, he agrees to let me buy him a drink.
When we go back to the table, Andie's eyes get big.

"Andie, Dave McKenna." They shake hands, and Dave sits down, ordering a brandy from a waiter who has instantly appeared.

In the brightly-lit room, it's easy to see the dark circles under his eyes, the road-weary look, earned from hundreds of gigs. For a moment I flash on my own future. McKenna answers Andie's questions politely and modestly accepts her compliments. People at nearby tables stare at us and whisper, but McKenna doesn't seem to notice.

He finally looks at his watch. "Well, guess I better go do this again. You ever get tired of playing?"

"Not yet," I say.

"No, I suppose not. You're too young. Well, thanks for the drink. Don't let him go on the road too much," he says to Andie. "It can wear you out."

Andie nods and glances at me. "Nice man," she says.

"Yeah, he is. Guess he thinks we're together."

"Well, we are, kind of. Does that bother you?" When I don't answer, Andie touches my hand. "Look, I know you wish I was Natalie tonight. I wish I could do something about that, but I can't."

I pull my hand away and wish I could light a cigarette. I can at least change the subject. "So what's on tap for tomorrow?"

"Well, we need to check with the San Francisco police unless you've got any more ideas."

I shake my head no. "Then back to L.A., right?"

"Yes, I don't know what else we can do here. We just have to hope Gillian, if she's keeping track, will be satisfied with this trip, that she'll call again."

"I'm not really looking forward to that." I signal the waiter for our check, but Andie grabs it when it comes. "This is all FBI expenses," she says, as she takes out a credit card.

I hold up my hands in surrender. "I'm not going to argue with the Feds."

"I wish I could believe that," Andie says.

I catch Dave McKenna's eye as we leave and wave good-bye. He nods, smiles at Andie, and continues to dazzle Moose's audience with more stride piano. Guy doesn't need a rhythm section.

I manage to smoke a whole cigarette while we wait for our car. We drive back to the hotel without saying much and once again find ourselves standing in front of our rooms. The air is chilly now, and a light fog is rolling in over the bay.

"You feel like talking?" Andie asks. She already has her key in the door.

"I don't think so. Feel kind of tired."

Andie nods. "Okay, see you in the morning, then." She goes into her room and shuts the door.

I stand outside for a few minutes, smoking, staring at the fog, the lights from Fisherman's Wharf winking back at me. The chilly air feels good on my face.

What the hell. Natalie and I aren't married. We're not even engaged. When I go into my room, I glance at the adjoining door to Andie's room, already knowing it isn't locked.

AT SAN FRANCISCO Police Headquarters, Andie and I sit at the desk of Inspector Gene Parello. He's a short, dark man in his early forties with a shock of curly hair and eyes that flick around the squad room as if he's looking for someone to arrive. He talks mostly to Andie, but he's checked me out pretty thoroughly already.

"I don't know what else I can tell you," Parello says, flipping through the file on Greg Sims Andie has brought along. "It was pretty straight up. Jumper off the Golden Gate. Hey, it happens. You a friend of Sims?"

I glance at Andie to get some cue from her. If I'm reading her right, we're going to play some version of good cop, bad cop with another cop. "Not really. Just following up for a family member."

"Sure," Parello says, "and you just bring along an FBI agent for company." He looks at Andie. "Something else going on here you want to tell me about?"

"I'm not at liberty to say," Andie says. "All I can tell you is, it's an ongoing investigation."

"Did you talk to any of Sims's family?" I ask

Parello nods. "Yeah, some woman, said she was his sister."

"She came in here? Do you remember what she looked like?"

Parello is already shaking his head no. "On the phone. She never came in, and she was very pushy. Kept asking how we knew it was her brother, how we knew it was suicide. Without a body, there wasn't much I could tell her. We had to go on the word of his friend. We didn't have a photo, and the sister didn't offer one." Parello shrugs. "Some friend, huh? Friends don't let friends dive into the bay. Guy was a total freak-out, but hey, we got 'em in San Francisco."

Andie and I glance at each other, both of us thinking the same thing. Parello hands back the file, and Andie looks like she wants to open it again right there.

"There is one thing," Parello says. "The sister never claimed his horn, and we didn't know how to contact her."

"His horn?" I shift forward on my chair.

"Yeah, the jumper was some kind of musician, I guess. Couldn't get much out of the friend. A space case."

"Can we see it?" I ask.

Parello pauses and looks at both of us.

"I can get a court order," Andie says.

Parello weighs his options for a moment. He says, "I'm sure you can, and I can still make lunch if I don't get hung up with you two. C'mon," he says, getting up and shoving the chair under his desk.

Parello leads us downstairs to the basement. After some small talk in the evidence room, a tall, skinny sergeant finally produces the horn from shelves crammed with boxes, suitcases, and an array of confiscated weapons that range from baseball bats and swords to automatic rifles.

I don't know what I expected to find. The case and horn are nothing special—just a tenor saxophone in a fiber case—but there is one thing. I take the horn out and look in the small reed compartment.

Lying on the bottom is a white feather.

I hold it up for Andie to see, then put it in my pocket.

"We need to take this," Andie says, looking at Parello and tapping on the horn case. "If you need—"

"I know," Parello says. "You can get a court order."

Andie signs a release form while I repack the horn. As we're leaving, Parello stands, hands on his hips, facing us. "Hey, sometime I'd like to hear what this is all about."

Once we're back in the car, Andie opens the file folder and points to the name. "Robert Wiley. The Robert at the church? I never connected that, did you?"

"I'd like to talk to him again." Something bothers me about the whole thing. If Gillian was so concerned about her brother, why didn't she come to San Francisco? Why only phone calls? And why didn't she claim her brother's horn? Maybe Robert has some answers, something to use with Gillian the next time she calls.

"How—back to the church?" Andie asks. "You think he hangs out there?"

"Maybe, but I want to do this by myself. If I do find him, I don't think he'll talk with you around."

Surprisingly, Andie doesn't give me any argument. "All right," she says. "I'll drop you off at the church and see if I can run down an address."

"Try the Veteran's Administration first. Robert had that look."

Andie nods and starts the car. We retrace our route from the day before down Divisdero. A half block from the John Coltrane Church, I see Sister Deborah locking the front gate.

"Let me out," I say to Andie. "See if you can find an address, and then pick me up in front of the church." I get out, and Andie drives off. I jog toward Sister Deborah as she heads for her car. She sees me coming toward her, stops, and smiles.

"Hello," she says. "I'm afraid we're not open until later. I just had to stop by and pick something up."

"That's okay." We stand on the corner, traffic rushing by, pedestrians brushing past us. We move over to the side against the building. "I wanted to get in contact with Robert, the guy that was here yesterday."

Sister Deborah's face clouds over. "Robert is very troubled," she says. "Is it something about your friend, the one who died?"

"Yes. I'd like to talk to Robert again."

Sister Deborah studies me for a moment. "Robert's not in any trouble, I hope?"

"No, nothing like that. He was the last one to see my friend. I just want to—"

"Well, I'm sorry, I can't help you," she says. "Robert hangs around the church a lot, but I don't know where he lives."

"Any idea where he works? Does he have a job?"

She shakes her head. "Sorry, I don't know. Sometimes he comes by for the meals we make, but if he has a job, I don't know where it is or what he does." She smiles again. "I'm sorry I can't help. If I see him, I'll tell Robert you're looking for him."

"No, that's all right, don't bother. Thanks for your time, Sister."

She nods and walks toward her car. I pace around in front of the church for a few minutes, scanning the street, wondering if Robert lives in the neighborhood.

Andie pulls up then. She leans over and rolls down the window. "Well?" I say.

"Get in," she says. "It's only a few blocks from here."

Andie turns off Divisdero at the next corner. A few blocks later, she turns again and pulls up near a row of run-down apartment blocks. She checks the number against a piece of paper and turns off the engine.

"You were right. A 'Nam vet. He gets a monthly VA disability check," she says, "so I think the address is good. It's number eight."

"Okay, I'll do this." I get out of the car and walk up to the building. There's a row of mailboxes, but no name next to number eight. I climb stairs to the third floor before I find Robert's. I knock several times, but there's no answer. I try a couple of other doors on the same floor, but no answer there either.

I go back to the car. Andie has found a better parking place across the street with a clear view of the apartment entrance. I get in and light a cigarette. "Not home," I tell her.

"Let's wait awhile," she says. She shifts in her seat so that she's leaning against her door, facing me at an angle. "I'm almost tempted to have one of those," she says, looking at my cigarette.

"Does it bother you?" I blow the smoke out the window.

"No, not really. It's just tempting."

We sit for a few minutes, watching traffic, keeping one eye on the building.

Andie gets some gum out of her purse, then leans back against the door, a slight smile playing on her lips.

"You know, I almost knocked on your door last night."

"Why didn't you?"

"I don't know."

"I'm glad you didn't," she says. "I would have let you in."

I look at her for a moment. "It's all about timing, isn't it?"

"Timing is everything."

I look away from Andie, not really ready to get into this, when I see a tall man, maybe thirty-something, go into the building, but it's not Robert. Andie follows my gaze. "If we find him, what are you going to ask Robert?"

"I don't know, but there's just something about the whole thing that doesn't hang together."

"You mean Gillian not coming here?"

"That, for sure."

Andie nods. "Maybe she was already planning, didn't want anyone to see her, much less the police." Andie sits up suddenly. "There, isn't that him?"

Robert comes down the street in the same clothes he had on yesterday. Scruffy jeans, the long shirt hanging loose outside. He stops every few feet, looks in storefront windows or stares at the traffic. Finally he turns in at the apartment entrance.

"Let's give him a couple of minutes," I say.

"You sure you don't want me to go with you?"

"No, it's better if I go alone." I get out of the car and walk up to the building. It's still very quiet as I climb the stairs. I knock again at Robert's door, but there's no answer. I listen at the door, knock again. A few moments later, Robert answers.

"Who is it?" Robert's voice is muffled, but he's close to the door. There's no peephole, so I know he can't be looking out at me.

"Robert? I was at the church yesterday. Remember? I'm a friend of Greg's."

Nothing. Then, "What do you want?"

"Just want to talk to you." I reach in my pocket and touch the feather. "I have something I want to give you."

More silence as Robert thinks it over, then the clicking sounds as locks turn. He opens the door a couple of inches and peers out. All I can see is eyes, the bushy beard, and wild hair.

"Hi, Robert. Can I come in? Just want to talk to you for a minute."

"Why? What do you want?" His eyes go over my shoulder, seeing if there's someone with me.

"I have something for you. It belonged to Greg." The door opens a bit more. Robert is wary, his eyes searching my face.

"What? Show me."

I hold up the white feather. "This," I say. "I think this was Greg's, wasn't it?"

Robert turns his head back inside but keeps his hands solidly on the door, then looks back at me. His eyes lock on the feather. "Where did you get that?" he asks. His eyes flick back and forth between me and the feather.

"Can we just talk for a minute? I have Greg's horn too."

Robert's eyes widen even more. "They wouldn't give it to me," he says.

"Who?"

"The police. They weren't nice to me." He turns his

head inside again. I can almost feel someone standing behind him. He steps aside then, and the door opens wider. The tall man we saw go into the building earlier is standing there.

"It's all right, Robert," he says. "Who are you?" He looks at the feather, a flicker of recognition passes over his eyes.

"Evan Horne. I'm—I was—a friend of Greg's. I'm just checking things out for his family. I wanted to return his horn."

"Where's the horn?"

"It's in my car."

"I don't know you," he says, "and you didn't know Greg." He sighs deeply. His head dips forward. He shakes it from side to side. He opens the door wider.

I feel a chill come over me. I want to say, Sorry to bother you, turn, and go back down the stairs, tell Andie there's nothing here. But it's too late. He looks at me, knows I know.

"Come in," he says. "I've been expecting you." He stands aside to let me in.

"I'm Greg Sims."

TWELVE

I STEP INSIDE. Greg Sims shuts the door and leads me down the hall, back to the kitchen. We pass a bedroom, and I catch a glimpse of unmade twin beds. "It's all right," he says, turning to Robert, who is close behind us. "Why don't you go watch some TV, okay?"

Sims is very soft-spoken, polite but firm, as if he were speaking to a well-behaved child. Robert nods, gives me one more wary look, then goes into the living room. A few seconds later we hear the television blare, tuned to some game show.

"Sorry," Sims says to me. "Robert's hearing is not too good. Coffee?" He fills up a kettle and puts it on to boil, then turns around.

"Sure." We stand facing each other in front of the stove. Sims shifts from one foot to the other, then gets a jar of coffee and two mugs from the cupboard. "Sorry, I only have instant."

"That's fine." I can't help staring. It's not every day you find someone you thought was dead. I feel like I've stumbled into a dream, disoriented by hazy unfocused images, confused feelings. Any minute I expect Rod Serling to appear and announce we're in the twilight zone.

Sims glances at me. "You're surprised," he says.

"I'm floored. I didn't expect to... Well, you know." I turn around and sit down at a small table while Sims waits for the water to boil.

He sighs again. "I guess I knew somebody would find

me eventually. Actually, I'm kind of relieved. I just didn't want it to be…Gillian. Did she send you?''

''No, I've never even met Gillian.''

''Who, then?'' Sims asks. He looks at me strangely, his eyes clouded with apprehension.

''I've only talked to her on the phone.'' He doesn't even ask if something has happened to her.

''I don't understand.''

''There's a lot to tell. It's a long story, Greg.''

He spoons coffee into the mugs. He knows, but he doesn't want to hear it yet.

''You told Robert you have my horn. Is that right?''

''Yes, I have it with me. Do you want me to get it?''

''Yes, would you mind?'' he says. He turns toward me. A light of interest flickers in his eyes.

''Be right back.''

Robert looks up when I pass the living room. I go out and back down the stairs two at a time, my mind whirling with questions. I dodge a couple of cars and run across the street to Andie. She's looking straight ahead, then does a double take when she sees me.

''What?'' she says. ''Did you talk to Robert?'' I get the horn out of the backseat.

''Yeah, and I also talked to Greg Sims. He's alive.''

''What?'' She starts to get out of the car, but I put my hand on the door.

''No, not yet. Stay here. I have to talk to him first. Let me see how it goes.''

''Evan—''

I dart back across the street before Andie can protest. Robert lets me in. He eyes the horn case, then returns to the living room, the television still blaring.

''Here,'' I say to Sims, handing him the horn. He looks at it for a moment, then takes it from me, sets it on the

counter, fumbles with the catches, and opens the case
slowly. He reaches out with one hand to touch the horn,
then steps back, unsure. He shakes his head and lifts the
horn out of the case like a child opening a gift Christmas
morning.

"Didn't think I'd see this again," he says. The apprehension dissolves into a slight smile. "Robert tried to get
it back for me."

The water is boiling then. He holds the horn under one
arm as all tenor players do, pours water into the mugs, and
hands me one with a spoon already in it. I stir my coffee
and watch him assemble the horn.

He pulls the cap off the mouthpiece, wets the reed, and
blows a few tentative notes. He laughs at the sound. "Been
a long time," he says, glancing at me.

He tries again, a few bars of a blues line. It's jagged,
erratic; most of the notes don't come out. He stops, shakes
his head again. His eyes flick over to me, then he blows
once again but stops, laughs halfway through, and sets the
horn down in the open case, stares at it for a moment.

Robert peeks around the corner at Greg. His eyes dart
from me to Greg and back again. Greg senses him, turns
around. "It's all right, Robert. I'm fine." Robert nods and
slips away.

Greg looks at the horn again. "Wow, been a long time,"
he says again. He joins me at the table and stirs his own
coffee, takes a sip.

I remember the feather, take it out of my pocket, and
hand it to him. "Why the feather?"

He takes it, spins it back and forth between his fingers,
then drops it on the horn. It clings to one of the keys.

"Kind of a good-luck charm. You know—Bird, Charlie
Parker." His eyes cloud over as he remembers. "You're a

musician, huh?'' He doesn't say "too," because he's not anymore.

"Yeah, piano. How'd you know? Robert?"

Sims nods. "He heard you talking about me at the church, Sister Deborah inviting you to come play. That's why I was expecting you."

"Is that the only reason?" I've known from the moment he let me in he was going to tell me everything, but it's going to be in his own time, his own way, a delicate balance I have to try and maintain.

I visualize Andie sitting out front, checking traffic, watching the entrance, getting more irritated by the minute. I don't want her charging up here and spooking Greg Sims.

"If it's not for Gillian, I guess I'm just kind of wondering why. Are you and Gillian—"

"No."

"No, I didn't think so." He turns and stares out the window, which opens onto a courtyard in back. There are a few trees and a small patch of grass. The window is like a mirror, sparkling clean like the rest of the kitchen.

"You know how long it takes, how much work, but no matter how much you put into it, how much you love it, there also has to be talent, a lot of it." He shrugs, smiles slightly. "I had some, but not enough."

"But is that a reason to—"

"I also had a driving, pushy, obsessed sister—Gillian. She's a few years older than me. Our parents split when we were kids, and our mother died shortly after. Never heard from my father again, but he left all his records. Quite a collection."

Sims smiles again as he remembers. "Lester Young, Coleman Hawkins, big bands, Dizzy, Bird, he had everything. God, I loved those records. I listened to them a lot, made me feel I had some connection with him." He speaks softly, in a detached kind of way, as if he's talking about someone else, but he looks beaten, used up. He looks at me. "Is that crazy?"

"Not at all."

"Thanks," Sims says. "Anyway, Gillian kind of raised me. She was determined we were both going to do well, despite what had happened."

"Gillian what? What's her last name?"

"Payne. She took it from my dad, pain, I mean, and she gave it out. That's the name she took. She always liked to play with words." He doesn't even pause. It's as if he's been carrying this around, wanting to let go of it, for a long time, and I'm the first to know.

"When I joined the junior high band, Gillian decided right then I was going to be a musician. It was fun at first, but I knew even then I didn't have that edge, that extra something, but she never let up."

Sims sighs and shakes his head. "I managed a scholarship to Berklee, but I knew the first day I was out of my league. I wanted to quit, do something else, but Gillian wouldn't hear of it. So I just took off, came out here, tried to disappear, but she found me. She's very good at that. Kept saying I just needed a chance, blamed it on the music business, how jazz had changed."

"Greg, did you know a musician at Berklee named Bobby Ware, called himself Cochise?"

"Sure," Greg says. "I knew him slightly at Berklee; he became a big star. He didn't learn that music at Berklee though. Not my kind of jazz. When I read about it, I couldn't believe someone I knew had been killed." Sims laughs nervously. "Everybody called me Zoot at Berklee because of my last name and all, but I was more into Trane."

I haven't touched my coffee. I push my cup aside and

lean forward. "Greg, listen to me. The killer was your sister, Gillian."

He looks at me. His eyes dart around, his mouth is half open. "What? What do you mean?" He rocks back in the chair.

"Greg, there were three others. Do you understand what I'm telling you?" I wait a moment, see the truth forming in his eyes. "Gillian has killed four people, all musicians."

His eyes are wide now, panicked. "Gilly? Oh God, no, that can't be." But I can see he knows it is. He gets up from the table and slowly walks around the kitchen as if movement will still the panic. "How can you be sure?"

"With two of them, she left a white feather. She wrote 'Bird Lives!' on the mirror of Ty Rodman's dressing room in L.A. It was Gillian. She's been calling me, pushing me to investigate your suicide."

He backs up a couple of steps, like he's been pushed. "I don't understand. Why? Why are you here?"

I sketch in the story, tell him about her threats, as quickly as I can, right up to finding him. Greg listens but doesn't say a word until I'm through. He sits down again, still shaking his head. "You'll never catch her," he says. "Never, she's too smart."

"We have to, Greg. You can help us, you know her, stop her from killing more. She needs help, Greg."

"Oh, no," he says, crossing his hands back and forth in front of him, like a referee calling time out. "I can't see Gillian again. She thinks I'm dead, and that's the way I want to keep it. I can't go through that again."

I reach across the table and touch his arm, keep my voice low and steady. "Greg, I know this is hard, but you're the only one who can stop her. Think about it. You don't want her killing anybody else, do you?"

"No, of course not, but...it's just so hard to believe." I

know he's wrestling with it. His fear of Gillian is real, though. "What would I have to do?" He asks, but he doesn't want to know.

"Look, I'm just a go-between here, Greg. The FBI is handling this, and one of their agents is with me. She's outside right now. Let's talk to her, see what's the best way to handle things, okay?"

"The FBI? I, I don't know."

"Listen to me, Greg. They'll protect you from Gillian." I take a deep breath, blow out air, and jump in with both feet.

"If they don't, I will."

Natalie was right all along. Deeper by the minute.

I DON'T WANT to leave Sims, but I know if I don't get Andie soon, she'll come up on her own. I've got to convince her this is the right thing to do.

When I get downstairs, she's standing by the car, fuming. "Goddammit, Evan, don't do that again. What is going on? You've been up there a half-hour."

"Get in the car. Please." Her eyes are blazing, but she gets in, and I join her in the front seat.

I recount my conversation with Greg Sims. She listens without interrupting till I'm finished.

"I don't think I even want to hear what you've got in mind," she says.

"Greg Sims is shaky. He's very afraid of Gillian. He'll help, I think, but we've got to protect him from her. He's got to know that. She could be up here in San Francisco now, watching us. If she sees Greg before we're ready, she'll freak."

Andie is watching me warily now. "What do you mean, before we're ready?"

"I mean we've got to keep Greg under wraps for now."

"We?"

"Look, I don't know or care how you do it, but you've got to fix it so we can keep Greg safe until the right time."

"And when will that be? Jesus, the man faked his own suicide."

"So what, that's not illegal. Remember Gillian's bargain. I've not only found him, I've found him alive. That might be enough to get her to come in."

Andie sits very still for a few moments, staring out the windshield, gripping the wheel. Finally she turns to me. "Wendell Cook will never go for this."

"He has to. C'mon, what else have you got?" I light a cigarette and watch Andie as she plays with the idea, and whether to trust me. I keep checking the apartment entrance, half expecting Greg Sims to bolt.

"All right," Andie says. She grips the steering wheel with both hands. "But I want to spend some time with Sims before I call anybody. Then we'll go from there."

"Fair enough. Let's get him out of here, back to our hotel."

"What about Robert?"

I already have my hand on the door handle. "Robert will be fine."

AT THE TRAVELODGE, Greg sits slumped in a chair while Andie talks to him softly, carefully, reassuring, spelling everything out, while she makes notes. She's good and has quickly established a rapport but been firm at the same time.

I listen but really don't know what to do. I imagine this is what it must be like debriefing a defector in a safe house. Andie glances up at me every once in a while until she finally has to say something to me.

"Evan, why don't you take a walk or something?"

"Yeah, maybe I will. You okay?" I ask Greg. He looks tired. I wonder if he knows how different his life is going to be from now on.

Back at the apartment, I watched him say good-bye to Robert and patiently explain that he was going to have to go away for a while. They shook hands solemnly, and Greg threw some things in a small bag and went down to the car. I turned back once and saw Robert watching us all the way down the stairs.

"Okay, I'll be back in a while." I start for the door.

"Here," Andie says, tossing me the cell phone. "Don't forget this."

I catch the phone, put it in my pocket, and get out, leaving Andie and Greg Sims to finish up.

I wander down to Fisherman's Wharf, dodging the crowd of tourists and try to find some sense of reality and optimism about finding Greg Sims. Even Gillian would have to consider this a success, actually finding her brother alive; but if I'm right, she's going to be very angry with Greg when she finds his suicide was faked and why. She'll feel betrayed, want to strike out at someone, and I'll be handy.

I walk to the edge of the wharf, lean on the railing, and look down into the cold, gray water. The sun has broken through, and most of the fog that shrouded the Golden Gate Bridge earlier is gone. Sightseers of all ages swarm around me. I watch one group of Japanese line up for the ferry to Alcatraz; I'm feeling the urge to join them, when the cell phone rings.

A little girl about eight or nine sees me grab the phone. "Look, Mommy, that man has a phone in his pocket." Her mother takes her hand and pulls her away.

I turn away from the railing and walk toward the middle of the parking lot. "Where are you, lover?" Gillian says. There's a click, then Chet Baker's trumpet eases into "The

Very Thought of You,'' frail, delicate, the air almost before
the notes.

"Don't you know?"

"Don't play with me, Evan. I've been busy, and I hope
you have been too.'' I look up at the sky. If she knew where
I was, she'd let me know; Gillian must still be in L.A.

"Yes, just like you said. Working on it.''

"Working on Agent Lawrence too.'' There's a smile in
her voice.

"What do you mean?''

"Oh, you know exactly what I mean, Evan. You're curious about her, aren't you? Natalie giving you a hard time?
Well, that's okay, I don't mind if you play a little, long as
you keep focused.''

"I'm not curious about her. She's an FBI agent.''

"Of course you're curious, Evan. She's an attractive
woman. Do you really think it was an accident they assigned her to you? She came to see you at Chadney's, and
your Natalie didn't. When two people are thrown together
like that, anything can happen.''

Chet Baker airily slides into the next phrase. A necklace
of poignant, almost blue notes, strung together on the
changes of his life. "Nothing is going to happen with Andie.''

Gillian laughs. "Oh, it's Andie, is it? Maybe not, but
you've been thinking about it, haven't you, Evan? Wondering what she'd be like.''

"I've got to go, Gillian. You want me to stay on this,
don't you?''

"Have fun, Evan. You better have something for me
soon.'' She's gone then, as Chet Baker surrenders to the
pianist.

AT SAN FRANCISCO airport Andie flashes her FBI badge,
and we bump three people to get on the flight. We're even

allowed to board first. Greg Sims remains quiet and withdrawn. Once we're airborne, he settles into the seat next to me and dozes. Andie is across the narrow aisle, reading from the notes she's made on Greg. I still haven't told her about Gillian's latest call, and I wonder if I should.

There was nothing in the call that pertained to the case, but I was unprepared for the impact Gillian's words had on me. She's right, of course. I'm very curious about Andie Lawrence, very attracted to her, and now very confused about my relationship with Natalie. What really bothers me is Gillian's suggestion that Andie was not assigned to me by accident. Did Cook see it too? Did Andie push for it?

I glance at Andie. Her elbow is on the arm of the seat, her chin in her hand. I lean across to her, my voice muffled by the drone of the engines and the conversation around us. "Why you?"

"Why me what?" She looks up from her notes.

"Why did Cook assign you to me instead of Ted Rollins?"

"Rollins?" Andie laughs. "You two didn't exactly hit it off."

I keep looking at her. I know the unlocked door to our adjoining rooms at the Travelodge is still on both our minds.

"Okay." She closes her notebook and sips from her Coke. I opted for Scotch when the attendant took our orders.

"That was only part of it. I guess I wanted to see if this was going to go anywhere." I still don't look away.

"You want it plainer?" She shifts toward me. "Okay, the first day you walked in, I knew I was interested. You had me at hello. How's that?"

"What about Natalie?"

"What about her? You're not married, you're not engaged, you don't even live together. She's not exactly standing by you in this, is she?"

I look away. Andie's only half right. Maybe I'm expecting too much of Natalie. I can't tell her everything, and she has little to go on except that I'm spending a lot of time with another woman, even if she is an FBI agent.

Andie reaches across the aisle and touches my arm. "I'm sorry, that wasn't fair." She smiles. "Remember what I told you before? Timing is everything. I shouldn't have to tell a musician that."

I finish my drink. The flight attendant comes by with a plastic bag collecting glasses, looking like she'd rather be anywhere than at twenty-eight thousand feet. She makes me think of Cindy Fuller, also a flight attendant, and how much a part of my life she'd been for a while, when she lived next door to me. I lean back on the seat and close my eyes. But twice, when I open them, I catch Andie glancing up from her notes, looking at me. I don't think she's really working.

We hit an air pocket, and the pilot announces our descent into Los Angeles. Greg Sims doesn't even stir. When we taxi to the gate, I have to wake him and get our bags out of the overhead compartment.

Andie has called ahead. Amid the mob of friends and relatives waiting at the gate at LAX, we have our own welcoming committee. Craning their necks for a first look, Wendell Cook and Ted Rollins might as well be wearing FBI warm-up jackets instead of the dark suits. Cook is pacing, scanning the lounge area, and Rollins is on his cell phone. I wonder for a minute if he's going to call Andie.

The only one I'm glad to see is Coop. He stands off to the side, looking cool as only Coop can, like he's just waiting to fly standby.

Cook nods at me, shakes hands with Greg, and then, one arm around his shoulder, walks him over to a deserted gate area where they sit down. Cook never takes his eyes off Greg's face. Andie and Coop follow and stand a few feet away, talking. I start to join them when Rollins pulls me aside.

"So that's the loony tune's brother, huh?" he says to me. "He looks a little wacky too. Maybe it runs in the family. How do we know he isn't in on it with her?" While he's talking to me, Rollins scans the faces. I bet he enjoyed flashing his badge to security.

"Sure, Rollins, that's why he faked his suicide."

"Well, he has possibly broken the law."

"Really? What did he gain? Since when is it illegal to disappear?"

"We'll have to deal with that issue. Any deals you made with him are subject to Bureau approval."

"Wouldn't have it any other way, Ted." I'm tired. I just want to get away from here, from everybody.

Rollins gives me a puzzled look. "I have to admit, that was pretty good work, Horne. You know, I've been thinking, maybe you and me, we could turn over a new leaf, since we're working together."

"A new leaf? Rollins, you'd have to replant the whole forest."

The muscles of Rollins's eyes twitch and pulsate. He just gets in "Fuck you, Horne," before Wendell Cook comes over.

"Nice going, Evan," Cook says. "This may be the break we needed."

"Ted was just telling me that, weren't you?"

Cook glances between the two of us, decides that isn't worth pursuing. "We're going to take care of Sims, get him fixed up somewhere safe."

"Just go easy on him," I say. "It may not look like it, but he's been through a lot."

"I can see that." Cook's big, round, sturdy face looks comforting. I'm sure Greg will be okay with him. Coop aside, if there's anyone I trust, it's Wendell Cook.

"Okay, we're out of here then. Coop will take you home, and we'll want to see you tomorrow. Gillian will expect you to go on with things, so do whatever you think." He turns to Rollins. "Ted, you come with us." He signals Andie, and the four of them start the long trek to the street.

I catch Greg's eye and give him the thumbs-up sign. I've already given him my number. Andie smiles at me once, pats her coat pocket, and points to me. I don't understand the gesture.

"Well, the prodigal son returns," Coop says. "You've got the FBI pretty heated up."

"Hey, Coop, tell me something good."

"I will. Tell you on the way."

"Where we going?"

"Somebody wants to see you."

THIRTEEN

WHEN WE GET to the street, I look around for Coop's car, but see only cabs, shuttle buses, and tired travelers loading suitcases into station wagons and sport utility vehicles.

"It's in the parking garage," he says.

"I thought you'd leave it at the curb with the red light on."

"Nah, you know me, never take advantage of my official law enforcement capacity. I leave that to Ted Rollins."

"Yeah, he's a real piece of work, always on my case." An airport security cop stands in the middle of the crosswalk and blows his whistle and waves his arms, signaling us to cross. We shoulder our way past the wave of people coming our way who can't wait to get out of L.A.

"Yeah, well, leave his girlfriend alone." Coop smirks as we cross the street and head into the garage.

"Andie? You're kidding?"

"Nope. He told me. She won't give him a tumble, though. She goes for musicians, it seems."

I remember Andie's gesture at the gate then and check my coat pocket. I pull out a scrap of paper with "Call me" scribbled in her hand. That I will do. We have a lot to talk about.

Once we clear the airport, Coop turns north on Lincoln. I roll down the window and light a cigarette. "So, any new developments?"

Coop shakes his head and glares at a Toyota that tries to cut him off. "Valet parking guy at Chadney's vaguely remembers a woman alone in a Lexus, but it's nothing we can take to the bank. Otherwise, zip. I told you if anybody takes this fruitcake down, it would be you. Finding the brother alive was a break. They'll start running Gillian through NCIC and DMV. Any more calls from her?''

"Yeah, one, while Andie was grilling Greg Sims."

Coop glances at me as he swings into the right lane and turns east on Wilshire. "And?"

"This one was different. She talked about me and Andie, wanted to know if I was interested. Playing with my head."

"Bet you didn't tell Andie about that one."

"No, I didn't. Where are we going anyway?"

"Somebody wants to talk to you." He pulls up in front of a coffee place Natalie and I have gone to many times. When he doesn't turn off the engine, I look at Coop. He nods his head toward the patio seating. Natalie is sitting at one of the outside tables. She glances up at the car and waves.

"If it goes well, Natalie will take you home. Otherwise, you can call me," Coop says.

"Does she know that?"

"You'll find out soon enough," Coop says. I get out of the car and shut the door. Coop leans over. "Tell Andie about that last call, or I will."

"Always the cop."

"That's me," Coop says, then he drives off.

I walk over to where Natalie is sitting. "Hi," I say.

"Hi yourself." She tries a smile but doesn't quite make it. She looks tired and drawn. There's a half-full cup of coffee in front of her.

"Want a refill?"

"No, I'm fine. Get something for yourself."

I go inside, get a large coffee, and bring it back to the table. I sit down and light a cigarette. "Why the secrecy?"

Natalie shrugs. "Coop thought it was best. He told me some of it."

"What? What did he tell you?" I sip my coffee, keep my eyes on her face.

Natalie looks away. "He told me you're helping the FBI catch a serial killer, you're the contact, that she's calling you and you've made some kind of deal with her."

"Is that all? Did he tell you what the deal was?"

"No, but isn't that enough? God, Evan, what are you doing to yourself? How did you allow this to happen? How long is this going to go on?"

"I didn't allow anything, it just happened. I told you before, I can't walk away from this."

"No, you never can." She pulls her jacket tightly around her body and stares at her coffee. More quietly now, she says, "How was San Francisco?"

"Fine. We maybe have a break in things."

"We? You and Andie Lawrence, right? She was with you?"

"You know she was."

"Did you sleep with her?"

I look away and let that hang in the air for several moments. "Come on, Natalie." I crush out my cigarette and lean forward with my arms on the table. "I had the chance, but no, I didn't. You'll have to take my word for it."

I watch Natalie. It's not much, but I see a flicker of relief graze her face, soften her eyes. Any other answer, and it would have been over right here, sitting on hard metal chairs at a coffee place on Wilshire.

I think back to our first days together, meeting in Las Vegas, driving back across the desert to L.A., and later, meetings at this very place that began as stolen moments and turned into long sessions, talking about everything. I never dreamed then we'd be having this conversation.

"Well, that's something," she says. She sips her coffee and sets the cup down carefully, but she won't look at me. It's as if she's been rehearsing, and now she's ready for a first reading.

"I've had a lot of time to think, Evan. I don't know what's happening with us, but I think we both need some time apart, at least until this, whatever this is, is over."

"You said that the other day."

"I was angry then. Seeing Andie at your place, listening to music—"

"I explained that. It had nothing to do with Andie and me. It's part of the case."

"I know, but now that I've had more time to think—she doesn't matter—I still feel the same way. I don't know what it is, Evan, but there's always been a part of you I couldn't get to. Maybe nobody can. You always seem to hold something back, and that's made me think about us even more."

I have no answer for that. She's probably right. Not many people get in all the way. Natalie has been the closest.

"Do you know how long this is going to go on?"

"No."

"What about the recording? The trio?"

"Why didn't you come to Chadney's? You could have heard."

"Was she there?"

"Yes, but that was also part of the case. I couldn't do anything about that." I feel my anger rising. This is old ground.

"Sure. Anyway, I've decided." She looks at me now. "I think you need to decide some things too, and we have to do that alone."

"So that's it?"

"For now, yes."

A kid in a white apron is wiping down tables, straightening chairs. He catches my eye and comes over.

"We're closing. Can I take these?" He points at the cups.

I look at Natalie. She nods slightly. "Yeah, we're finished." I wait till he's back inside.

"Natalie, don't dangle this in front of me. It would be nice to know that you're behind me on everything too. If you're not, I need to decide what to do about it."

"Yes, you do." Her voice is firm but so quiet I almost can't hear. She stands up then. "Let's see how we do on our own, okay? I want you to be sure."

"If that's the way you want it."

"It's not the way I want it, Evan. It's the way it is."

She touches my shoulder, gives me another half smile, then turns and walks off, slowly at first; then she gathers speed as I watch her go, head down, shoulders slumped, hugging herself, all the way to her car. I wait to see if she turns around, but she doesn't, and I don't go after her.

I sit there for a long time, thinking, smoking, long after the lights go off and I'm left in the darkness.

Then I call Coop.

IT'S RAINING AND DARK when I wake up. A slow, fine drizzle, just enough to keep an oily sheen on the streets, reflects headlights and neon and makes driving an exercise in tension. I lie still for several minutes, listening to the rain, listening for the phone, listening to my own heartbeat.

A little over a week ago I was well on the way to a comeback, a recording contract in the offing, my hand better than ever. Now I'm helping the FBI, getting calls from a psycho serial killer; and Natalie, if she isn't already gone, is rapidly slipping away.

Maybe she was right. We need time alone, time for me

to decide what I want. Maybe I need to really see what Andie Lawrence is all about. Was Gillian right? How interested am I? Enough to cross that line? How did I let Gillian get into my head? There's no turning back if I do, not with Natalie. Keep up with things as usual, Wendell Cook had said. I don't even know what that means anymore.

I get up, make coffee, and call Jeff Lasorda. "Hey," Jeff says, "everything still cool?"

"A few complications, but otherwise no problem." Jeff is silent for a moment, not sure what to say. "Any chance we could get together this afternoon?" I need to play, keep up some semblance of normality until Gillian's next call.

"Sure, fine with me," Jeff says. "Want me to call Gene, see if he can make it?"

"Yeah, let's do that. Thanks, Jeff. Your place?"

"I'm here."

Next I call Andie Lawrence. "How's it going?"

"It's not. She's a phantom. Gillian Sims, Gillian Payne, there's nothing on her anywhere, but we're still looking."

I sigh. How can anyone elude the FBI like that? "How's Greg?"

"He's fine, don't worry about him."

I think of something else then. "Has he played his horn at all?"

"Yeah, he had it out, fooling around with it. He seems embarrassed, though. Why do you want to know if he's been playing?"

"I've got an idea, to push things along."

"What?"

"When Gillian calls, I want to tell her I've got Greg's horn, see if she'll meet with me."

There's silence for several moments on Andie's end. "I

don't think so. She'd never go for it, and neither would Wendell.''

"Andie, I want this over. It's worth a try, isn't it?"

"All right, I'll run it by Wendell. Evan, I want to see you."

"I want to see you too. I'm rehearsing this afternoon. I'll call you later."

"Do that." She hangs up then.

The line has been drawn.

GENE, IT TURNS OUT, can't make it, but at Jeff's house, he and I go over a number of tunes, rewrite some chord changes, and decide on some sketchy arrangements for the recording.

For some reason I feel more relaxed, as if I've turned a corner somehow. Jeff notices and rises to the occasion, literally reading my mind. The musical bond between us grows as the afternoon wears on.

"You're playing in the zone, man," Jeff says, after over an hour. "Especially on 'The Very Thought of You.' What made you think of that one?"

I shrug. "Don't know. Just heard it again recently." I look at my watch. "I have to go. Thanks, Jeff. This was a good session. I'll call you." He lays down his bass and walks me to my car.

"My offer is still good, you know, if things get too weird."

"Thanks. Don't worry. Things ain't what they used to be, but they're going to get better."

"Now there's a tune," Jeff says.

As soon as I hit the Ventura Freeway, I call Andie. "I'll be a while," The rain has quit, but the oil-and-water slick makes for slow going. I circle around two fender benders before I merge onto the San Diego Freeway.

"Okay," Andie says. "I'm leaving the office now. How about if I pick up some Chinese?"

"Sounds good to me. See you then." I break the connection and crawl over the Sepulveda pass behind a snarl of winking brake lights, all of us packed together in five lanes. I manage to squeeze over, take the Sunset exit, and make it to Andie's without any mishaps or calls.

She comes to the door in jeans and a soft white turtleneck sweater, a whiff of perfume trailing after her. Inside there are cartons of rice and a variety of dishes on the table. Carmen McRae is singing Monk on her CD player. "Thought we could share," Andie says.

I hang my coat over the back of a chair, feel the weight of the cell phone I'm never without now. "Great, I'm hungry."

She brings two bottles of Henry Weinhard and plates to the table, and we dig in with the plastic chopsticks. We eat, listen to Carmen McRae, and sneak glances at each other, relative strangers, circling, investigating. It's unspoken, but things have changed now, and we both know it.

"You're different tonight somehow," Andie says.

"Am I?" I push my plate aside and drain the last of my beer.

She nods, drinks from her own. "Rehearsing must agree with you. How did it go?"

"Fine, it's coming together well. What about you?"

Andie sighs and sets her bottle on the table, turning it in circles. "No luck on Gillian, but I didn't expect any." She holds my gaze for a moment. "Wendell didn't think much of your idea about meeting with her."

"But?"

"He's weakening. Hell, he's desperate. We just have nothing else. Are you sure you want to do this?"

"I don't see that I have much choice. I told you, Andie, I want this over."

She looks away. "I know, I know. There are just so many ifs. Gillian has to call again, she has to agree, and I don't know how we'd handle it."

"What do you mean? Handle it?" I reach for my cigarettes. "Come outside with me."

I go out on the patio. Andie joins me and brings another beer. I lean on the railing, feel Andie brush against me as she hands me a bottle.

"I mean we can't just let you go off alone. Gillian's too unpredictable. She'd spot surveillance a mile away. She's too smart. We wouldn't have any control."

I take a deep drag of my cigarette and look out toward the pool. "We'll just have to figure something out, won't we?"

"What have you figured out about Natalie?"

I turn and look at her. "Wow, that's quite a segue."

"Sorry, it's just on my mind. If you don't want to talk about it—"

"No, it's okay. We met last night, kind of a showdown. She thinks we need some time away from each other."

"And what do you think?" Andie moves away, not closer.

"I think she's right."

"Is that why you're here?"

Before I can answer, we both hear a muffled phone ring. "That's mine." I go back inside, take my phone out of my coat, and press the call button. Andie turns off the stereo and stands in the middle of the room.

It's Charlie Parker with strings this time, "Embraceable You." I nod at Andie and sit down on the couch. Andie sits close, at my left. I can feel the warmth of her leg on mine.

"Hello, lover," Gillian's low, languid voice says. "Have you been busy on this rainy day?"

"Very."

"Tell me." The volume of Bird's horn drops down. I hold the phone slightly away from my head, and Andie leans in closer so she can hear.

"I'm back from San Francisco, and I've got your brother's horn."

I press the phone hard to my head. For several moments there's nothing but Charlie Parker's dizzying run of the changes. Then a click—Gillian's lighter—and the sound of exhaling.

"What about Greg?" she asks. There's no playfulness in her tone now. Andie pulls at my arm, signals me to tilt the phone so she can hear.

"I saw the police in San Francisco, Inspector Parello. There was nothing more from them than what he told you." Gillian is quiet again for a moment. "I thought you might want the horn."

"Let me guess. We meet someplace crawling with FBI, I'm captured, you're a hero."

"It doesn't have to be like that. I don't want to be a hero, Gillian. You can call me at the last minute, name the place. There won't be time for them to get there."

Andie's eyes widen. She's shaking her head no.

"How do I know you'll do that?"

"You'll have to trust me."

Andie is gripping my arm hard, her fingers digging in. The volume comes up again as the strings struggle to keep up with Bird.

"I'll call you," Gillian says. "You won't know when, but be ready."

She hangs up. I set the phone down, pry Andie's fingers off my arm, and lean back on the couch. She gets up and begins pacing around the room. Suddenly she stops, looks at me.

"Okay, this is how it can work. One car, maybe two at most, far enough back from you but close enough so we can move in." I get up and walk back out on to the patio, light a cigarette. Andie follows me. "That's the way it's going to have to be, Evan."

I turn around, lean against the rail. "Whatever you say, but I have to get that horn now. There won't be time later. You heard her. She could call anytime."

"Yes, the horn." The rush comes over her, colors her face. "All right, we'll go now."

"One more thing."

"What?"

"There was another call, in San Francisco." Andie stands staring at me. "While you were talking to Greg."

"Yes?"

"I didn't tell you then. It was mostly about you and me, kind of a playing-with-my-mind call."

Andie nods. "That's what the conversation on the plane was about, wasn't it? All those questions about why I was assigned to you."

"Yes."

"She got to you, didn't she?"

"Does it change anything?"

"No, I would still have had the same answers."

I turn back toward the pool, feel Andie reaching out. "Are you going to stay tonight?"

"I don't know. Let's get the horn. Where is Greg?"

She hesitates just for a second. "Rollins is with him. Not far from here."

We go in my car to a motel on Santa Monica Boulevard near the Mormon Temple.

"Wait here," Andie says, getting out of the car. I watch

her walk across the parking lot, glance around, then stop in front of one of the first-floor doors.

I can just make out Rollins, standing in the shaft of light coming from inside. He takes the chain off the door, opens it, and Andie goes inside. She comes out a few minutes later, carrying the horn case. Rollins watches her walk to my car, then shuts the door. Andie gets in, shoves the case in the backseat.

"Let's go," she says.

I pull out and head back for her place. "How's Greg?"

"He was asleep. Rollins is the problem. He wanted to know what's going on."

"Did you tell him?"

"I said we'd meet tomorrow."

I glance at Andie. She's staring straight ahead. When I pull in her parking lot, I don't shut off the engine.

"You're not coming up?"

"Not tonight."

She nods, then leans across and kisses me lightly on the lips, touches the back of my neck. She gets out of the car and walks toward her apartment. She turns and looks back once, smiles.

I sit for a moment, knowing all I have to do is turn off the engine and go upstairs. I won't even have to knock. Her door will be unlocked, at least for a while.

I'M HALFWAY HOME, stopped at a red light, when Gillian calls.

"Where are you?" There's no music, just Gillian's voice.

"Wilshire and Lincoln in Santa Monica."

"Turn on seventh and go down into Santa Monica Canyon. When you get to the beach, park in the lot across the highway and wait."

The light changes to green. I cross the intersection and pull to the curb. "What then?"

"I'll call you. It better be just you and me, lover." Then she hangs up.

I turn north on Seventh, cross San Vicente, and wind down into the canyon with one eye on the rearview mirror. At the Pacific Coast Highway, I turn right, pull into a beach lot, and park close to the sand. I turn off the engine, roll down the window, light a cigarette, and wait. The surf seems louder in the darkness

There are two other cars, lots of space between them. Probably high school kids. In the rearview mirror the PCH traffic rushes by, but no cars turn in the lot or even slow at the entrance.

Maybe she's not coming; maybe this is a test to see if it's a trap. There's no figuring Gillian Payne at this point.

I flip my cigarette out the window and jump when the phone rings.

"Santa Monica Pier," Gillian says. "Walk to the end of the pier and just keep looking out over the water. Don't turn around."

"Wait I—"

"Just do it. You have fifteen minutes." I drop the phone and start the engine and roar out of the lot, turning south on PCH.

Fifteen minutes. No time to get anybody in place, not Andie, the police, just me. I weave in and out of lanes, pushing it all the way. At the California Incline, there's a long light. I hesitate for a moment, then grab the phone and punch in some numbers. It's four rings before I hear a voice.

"Coop. Santa Monica Pier right now. She's coming." I break the connection and shoot up the incline onto Ocean

Avenue. I turn onto the pier, nose down the steep hill, past the carousel as far down as I can go, and park.

There's a couple of restaurants open but few people. I grab the horn case, jump out of the car, and walk to the end of the pier, studying faces. At the end I look around once more, set the case down beside me on its end, and lean on the railing.

I can hear the water lapping against the pilings and smell the ocean, and I wonder if Coop can get here fast enough. Cupping my hands around the flame, I light a cigarette and wait, straining to hear footsteps behind me, but there's nothing but the distant hum of traffic.

"Don't turn around; I don't want to hurt you, Evan." Her voice is even lower than on the phone and right on time.

"Gillian?" My voice is lost in the air.

"Slide down the railing to your left."

I move over several feet, sense her behind me. I grip the railing with both hands. If I have to, I'm going over, into that cold black water.

Gillian drags the case back. One hand busy. What's in her other one? A gun? The knife she used to kill four people? Where is Coop?

I hear the snap of the case pop as she opens it. I picture her kneeling, looking inside. Then the case slams shut, the catches going home, the case being dragged away. Come on, Coop, where are you? Have to keep her here.

"Thank you, Evan."

"Wait. There's more, Gillian."

"More? What do you mean?"

I want to turn around, see her face. "Your brother is alive. I've talked to him, seen him."

Gillian laughs, like she did on the phone. "I expected

more of you, Evan. Please don't tell me I'm surrounded, or the police are on the way."

"It's true. I've talked to Greg. We brought him to L.A."

"You're lying. Did they tell you to say that?"

"No, it's true. He told me everything, about your father, the record collection." I wait a moment but there's no reaction. "He faked his suicide, Gillian. To get away from you."

"No, that's not possible." Her voice breaks slightly.

"You pushed him too far, Gillian. He had to get away from you. He can't play that horn now. I heard him."

"You bastard." She spits out the words. I can feel her coming closer. I grip the railing tighter, brace myself to spring over.

"Hold it right there." Another voice, quiet, hard. Coop, somewhere behind Gillian. "Don't move."

I spin around then, but too quickly. Just a glimpse of Gillian from behind, a blur in a light raincoat, long, dark hair. She swings at Coop, crouched behind her, his gun in both hands. Something gleams and flashes in the light as she slashes at Coop's arm. He falls back, trips over the horn case.

Gillian turns, briefly glances at me, then she's running up the pier. I go over to Coop. He's up on one knee, holding his arm, the blood seeping through his fingers, dripping on the pavement.

"Fucking bitch cut me," he says. He tries to stand up but doesn't make it. "They'll get her."

I look up toward the other end of the pier, see two black-and-whites, red lights flashing, blocking the street at the top of the steep incline at the pier's entrance.

I kneel down beside Coop. Blood pumping out of his shoulder. I rip off my jacket, wrap it around his arm, near the shoulder. Even in the dim light I can see his face drain of color as he slips into shock. I dig my phone out and press 911.

"The end of Santa Monica Pier," I shout into the phone. "I need an ambulance, tell the cars at the top of the pier. Hurry."

My coat is soaked with Coop's blood. I sit with him, talking, cradling him. "C'mon, man, hang on." It's only minutes, but it seems like forever before I hear sirens, see the ambulance. Two paramedics pry me away from Coop and get him on a stretcher.

Before I jump in the ambulance, one of the uniform cops sees the blood on me, asks if I'm okay.

"What about the woman?"

"What woman? We didn't see anybody."

FOURTEEN

BAD THINGS HAPPEN at hospitals. They've always made me uncomfortable, even as a visitor. With my accident and therapy, I've had my fill of the cloying smell of antiseptic, the casual attitude of the nurses and doctors, the haunted eyes of patients awaiting their fate, and the grim faces of friends and relatives waiting for news.

Now I'm one of those grim faces, sweating it out for Coop, jumping up every time the ER door opens, wondering if there's time to go outside for a smoke, waiting for the first news. When the doctor finally comes out, I study his expression for some sign that this time it's okay.

Despite the deep slash and loss of blood, he assures me that Coop will be okay. My jacket stopped more blood loss. "What was that, a scalpel?" he wants to know. "Jesus, that was deep." He stands, looking over my shoulder as someone is rolled by, shifting his weight from one foot to the other, impatient to go on to the next disaster, and looking far too young to be a doctor. His greens, the stethoscope around his neck, and his tired eyes are his credentials.

"I don't know what it was. You're sure he's okay?"

"Sliced a bit of the muscle. He's weak, but okay," he says, in that maddening matter-of-fact tone. "I've seen worse. Give us a few minutes to get him in a room, and you can see him."

"Thanks, thanks a lot."

"Sure," he calls over his shoulder.

I dial Andie from a pay phone, but before it rings twice, she, Ted Rollins, and Wendell Cook spill out of the elevator. Rollins is in the lead, flashing his badge at the two uniformed cops, demanding an explanation. He glances at me, doesn't even ask about the blood on my clothes.

"Shouldn't you be with Sims?" I ask.

"Don't worry about the fruitcake's brother. I've been relieved. You've got some talking to do, pal."

Andie puts her hand to her mouth when she sees the blood on my shirt but manages not to grab me. Wendell just glares and goes off to check with the doctor on Coop's condition.

Andie and I walk down the hall a ways to get away from Rollins.

"What happened?"

"Gillian called right after I left you." I fill her in on everything. "Coop was the only one I could think to call." I see anger flicker in her eyes for an instant, then quickly fade. "How did they miss her? The pier was blocked." I still can't believe she got away.

Andie shakes her head and shrugs. "There are some stairs on the side of the pier. Apparently she came by boat, escaped the same way." Andie stops, touches my arm. "Listen, we're going to get a lot of static for this. Wendell wants a full report. It's up to you how much you want to tell him."

I nod, knowing what she means. We turn back toward the waiting room where Wendell and Rollins are waiting.

"Doctor says you can see him now," Wendell Cook says to me. "Room 360."

I start to walk away, but he stops me, grabs my arm. "I want to talk to him too, if he's up to it. Then I'll start on you."

I nod and pull away. Coop's room is dimly lit, the bed slightly inclined. His left arm and shoulder are encased in bandages. I walk over to the bed. He blinks, looks at me.

"Hey, sport. How you doing? I'm flying. Gave me some good drugs. You okay?" He looks at my shirt.

"This is your blood. You owe me a jacket."

He manages a slight smile. "Soon as I get out of here. Something from Abercrombie & Fitch? Hey, thanks, man."

I look at Coop lying there, think how close this was, and bite my lip. "No, Coop, I fucked up."

Coop shakes his head. "There was nothing you could do. I should have blown her away, this would all be over. Didn't want to hit you." He closes his eyes for a moment. "Wendell out there? I need to talk to him."

"Yeah, I'll get him. Take it easy, okay. I'll see you tomorrow."

"Don't plan on going anywhere."

I go out, find Wendell waiting in the hall just outside the door. "Go ahead, the drugs are kicking in."

"You wait here," Wendell says before he goes inside.

I wait, lean against the wall, and breathe a huge sigh of relief for Coop. In the reception area, I can see Andie and Rollins in a heated discussion. I can imagine what that's about, how much Rollins is getting off on my mistake.

Andie glances my way, waves, and disappears in the elevator. Wendell Cook comes out. "Okay, let me get rid of Rollins, and I'll take you back to your car."

I ignore Rollins's hard looks and follow Wendell out to the parking lot. He doesn't say anything till we're in his car.

"I don't know if Coop's covering for you or not, but he says there was nothing he or you could have done different." Wendell sighs and starts the car. "At least we have a partial description."

"I could have not met her, but there wasn't time to do anything else."

When we stop at a light, Cook slams his hand against

the steering wheel. "A goddamn boat. Who would have thought of that?"

I remember now. I spent enough time on the pier as a kid. There were creaky wooden stairs, landings for small boats, on both sides of the pier. I just never thought about it until now.

Cook eases down the steep incline to the pier and pulls up next to my car. He looks at me. "You know, Horne, this is really out of hand. Coop gets cut, Gillian gets away, and all we've got is you and that stupid saxophone."

"Yeah," I say, "but she wanted it. She'll be back."

AT HOME, I strip off my clothes and toss them in the trash. I take a long shower, fix a drink, and wait for the phone to ring. Gillian will call, I know it. I put on some music, picking a Keith Jarrett recording that includes "Moon and Sand." I'm ready for her; I can play her game. When the phone rings, I turn up the volume, press the record button on the phone machine. I let her listen for a moment before I say anything.

"You lied to me, Evan. You broke our bargain." There's nothing languid about her voice now. It's full of bitterness and betrayal. This is the manic side Andie talked about.

"I didn't lie about Greg. I couldn't have known about the things I've told you if I hadn't talked to him. You know that."

"I don't care about that. You lied to me. You figure out who's next."

"I'll be waiting, Gillian. Come and get me." I slam down the phone, feel my heart beating.

The phone rings again, but I don't pick up. I hear my own voice on the answering machine, but there's no music, no message. Gillian's already got mine.

I finish my drink, listen to some more Keith Jarrett, then collapse into bed and sleep better than I have in days.

"THIS IS HOW it lays out," Wendell Cook says. "We've listened to the tape from last night's call. You pushed her hard, so we think she's going back on schedule."

I'm in Cook's office with Andie and Ted Rollins. Coop's absence makes me miss him even more, but when I checked with the hospital this morning, they told me he was resting comfortably, whatever that means.

"Yeah, I went too far, I guess. I was thinking about Coop."

"You should have thought of that before you called him. That was a real bozo move," Rollins says. He gives Cook a challenging look, but Cook doesn't react.

"The point is," Cook says, "you might have done the right thing."

"What do you mean?" I'd spent the morning regretting my actions, but at the time, all I could think about was Coop lying on the pier, bleeding to death.

"She's angry," Andie says; "this is when she'll make a mistake. She's been in control so far, but now that's changed. She's going to get careless. She would never have shown herself if it wasn't for Greg's horn. Now she says the bargain is off." Andie looks at her notes. " 'You figure out who's next.' That's what's on the tape."

"So, how does that help?"

"We think we know who it might be. We've been tracking concert appearances of any groups that fit her target profile." Andie pauses and looks at Cook. "Do you know a group called Moontrane?"

"I've heard of them, can't miss them on the radio sometimes."

Andie looks at Cook, passing the ball to him. She looks

uncomfortable. They both know something I don't, and they're about to break the news. "We've already alerted the leader," Cook says, "given him the option to cancel without telling him too much, but he's adamant about going on. So—" Cook scratches his head, then continues. "Gillian wants you too. If she's thinking about Moontrane, you'll be a bonus."

"I don't understand."

"We want to put you with Moontrane for that concert. I'll be there, so will Ted, a lot of our people. We'll have it well covered if Gillian shows."

"What does the leader say about this?"

Cook smiles. "Well, it seems he knows you, says he'd like to have you with the group, even under these circumstances."

"He knows me? Who is it?"

"Guy named Nicky Drew."

I don't say anything for a moment, just look away. Playing with Moontrane will be bad enough, but Nicky Drew? My luck just keeps getting worse.

"You do know him, right?" Cook asks. "Is there some problem with that?"

"Yeah, I knew him. Look, I don't know if this will work. Drew and I didn't get along very well. We both went to Berklee, played in a group together there, and—"

"So what's the problem?" Rollins wants to know. "Your friend is lying in the hospital, and that's on your head." He gets up and walks over to me, leans on the table.

I look up at him. "I don't need you to remind me of that, Rollins."

"Well, maybe you'd like it better if it came from Andie."

I glance at her. She colors slightly but doesn't look at

Rollins. Cook looks at all of us, his gaze raking across all our faces and finally coming to rest on me.

"I don't know what's going on here," he says, "but at this point, I don't care either. We've got a lot to do before Saturday, so let's get to it." He looks at Andie now. "You work this out with Evan, set up a meeting with Nicky Drew, and we'll go from there. Do I have your cooperation on this, Evan?"

"Yeah, sure. I'm in. Where is this concert?"

"Las Vegas."

AT THE HOSPITAL Coop is sitting up, smiling, watching TV, talking to Natalie. There's a frozen moment when she sees me walk in with Andie. The three of us stand still and look at each other. Only Coop is amused, and he does his best to break the tension.

"Well, you're probably all wondering why I've called you here today," he says.

Andie and Natalie lock eyes for a moment. "I'll wait outside," Andie says, and leaves before I can say anything.

I wait until the door is shut, then walk over to the bed. "How you doing, guy?" Except for the bandages and IV, Coop almost looks like his old self.

"Okay, sport, they're treating me well. Got this little pain in my shoulder, though. Can't think what that could be."

"He was very lucky," Natalie says. Her look is accusing. She holds it for a moment, then turns away.

Coop rolls his eyes. "Hey, Nat, thanks for coming by. I need to talk to this piano player for a minute, okay?"

"Sure," Natalie says. "You get well fast." She bends over the bed and kisses Coop.

She starts out of the room, but I stop her. "Can you wait for me a few minutes?"

"I don't think so," Natalie says. "You look pretty busy." She goes out without looking back.

"Do I sense a little tension between you two?" Coop shifts in the bed and puts his right hand behind his head.

"Yeah, you could say that. Our little talk didn't go so well the other night. She thinks we need some time apart."

Coop raises his eyebrows. "Wish I could tell her the whole story. So, bring me up to date. What's the next move?"

"Andie has been tracking the list of potential victims. A band called Moontrane is doing a concert in Las Vegas on Saturday. They look like the best bet. They want me to go undercover with the band, draw her out."

"Not your kind of music?"

"It's worse than that. The leader is a jerk I knew in school."

Coop shakes his head. "You do pay some dues. Saturday, huh? Well, I should be out of here by then. Haven't been to Las Vegas in a while." He sees me start to protest. "Don't even think about it. I want to be in on this, even if it's just to see how things come out. You think she'll show?"

"Oh yeah, she'll show. I pissed her off good." I look at my watch. "Well, I have to go, Coop. Take care."

"You too."

In the hallway, I see Andie leaning against the wall, her arms crossed in front of her.

"Did Natalie come by here?"

"Yes, she did," Andie says. The corners of her mouth turn up in a slight smile.

"She say anything?"

"She said, 'He's all yours.' "

ON THE DRIVE OUT to Malibu, Andie reads from a press release about Nicky Drew and Moontrane. The rain has stopped as quickly as it came, and now the coastline looks like a postcard.

"There's more to Nicky Drew and Moontrane than gold records," Andie reads, "and his upcoming concert in Las Vegas is a good example. Drew, one of jazz's premier artists, has rededicated himself to the music that's brought him fame and wealth. 'This one is going to be a gift for my true jazz fans,' Drew said in a recent telephone interview. 'We're going to do more acoustic music. I'm going back to genuine roots for a more organic sound, the sax featured in its full glory.' " Andie looks over at me. "Should I go on?"

"You mean it gets worse?"

"Afraid so," Andie says, continuing. " 'I truly feel this sound found me, and to prove it, I'm bringing in my old friend Evan Horne from my Berklee days, a really great piano guy, for the Las Vegas concert.' "

"An organic sound? Who wrote that?"

"Drew did most of it. He insisted," Andie says as we pass Malibu Pier. "Keep going, it's past Zuma on Broad Beach Road."

We ease up the incline past Pepperdine University on our right, the Pacific shimmering blue on the left. I roll down the window and breathe in the sea air.

"So tell me about this bad blood between you and Drew."

I shrug. "Not much to tell, really. We had some classes together, played in a couple of groups. He was cocky, even then. Thought he was the next Cannonball Adderly. He organized a group, got some gigs around Boston, but got pissed at me because I wouldn't play the electric piano. After that, we went our separate ways."

Andie looks out the window as the road dips down nearer the ocean. "You never compromise, do you?"

"Is that so bad? Look, what I do has nothing to do with Nicky. He made his choice, I made mine. I couldn't do what he does."

We're both silent for a while, until we reach the light at Trancas Canyon. "That's Broad Beach over there," Andie says, pointing to the left.

I turn off the coast highway onto the narrow beach road, past multimillion-dollar houses that from the rear look like nothing but carports and garages and mailboxes on pedestals.

"Slow down," Andie says. "It's right along here." She checks the numbers and points. "There, that's it."

The house is all white, kind of art deco; it would look more appropriate in Miami Beach. I turn in, veer down the steep driveway, which curves to the left at the bottom of the incline, and park alongside a Dodge Viper and a Porsche.

I shut off the engine and grip the wheel. I'm not looking forward to this. We get out, walk to the huge, ornately carved door, and ring the bell.

Nicky Drew, in shorts and a designer sweatshirt with the sleeves cut off, comes to the door himself, a bottle of beer in one hand. With the other he brushes his long blond hair back on his head.

"Evan Horne." He grins at me, and I know he's going to enjoy this. "Man, you haven't changed a bit."

"Neither have you, Nicky." We shake hands briefly, but his eyes are already on Andie.

"Please, tell me who this is."

Andie goes official. She takes out the thin wallet and holds up her ID card. "Special Agent Andrea Lawrence, Mr. Drew. Can we come in?"

"Whoa," Drew says. He grins at her and puts his hands over his head. "I didn't do it, honest." He winks at her and backs up. "Come on in."

We walk down two steps into the living room. The opposite wall is nearly all glass, affording a spectacular view of the beach and ocean beyond. Drew waves us to an enormous white leather sofa that faces the window. He flops in a black leather recliner. He fiddles with a switch on the side till he's almost horizontal.

"Hey, you guys want a beer or something?"

"Yeah, beer sounds good."

"How about you?" Nicky asks Andie. "Do I have to call you Special Agent Lawrence?"

"Andrea will be fine. Just a Coke for me."

"Oh, I don't do coke, honest," Nicky says, then laughs uproariously. When he recovers, he says, "Sorry, you mean the liquid kind." He twists in his chair and yells toward the other room. "Hey, baby, bring my man Evan a beer, and a Coke for Special Agent Andrea."

A few moments later a tall brunette, her hair tied back in a ponytail, wearing a bikini, floppy sandals, and an unbuttoned man's denim shirt, comes in. She can't be more than nineteen or twenty. She sets the beer and Coke on the glass coffee table in front of us and stares at Andie.

"Nicky told me you were coming," she says. "Are you really in the FBI?"

"Yeah, that's right, baby," Nicky says. "Say hello to Evan Horne and Andrea Lawrence."

"I'm Karen," she says and shakes hands with both of us. "Nicky says you're a great piano player and you're going to do the Vegas thing with him."

"I guess that's true," I say.

"Get out!" Karen says. She claps her hands together. "I've never been to Vegas. I can't wait."

"Yeah, well, we'll see," Nicky says. Karen doesn't see him roll his eyes at me.

Andie scoots forward on the couch and takes a drink of her Coke. "Mr. Drew, Nicky, we need to talk." She glances at Karen and smiles, then looks back at Nicky. It takes him a moment to get it.

"Oh, right. We got some business, baby," he says to Karen. "Why don't you go down to the beach and work on your tan?"

Karen pouts for about three seconds, then gets up. "It was nice meeting you both," she says. Her nails are lacquered bright red. She wags one finger at Nicky. "I'll talk to you later, Mister Moontrane."

"Yeah, whatever, baby," Nicky says, then watches her walk out of the room. "She's one of the Laker cheerleaders," he tells us. "Got courtside seats, Evan, right near Jack Nicholson. Have to join me sometime."

"Mr. Drew," Andie says, "I want to impress upon you how serious this is, the Las Vegas concert. We don't want to interfere with your music, but we're dealing with a very dangerous person, and the security arrangements are going to be very tight."

Nicky glances at me, then back to Andie. "Hey, the FBI has my full cooperation, don't worry. Long as we don't have your guys standing around on the stage in black suits with earphones or anything like that."

Andie allows herself a slight smile. "We thought we could have some people to help your road crew, have them dressed the same, help with unloading, setting up, that kind of thing."

"Yeah, that could work," Nicky says nodding. "No bullet-proof Plexiglas, though. My fans want to see me."

Andie stares at Drew for a moment. "She doesn't use a

gun, Mr. Drew. She uses a knife of some kind. I'm sure you've read about the other victims."

"Yeah, right, I did," Nicky says. "Can't believe it. Ty Rodman and Cochise, both gone." He shakes his head. His pensive expression almost looks genuine, but he recovers quickly. "Course I'll have my man, Evan here, right with me."

"Evan is a decoy, Mr. Drew. Nothing more."

Nicky starts to drink from his beer, then stops with the bottle in midair. "You really think this woman you think might be the killer is going to show?" There's no fear in his eyes, but then Nicky Drew wasn't on Santa Monica Pier with Gillian. To him it's a news story, and he was far removed from it. This is some kind of extra excitement for him. I think he likes the idea of brushing up against danger.

"We hope so," Andie says.

Nicky takes a long slug of his beer and turns to me. "Okay, then, I got a tape I need you to hear, man, so you have an idea of what we do. I don't suppose you're familiar with Moontrane, are you?"

"Not a note," I say. Nicky nods and smiles and shakes his head. "Evan the purist. No, man, you haven't changed at all."

Andie stands up. "Well, I'll leave you guys to it. I think I'll walk down to the beach and talk to Karen."

"Cool," Nicky says. "Right through the sliding doors off the den. You'll see her. C'mon, man," he says to me. "Let's hear some music."

Nicky takes me down to a room on the lower level of the house. It's jammed with recording equipment and wall shelves holding hundreds of CDs. There's a small wet bar complete with a mini-refrigerator, and on the wall behind it, framed behind smoky glass, are Nicky's CDs. A collection of photos of Nicky in action at concerts adorns the other wall. In one corner, two alto saxophones rest on stands.

"Another beer?" Nicky asks. He goes behind the bar and pulls one out for himself.

"No, thanks. Mind if I smoke?"

"No, just quit myself, but if you want a little toke—" He slides a round glass ashtray across the bar, the label from one of his CDs imprinted on its bottom. He opens his beer and leans on the bar. "So how have you been, man? Long time since Berklee."

"Yes, it has been. You seem to be doing pretty well."

"Your hand okay and all? I read about that. What a drag."

"I'm fine, got a trio, new record contract with Quarter Tone Records."

Nicky shakes his head. "Never heard of them. Small outfit, huh?"

"Very, but a lot of freedom to do what I want."

"And what's that?" Nicky almost smirks. "To keep chasing Bill Evans, Keith Jarrett?"

"That's what I play, Nicky. Maybe someday I'll catch them."

"But why, man? Shit, let your hair grow a little more, get funky, and I could get you into some big bucks." He gestures at me with the beer bottle in his hand. "See, you just don't get it, man. Bebop is dead. Smooth is where it's at. It's on the radio, it's in Tower Records. Hell, I'm doing a TV commercial next week. Most of the people who buy CDs don't even know who Cannonball is, much less Bird."

"All good reasons to keep bebop alive. That's the trouble, too many of those people think jazz began with you and Kenny G and Ty Rodman and Cochise. You're not playing jazz, Nicky, you're playing *at* jazz."

I hear my own words and suddenly realize how much I sound like Gillian.

"Yeah, well, wait till you see and hear that crowd in Las Vegas. You might change your tune."

Both hands on the bar, I lean forward. Nicky backs up slightly, but the nervous smirk is still on his face. He covers it by brushing his fingers through his hair. "What?"

"You listen to me, Nicky. If it wasn't for the FBI, I wouldn't be within ten miles of you or Moontrane—and by the way, calling it that is an insult to Woody Shaw. Four people have died so far, and my friend got hurt badly the other night. Do you understand that? Four people. Now, if playing with you helps stop it, that's what I'm going to do. That's the only reason I'm here. Are we straight on that?"

Nicky's face has gone ashen for a moment. "Yeah, sure."

"Fine, let's get to the music." Nicky watches me as I crush out my cigarette in his CD ashtray.

"Whatever," Nicky says. He goes to the sound system. "This is the final mix of my new one. I'll do a couple of these Saturday. Mostly blues lines or some sexy ballads. All you have to do is play the chords for me." He presses the play button, and we hear a voice say, "Blue You, take seven."

I glance at Nicky. He shrugs. "Hey, there was a technical problem."

It's mostly Nicky's alto over drums, bass, guitar, and a couple of keyboards. Heavy backbeat, some wah-wah guitar chording, a few short solos from the piano player. He lets the tape play through three tracks before I stop him.

"Are they all like that? Is that your organic sound?"

Nicky grins. "Like that, huh? Make a good title, don't you think? Organic Drew? Organic Drew's Blues?"

"Killer. Just tell me the keys, and we'll be fine."

He pulls a half-dozen CDs from one of the racks and hands them to me. "You maybe want to check these out too."

I look at the top one. *The Essential Nicky Drew* is the title.

We go back upstairs to the living room. Outside, down on the beach, I see Andie talking with Karen. Nicky follows my gaze.

"So what's it like balling an FBI agent?"

I turn and glare at Nicky. "I wouldn't know."

"Okay, man, chill out. If you haven't been there yet, that's cool, but she's hot for you, man. Anybody can see that. I know something is happening."

I let that one go. "I'll be flying up with you, I guess, Saturday morning, just so it looks good."

"Sure. LAX at nine. Tell your special agent she can put a couple of her people with the sound guys. Nobody will notice that. They never get the fucking sound right anyway."

"I'll tell her."

"When you go home tonight, to your little apartment or wherever it is you live, think about where I live, what I've got. You might change your mind about my offer."

"I already thought about it, Nicky. The minute I walked in here."

FIFTEEN

AT HOME I find a message from Paul Westbrook. It's one I almost don't want to return. "Evan," Westbrook says. "I've got studio time booked for next Tuesday and Wednesday. You guys ready? You can put it off if you want, but it'll be months then."

I mentally breathe a sigh of relief. "No, I'm ready, we're ready. We're going to have one more rehearsal."

"All right," Westbrook says. "I'm looking forward to it." There's a couple of moments of silence. "Everything okay?"

"Yeah, nothing to worry about. Everything is fine."

"Okay then, see you Tuesday."

I call Jeff Lasorda and arrange for the rehearsal. "Tomorrow or the next day," I tell Jeff. "I'll be out of town over the weekend."

"No problem," Jeff says. "All that other stuff cleared up?"

"What stuff?"

Jeff waits a moment for me to elaborate. "Okay, I won't go there." Jeff, always the diplomat.

"It's okay, Jeff. All I want you to worry about is the music."

"I know, man, this could really be a good one. Tomorrow afternoon should be cool. I'll call you back."

"Thanks, Jeff." I hang up and wish the music was all I had to worry about, but two pieces of mail remind me there's more.

The postcard is unsigned, but it's from Gillian. On the

front is a photo of Charlie Parker, one of the hundreds of him taken over the years. On the back is another of her poems.

Fables of Faubus
Better Git It in Your Soul
Good-bye Porkpie Hat

I don't need Ace to tell me about the porkpie hat. It was Lester Young's trademark as much as the way he held the tenor sideways. The three lines of the haiku are Mingus song titles, all from the album *Mingus Ah Um*. But Lester Young, the Prez, played tenor; Mingus was a bassist. What's the connection? Maybe Moontrane and Nicky Drew are not Gillian's target.

I go through my collection, dig out the album, and scan the titles. One of Mingus's tributes to Parker, "Bird Calls," opens the second side, but that doesn't seem enough. What then, something in the song titles? "Git It in Your Soul" is almost a gospel piece. "Porkpie Hat," for Prez, is a haunting ballad. "Fables of Faubus" is as complex as the civil rights movement for which it was written. I put on the album and listen to both sides, but nothing occurs to me, just renewed respect for Mingus as a composer and for the level of the players.

Maybe I'm trying too hard. Something else nags at me, something I've seen in the last couple of days, but I can't nail it down.

I go out and walk down to the beachfront, perhaps now for one of the last times: The other letter is an eviction notice. The developers that have been after my neighborhood have finally won. I've been given a thirty-day notice on my apartment. It's all very polite and businesslike, but the upshot is, I have to move. Somehow, it doesn't have the impact I thought it would.

I head north, trying to work it out, knowing every communication from Gillian drives me closer to Andie Lawrence. Is that the only thing pushing me toward her? I feel like I don't know anything anymore except how much I want this to be over.

I turn back after a mile or so, deciding I want to talk to Cal Hughes about the record. He's home and greets me with little surprise. For once he's not reading. He's got an old movie on, Hitchcock's *Rear Window*.

"Don't let me interrupt you," I say as we watch Jimmy Stewart point his camera into the windows across from him.

"You're not. I know the ending," Cal says. "That's how the FBI does it, gets into people's lives without them knowing it until it's too late."

"What do you mean?"

"How are you getting along with the government?"

"What are you talking about?"

"I've seen that agent, what's her name? Lawrence? Are you two an item now?"

"We're not, but we could be."

Cal stops the tape as Jimmy Stewart zooms in on Raymond Burr. "Just watch yourself. They know a lot about you now."

"Andie Lawrence has been straight with me."

"Has she? You're forgetting that long before they brought you in, they combed through your life and the life of everybody you're connected with. They're thorough if nothing else."

I look at Cal and suddenly know what he's talking about. "They contacted you?"

Cal shrugs. "Didn't have to, except to update my file. I go way back with them. Oh, don't worry, it wasn't anything subversive, unless you call offering piano lessons in Watts un-American.''

Cal lights a cigarette. "I got some heat about it; they thought it was recruitment for the Black Panthers, white guy working with black kids in Watts. Some of my dates dropped off, and I couldn't figure it out at first. Then a few friends called me, said they'd been questioned, wanted to know about my motives. Hell, I thought I was doing good. Anyway, it's history now, long before your time." Cal studies me for a moment. "You didn't know, I guess."

"No, I didn't. How do you know they checked on you again?"

"Same friend called me, told me, 'They're lookin' at you again, Cal.' "

"I'm sorry, Cal. I can speak to her if it's a problem for you."

"Don't worry, there's nothing they can do to me now. Don't cut any deals with them over me." Cal gets up and goes to the kitchen.

Andie has some explaining to do. I want to know how much an act it was for her to go after me. Cal comes back with a drink for both of us.

"How close are they to catching this weirdo?"

"Very. Maybe this weekend. I'm going to Las Vegas, playing with a group called Moontrane. They think she may try something there."

"Never heard of them—of course, I'm a little out of step with mainstream America."

"Cal, there's a favor I want to ask you."

"Ask."

"The record date is still on. I want you to be there when we record."

He reaches down and rubs Milton's head. "I don't leave the house much these days."

"I'd feel better if you were there, help me pick the takes, that kind of thing. You know my playing better than anyone."

"You don't need me, Evan. Just go with your gut."

"I know, but I'd like it just the same."

Cal lights another cigarette and sets his drink down. "Let me think about it."

"Please."

"This is really twisting you up, isn't it?"

"I guess it is."

"Get your mind clear before you go into that studio."

I nod. "I know, I have to do that."

I STOP AT ANDIE'S on the way home. She opens the door, smiles, and doesn't seem surprised. "Come in," she says. "I'm just doing some paperwork."

I follow her inside, hand her Gillian's postcard. "Just came today."

She takes it from me, looks at the photo of Bird, then turns it back over to read the poem. "She's back on track with the form—five, seven, and five syllables."

"Those are Mingus song titles. I went over the album, but I can't come up with anything that connects with Nicky Drew."

Andie keeps her eyes on the postcard. "There's beer in the fridge if you want one."

"Actually, I'd rather have some coffee."

"Sure, I'll make some."

She goes to the kitchen and fills up the Mr. Coffee. "Maybe we're going too far," she says. "Maybe it's not the message but the haiku, the syllables."

"I don't follow you."

"The number seventeen, or seven plus one—eight. A birthday, something like that. An area code, a zip code?"

"No, I think that's a stretch. It's something in those song titles. Anyway, we'll know Saturday."

Andie pours two mugs of coffee and brings them to the table. I watch her sip hers and study the card some more.

"Tell me about Cal Hughes, Andie."

"Cal Hughes?" She looks up, but not quick enough for me to see the change in her expression.

"Yeah, old friend of mine, a piano player, one of the best in his day."

She sets the cup down and looks at me. "Evan…okay, I've read the file. It was put together a long time ago."

"But you had to check again, didn't you?"

"Evan, it's not what you think."

"Isn't it? What about my file, Andie? Isn't there one on me too?"

"You know there is. The first time you came to the Federal Building, Wendell told you things, things about you and Natalie. You must have guessed."

"And think back to the first time we had dinner at the beach. You asked me all about myself, like we were just getting acquainted on a first date, but you already knew the answers. You asked about my family, and when I didn't respond, you said, 'Okay, I won't go there.' Remember that?"

She looks down. "Yes, of course I remember. But I didn't know then that we'd…what happened between us would happen."

"I'd like to believe that, Andie, I really would."

"Believe it, Evan. When you walked in that office, I didn't know what to expect, certainly not that I was going to—"

I get up and go out on the patio to have a cigarette. Andie follows me out. "We were asking you to help us. I had to know as much as I could about you. That's Bureau policy. I won't apologize for that."

"No, I guess you shouldn't have to."

"We had to have your trust too," she continues.

"And Ted Rollins didn't quite fit the bill, did he?"

"No." She laughs. "I'm sorry."

"What?"

"I'm just trying to imagine you and Rollins having dinner together."

"Well, that is hard to imagine."

"So, are you rethinking us?"

"I'm rethinking a lot of things, Andie."

"Will you tell me when you've got it sorted out?"

"You'll be the first to know."

AT LAX, THE MOST welcome sight is the bass player sprawled in one of the seats at the United gate. A bag of tortilla chips, a Coke, and his electric bass are all within arm's reach. Still long and tall, Buster Browne hasn't gained a pound despite his junk food diet. He has headphones in his ears, and his head nods slightly to the music from the portable CD player as he focuses on a book in front of him.

I tap him on the shoulder. He looks up, grins, and takes off the headphones. "Hey, man, just heard you were on this gig," Buster says. "I don't know why, though. Heard you were smokin' at the Bakery."

"Hi, Buster." I look at the book, a novel by Thomas Pynchon. "Heavy stuff, Buster."

"Yeah, reading Pynchon is like listening to Ornette Coleman. So what are you really doing here?"

"It's a long story. I'll fill you in on the flight." I set my bag down and drop into a seat next to him.

"Cool," Buster says, but his grin dissolves. "Nothing

hinky going down on this gig, is there? I want to know when to fade."

"Don't worry, I'll let you know. You been with Nicky long?"

"Couple of months. Heavy bread, but heavy dues too. You'll see. We vamp for twenty minutes sometimes while he dances around. He's like Kenny G on speed. The drummer will kill you, man. He plays a backbeat like somebody driving spikes into train tracks. Hope you got some ear plugs."

"I can't wait."

"See the blond guy over there?" Buster points to a tall, thin man with straw-colored curly hair. "Guess what his name is."

"Golden?"

"You got it. He calls himself our blues coordinator." Buster glances over my shoulder. "Cool it," he says. "Here comes the man."

Nicky Drew walks up, dressed for the road in all black. A Rolex watch peeks from beneath his cuffs, but for a moment it's his hat that gets my attention. Now I know the connection.

"See you two know each other," he says. "Everything okay, Evan?" He notices my look. "Like the hat, huh?"

"Everything's fine. Yeah, very stylish." I glance at Buster. "You're lucky to have Buster here on bass."

"Really. Thought it was the other way around. Where's your special agent folks?"

"Don't worry, they'll be here."

"Soon as we check in the hotel, we go out to the park for a sound check." Nicky tips the hat back on his head and wanders off to talk with Karen, the focus of all male eyes in the area. Black leather miniskirt and a bright gold blouse with the top buttons undone is her outfit for the day.

"What a guy, huh? Least it's not John Tesh," Buster says. "What does he mean, special agent folks? Are we talking FBI?"

"Just some extra security for the concert. You been reading the papers?"

"You mean Cochise and Ty Rodman? Sure." Buster studies me for a moment. "That's why you're really here, isn't it."

"Don't worry about it, Buster."

"Yeah, I bet that's what they told the bass player on the *Titanic*." He looks at me again. "Well, I think that's all I want to know." He puts his headphones back on and reaches for the chips and his book.

I spot Andie emerging from the crowd, but she's alone. I walk over and intercept her. "Where is everyone?" She's looking cool and official in a dark pants suit.

"They took an earlier flight," she says, "and Coop talked them into taking him too. Says he knows the local guy there and will run interference. Lieutenant John Trask. You know him?"

"Great. He'll be glad to see me. We crossed paths before—last year—over the record collector's murder."

Andie smiles. "You do get around, don't you?"

"Yeah, that's me, the traveling detective."

"I need to talk to Drew. Want to join me?"

"I don't think so. The more room I give him, the better. But check out his hat."

"His hat?" She looks across the lounge and finds Drew. "Oh, God," she says. "Porkpie hat."

"I remember seeing some photos at his house the other day. Didn't think anything about it at the time."

I leave Andie to Nicky Drew and present my driver's license for check-in.

"Have a nice trip, Mr. Horne," the attendant says as she

hands me a first-class boarding card. I should have known. We board a few minutes later, with only a slight delay while Nicky signs a few autographs for the flight attendants. He and Karen take the first two seats; I sit with Andie. Buster and the rest of the band are in coach. Buster was right. What a guy.

I buckle up and close my eyes during takeoff, losing myself in the whine of the engines, glad for the escape, if only for an hour. Since Tuesday I'd managed one more rehearsal with Jeff and Gene and finalized the recording date with Paul Westbrook. We had decided on a list of tunes, and the trio is as ready as it's ever going to be. If I can survive this concert, if Gillian shows, if Gillian is captured. If, if, if.

When I open my eyes and turn to look at Andie, she's watching me. "Thought you were asleep," she says.

"No, just thinking."

"It's almost over, Evan." She reaches across and squeezes my hand.

"You really think Gillian is going to show?"

Andie nods. "If she does, we'll be ready for her."

"Are you going to tell Drew about the hat?"

"No. Would it do any good?"

"Probably not."

We get coffee, and almost before we level off, I feel the first gradual descent into Las Vegas. My only time in first class, and it's too short.

Coop is waiting with Wendell Cook at the gate, along with John Trask, who gives me a quick look and then ignores me completely. Maybe he thinks I'm just with the band.

The only sign that Coop has been injured is the thick bandage on his arm, which won't fit into the sleeve of his jacket. He holds it up with his other hand and waves it at me.

"Hey, sport. Traveling in the big time now, huh?"

"Good to see you up and around, Coop."

We make the long walk to the baggage area past the slot machines and get on the moving walkway, where announcements from the stars tell us to stay to the right.

Outside, there's a white stretch limo for Nicky and Karen, a truck for the instruments and other equipment.

"High noon, guys," Nicky Drew says. "At the park."

Andie goes with Cook for the short drive to our hotel. Two of Trask's men get in the limo with Nicky and Karen. Buster and the rest of the band pile into taxis. Coop and I get one of our own.

We're at a chain hotel just off the Strip. I just have time to explore the room a little when the phone rings.

"Evan, Ace. Tell me it isn't true."

"Afraid so. Stay away, Ace. This is not for you. I'll call you after."

"Oh, shit," Ace says. "You're really going to do it aren't you? They've made you a decoy."

"I don't know what you're talking about, Ace."

"Nothing else would get you with a band like Moontrane." He pauses for a moment. "Well, I hope I don't see you on the six o'clock news. Good luck."

"Thanks, Ace. I'll call you later."

I go downstairs. Nicky's limo is already gone, but there are a couple of cars to take us to the park. I grab Buster. "C'mon, ride with us." We get in one of the cars with Coop, and I introduce Buster.

"Ah, so this is Buster Browne," Coop says, remembering the Lonnie Cole case.

"What happened to your arm?" Buster asks.

Coop winks at me. "An unknown assailant. Got in the way of a knife."

Buster glances at me. "Jesus. I should have gone out with John Tesh."

We go west on Tropicana past the New York, New York, one of the newest hotels, and merge onto I-15, passing behind the Strip hotels. In daylight there's a surreal quality about Vegas. At the 95 interchange we head north and are soon on the Summerlin Parkway and the turnoff for Hills Park.

The cars pull in beside Nicky's limo and a motor home that will serve as a portable dressing room. The park itself is large, flanked by an elementary school and a baseball diamond. Seating is on grass in front of the circular cement stage. A white canopy covers the top and back. The stage is a blur of activity, with sound techs running cables, setting up microphones. Too many people, too open, I think. Gillian will never get close to this.

I spot Ted Rollins in a yellow jacket with "Security" printed on the back, briefing a similarly dressed group. They fan out over the grounds. One of them shows us to the motor home parked behind the stage, and I flash on Ty Rodman's dressing room at Santa Monica Civic. There are two guards outside, scanning everyone who comes near.

I wander back to the stage, where the electronic piano is being set up. "Want to try this out?" the tech asks.

"Not really." I sit down and turn it on. We're flanked by six-foot-high speakers and large monitors in front. I try a few chords, but it feels funny. Touch doesn't matter with these. No matter how hard or light you hit the keys, the sound is the same. The action is too easy.

I glance up at the drummer as he sits down behind a massive kit, quickly obscured by half a dozen cymbals. A tech with a headset speaks into a microphone and looks

toward the center of the park where the soundboard is lo-
cated. He reaches over my shoulder and taps on a key.

"Let's see what we got," he says to me.

I run through some chord changes, trying to get used to
the keyboard's action. The sound echoes back at me from
the monitor speakers. I see the top of the drummer's head
nod. He peeks at me from beneath a cymbal and smiles.
Buster joins us and plugs his bass into a huge amplifier,
and we check each instrument for twenty minutes or so.
Only then does Nicky turn up in jeans and a T-shirt, his
alto hanging from his neck chain.

He walks to the front microphone and blows a Bird-like
flurry of notes, mainly for my benefit, waves toward the
sound booth, then turns to face us.

"Okay, let's do one," he says. " 'New blues.' " He
stamps his foot for the tempo, and I'm nearly deafened by
the sound of Buster's bass. It churns and rumbles around
the stage and comes to rest in my stomach. Buster glances
over at me and mimes, "Sorry."

The drummer bashes away as the stage lights come on
and catch the gleam from his cymbals, swaying precari-
ously on the stands. Golden, the guitarist, dips the neck of
his guitar toward Nicky, then bends backward and stomps
the wah-wah pedal as his strings scream to life. Welcome
to fusion.

Nicky walks around the stage, blowing easily, stopping
by each of us to listen. When he gets to me, he stops and
leans in. "Cool, man. You're going to like playing this
shit." He roams around the stage, then ambles back to the
microphone and blows two choruses before pivoting toward
us like a basketball player, holding up his hand to stop.
Suddenly the cacophony ceases, but the echo lingers for a
moment.

Nicky steps forward and pushes his sunglasses up on his

head. "Hey, didn't I tell you, this guy can play." He lets the horn dangle and claps his hands together. "Great, Evan, great. We'll smoke 'em."

I stare at Nicky for a moment, then glance at Buster. "I didn't do anything, Nicky. I couldn't even hear what I played."

Nicky manages to keep his grin in place. "Cool, man, really cool. Guy doesn't even know how good he sounds." He looks at his Rolex. "Okay, guys, we got an hour. Loosen up. We hit at three."

On his way offstage, Nicky stops and speaks quietly to me. "That sucked, Evan. You can't just sit there hunched over the piano like you're Bill Evans at the fucking Village Vanguard. You've got to get into this shit, man."

"Is there a problem?" I'm halfway up off the piano bench, and neither of us has heard Andie come up behind us.

"No problem," I say.

Nicky turns to glare at Andie. "I don't care if you're FBI or not," he says. "Nobody fucks with my concert. Everybody has to be into it, or it doesn't work."

Everybody onstage freezes for a moment at the sound of Nicky's voice. "Don't worry, Nicky. I'll figure out some way to make it look good."

"And you understand something, Nicky," Andie says. "We'll shut your concert down if necessary. We're here for two reasons. To protect you, and to make it look as normal as possible."

"Yeah, yeah," Nicky says. He turns and walks off. "Well, what are you all looking at?" he yells.

"Charming," Andie says. "You going to be able to get through this?"

"Yeah, if I can figure out how to turn up this thing," I

say, pointing at the piano. "If you can't beat them, join them. In this case it'll be self-defense."

"Want to go for a walk?"

"Sure. I need to clear my head."

We walk down steps, out onto the grass. A section right in front of the stage is roped off, and Rollins and several other security people are talking. Scattered about are some early arrivals, staring up at the dark, cloudy sky, blankets spread, lunches laid out, unaware perhaps they'll be blasted by the speakers. Or maybe they don't care.

Andie and I walk around the perimeter toward the far end of the park. "Hang on a minute." I jog over to the sound booth, which today is a board on a table in a picnic area taken over by Moontrane for the concert. There's one guy in a security jacket and two guys at the board in jeans and T-shirts. One of them listens to something through headphones.

The security guard gets up as I approach. "I'm the keyboard player," I say, holding up my hand. "Can you guys give me a little more monitor?"

The first guy taps the one with the headphones. He lifts them off and glances at me. "He wants more monitor, Steve."

"I'll try," Steve says, "but we'll get into feedback if we punch it up too much. It sounds okay out here. Take a listen."

He hands me the phones, and I put them on. It's the blues we did during the sound check. Nicky's alto dominates, of course, but the keyboard comes through clear, an almost professional mix.

"I'm impressed. Just having trouble hearing up there."

"You'll get used to it," Steve says. "If it's still a problem, just give us an up sign."

"Thanks."

When I get back to Andie, she's talking on her cell phone. "All right, we'll keep an eye out for him here," she says and hangs up.

"Who was that?"

"One of the guys back at the hotel. Greg Sims wandered off. He was with Coop."

"Greg? He's here? Why?"

Andie shrugs. "Wendell thought he might be useful if Gillian shows." Andie sees my apprehension. "Don't worry, we've got everything covered. I'll be in the wings and in communication with Wendell at all times. Rollins and his people will be right in front of the stage. We have people at all the entrances. Nobody will get through."

"And the—"

"Motor home? We've already got two men on it."

I nod. "Let me know if Greg shows up here. I'd like to talk to him."

"All right," Andie says. "I'm going to check at the main entrance."

"Okay." I walk back to the stage area around back to the motor home. The park is filling up quickly. Looks like a sellout; Nicky should be happy. I find Buster Browne leaning against the wall in a black shirt and black pants.

"What's with the Zorro outfit?"

Buster smiles. "Welcome to rock 'n' roll. There's one for you too."

"You're kidding."

"Audience has to know Nicky is the good guy. He'll be in white. Hey, it'll be over soon," Buster says.

"Yeah, like a root canal."

I leave Buster and head for the dressing room. My black outfit is hanging on the back of the door with my name pinned to it. Nicky has thought of everything. I change, check myself in the mirror, and shake my head. How will I ever live this down?

On the way to the stage, I run into Nicky. Buster was right. He's all in white, some kind of jumpsuit. "Hey, Evan," he says. "I'm just going out to the limo for a minute. Want a little toot?"

"No, thanks."

"Suit yourself. Few minutes, man, and I'll be making history once again."

I watch Nicky leave and listen for a minute to the taped music playing through the speakers. Outside I can see the park is now nearly full. Some people are up and dancing around in anticipation of the concert. In the wings a guy in a KUNV Radio T-shirt is smiling, nodding his head to the music, one of Nicky's recordings.

He sees me come up and sticks out his hand. "Hey," he says. "Don Gordon, I'm emceeing today. You guys are great, you know." He almost sounds genuine.

"Thanks."

Buster, the drummer and the guitarist come up behind me. "Guess this is it," Buster says.

We walk out onstage and take our places. I look for Gillian. Buster turns on his amp. "We vamp till he comes out," he says. "We might be a while."

"I can't wait," I say, sitting down at the piano. There's no music to worry about, so I look for Gillian.

SIXTEEN

"ARE YOU READY, Las Vegas?" shouts the emcee. He paces around the front of the stage with a cordless mike, glancing at us to make sure we're ready.

"Yeaaaaaaaah," the crowd responds. It's dark, and rain threatens, but that hasn't kept the people away. With the stage lights I can't see very far back, but by the sound the park is probably full.

"All right then, Las Vegas, give it up for Nicky Drew and Moontrane, right here!"

Buster stomps his foot for the tempo, and we're under way. I see my hands on the keyboard, but between the crowd noise and the roar of amps and speakers, I can't hear a note. The earsplitting guitar screams, the drums pound, and the drone of Buster's bass resonates and slaps against the plastic canopy covering the stage. A three-chord vamp is all we have to play while the guitarist bends strings and sends his body into quasi-convulsions for nearly five minutes.

The keyboard is facing at an angle, so I can see Andie opposite me, standing in the wings, the radio transmitter in one hand, the other covering her ear. Coop is just behind her. He holds his arms out to his side in a shrug, meaning there's no sign of Greg Sims, and for the moment anyway, no sign of Gillian.

Golden shuffles toward me, pointing the neck of his guitar like a shotgun, then swings it wildly upstage and mercifully lets go with both hands to the roar of the crowd. My turn to solo?

Buster and the drummer look toward me, Buster like he's wondering what I'm going to do and hoping it's not going to be anything he'll be sorry for. I raise my head, then slice my arm through the air, cutting them off, and continue alone. Dropping the volume to a whisper, I work my way through the vamp, playing off the three chords. I sneak a look at the Golden, who is staring at me dumbfounded, feet flat, hands on his hips. He spins around, looks toward the wings for Nicky. This is not part of the plan, but Nicky is not there.

I ignore him and pull out every funk lick I've ever heard, gradually increasing the volume, then give another arm signal, my palm flat, to Buster and the drummer to join me but lightly. I catch a grin from the drummer. Buster fingers his bass lines and nods his head slightly as the three of us hit a groove and lock in. I keep it up till I hear the crowd start to catch on to what we're doing. When we're back to nearly full volume, Golden jumps in and joins us. In the wings I can see Nicky Drew now, talking to Andie, his alto around his neck, his body rocking, pointing at me.

He takes the cap off the saxophone, rocking more now, his eyes locking with mine for a moment, then starts shuffling onstage. He comes straight toward me. A TV crew tracks him onstage, a cameraman and a bleached blond with short hair and dark glasses guiding the cable trailing him. A few people catch sight of Nicky, and the roar goes up.

At center stage, Nicky pivots to his left and strolls toward the front microphone, the porkpie hat tilted back on his head, the horn held out in front of his body, blowing off the three chords. By the time he reaches the mike, the crowd is on its feet, chanting, "Moontrane, Moontrane," almost in tempo.

Nicky, rocking back and forth, rips off line after line on the vamp; then, as he holds one long note, his fist goes in the air. He drops it to his side, cutting us all out. For a moment the last note echoes in the silence around the stage. Buster and the drummer wipe their faces with towels. Buster leans toward me and says, "Big chords coming up."

Nicky's cadenza probably includes everything he learned at Berklee, every lick he's heard. He finally runs out of gas and half turns toward us. He jumps in the air, and we hit three chords each time his feet hit the stage. The only thing he doesn't do is drop to his knees and bend over backward, but maybe that's coming later.

Nicky backs up, bows from the waist, waves a hand in our direction, and basks for nearly a minute in the crowd's ovation. It's a carefully choreographed performance, and this is only the opening number.

"Thank you, thank you very much," Nicky says to the crowd. "All right, Las Vegas, are we having fun yet?" He puts his hand to his ear for the predictable response of the crowd, as if he can't hear them. While they get control of themselves, he turns toward us and shouts, "Flowers."

It's a fast Latin number, almost a samba. Buster sets the pace while the drummer hammers out the beat on the bell of his cymbal like a blacksmith on an anvil. I play the changes down while Nicky dances around in a mock samba step, Golden hovering at his side. After three choruses he steps aside, waves at the crowd, and points at me. The crowd settles down during my solo, then Nicky rejoins us and takes it out.

We do two more up numbers. Nicky whips the crowd into a frenzy, then takes them down with the kind of slow, mournful blues that David Sanborn has made a career of. I'm still having trouble hearing anything but Nicky's horn, the drummer's bashing, and Buster's throbbing bass. When we end the blues, Nicky steps up to the mike and introduces Buster, Golden, and the drummer.

"I've saved this keyboard guy for last," Nicky tells the crowd. "This is a special night for me, to have an old friend playing with me again. Give it up, Las Vegas, for one of the great keyboard players in jazz, Evan Horne."

Nicky turns and claps his hands, then turns back to the front. "I'm so excited I'm going to let Evan have it while I cool down." He takes a few steps toward me. "Anything you want, man."

I nod, guessing he was going to do this. Over the crowd noise I cup my hands over my mouth and shout, " 'Mercy, Mercy,' " to Buster. How can I go wrong with Cannonball Adderly? Buster nods and passes the word to the drummer. I start with Joe Zawinul's intro. Buster joins in, and the drummer picks it up till we're all in synch.

I glance up at Andie, who is shaking her head no. Nicky has backed off to the side listening, fiddling with his horn. This would be the perfect time for someone to grab him, but I don't see anyone or anything out of the ordinary.

I play two more choruses with the cameraman kneeling to the side, pointing the lens up into my face. Out of the corner of my eye I see the blond girl, her eyes on me, crouching behind him, letting out cable as she duckwalks around the keyboard. She seems to be paying more attention to me than to the cameraman.

Nicky jumps in and does his Cannonball impression for two more choruses, then suddenly, from offstage, we hear another horn. It's coming from behind me, loud but off-key. I glance across at Andie and Coop. Both are leaning forward, pointing. I look over my shoulder. Greg Sims is walking on from the wings, blowing his tenor. He sidesteps the girl holding the television cable. She slips, falls backward, and stares after him.

Nicky hears Greg's horn too and looks behind him. His eyes get big as he spots Greg, who now stands next to him, blowing hard, desperately trying to negotiate the changes but not making it. Nicky shoulders him aside and takes it out. The crowd applauds, but they're as confused as we are. Rollins and three security guards are already onstage, escorting Greg off past me.

Buster looks at me. "Who was that?"

Nicky recovers and makes another announcement. "Well, that's jazz. Never know who's going to drop in. Now I know why I love Las Vegas so much," he says, "but hey, we gotta take a little break. Just kick back, have a brew, and we'll be back shortly."

The crowd cheers again as the emcee runs onstage to remind them who they've been listening to and starts a pitch about CD giveaways.

As I stand up from the piano, Golden unplugs and runs over to me. "Man, that was so fucking cool, what you did on the opener. How did you think of that, man?" His eyes are glazed, and the long blond hair is falling over his face.

"Just lucky, I guess." I brush past him and head for Andie. Nicky gets there at the same time and he's livid.

"Who was that? Horne, if you had anything to do with that—"

"Shut up, Nicky." Andie's on the two-way radio. "Okay, okay," she says into the radio. "Well, we know where Greg is."

"Who the hell is Greg?" Nicky shouts. "Goddammit, somebody talk to me."

Coop steps forward and pulls Nicky away. He jerks out of Coop's one-handed grasp and walks off.

Again something nags at me, but I can't place it. I look back at the stage. The television cameraman has set down his gear. He's talking to one of the sound techs, but his assistant is gone.

Andie sees me staring at the cameraman. "What?" she says.

"The blond girl, with the cameraman." I push aside some sound techs and get to the cameraman. "Where's your cable girl?"

He looks around. "I don't know, she was here a minute ago. She's a sub, and—"

I start running backstage, toward the motor home, knowing I'm going to be too late. The door is shut but not locked. I listen for a moment, then open it slowly.

She has Nicky in a chair, her arm around his neck, a glittering blade held to his throat. Her eyes burn into mine. "Get out of here, Evan," she says.

"Gillian, don't do this." I close the door behind me and try to push the lock button.

Greg stands to the side, staring at Gillian. His saxophone lies on the countertop. Nicky Drew, his eyes squeezed almost shut, his body stiff, grimaces in terror. He tries to say something. Gillian tightens her grip, touches the blade against his throat. A thin trickle of blood oozes out.

"We're going out, Evan, Greg and me."

"No, Gilly, you can't do this," Greg says. "Let him go."

"Shut up, Greg, just do as I say."

Greg takes another step forward. "No, Gilly, I'm not doing that anymore."

"Greg, don't move," I say. Nicky's eyes search out mine in panic. Greg hesitates, looks at me, then back to his sister. "Gillian, I can get you out of here, just let Nicky go."

Behind me, someone is pounding on the door. Gillian's eyes glance toward it, but her grip on Nicky tightens. One slip of that blade, and Nicky Drew joins Ty Rodman and Cochise.

"Call them off, Evan," Gillian says. "You're going to

get us both out of here. Greg, you come with me now, or I'll cut his throat right in front of you.''

"She'll do it, Greg. You better do as she says.''

Greg stops, glances at me. He doesn't know what to do. He looks at his saxophone, then back to Gillian.

The pounding on the door stops, but someone is shouting. "Evan, we're coming in.'' It sounds like Wendell Cook, but I know Andie, Coop, and probably Ted Rollins and half the FBI are all out there.

"Wait!'' I shout at the door. "Let Nicky go, Gillian. That's the only way they're going to let you out.''

Gillian looks at Greg. "You're going with me. It's not too late for you. You heard the crowd out there. They loved you. It'll take some time, but you'll get it back.''

"No, Gilly, there's nothing to get back. Listen.'' Greg grabs his horn and starts to play. Long, painful notes seep out of the horn. He points the bell of the horn at Gillian and moves closer until he hovers over Nicky's trembling body.

Gillian stares at him, mesmerized by the sound as he struggles to make something come out. The horn is so close it's almost touching Nicky. Then everything happens at once.

As the door bursts open, Greg lunges toward Gillian and shoves the tenor into her face. She puts her hand up to ward him off, just enough for Nicky to squirm free. He slides under Greg to the floor and crawls away, his hand going to his throat.

Somebody pushes me aside. As I go down, I see Greg reach Gillian. There's a flash of the blade. Gillian trips, falls toward Greg, and catches him in the neck. A stream of blood spurts out over her as she screams.

Greg collapses to the floor as if the air has been let out of his body, his feet cut from under him. Gillian stares for a second as Ted Rollins and three agents slam into her. They throw her to the floor on her stomach, yank her arms behind her, and have her cuffed in seconds. Rollins kneels on her, his knee in her back, holding her by the hair as she screams.

"Somebody help him! Help him!"

I get up to my feet and watch three agents kneel over Greg. One grabs a towel and presses it like a compress to his throat, but it quickly soaks through, bright red. Another agent radios for paramedics. They arrive shortly and take over, but he's losing a lot of blood.

Rollins and the other agents pick up Gillian and carry her out past me. She's still screaming and trying to get a look at Greg as he's loaded onto a stretcher.

"I didn't mean to, I didn't mean to," she sobs.

Rollins glances at me. "Well, we did it, Horne. We got our loony tune."

"How did Greg get in here?"

Rollins shrugs. "Security thought he'd be safe in the trailer."

I sit down in a chair and stare at the puddles of Greg Sims's blood on the floor. Nicky Drew crawls out from under the counter and wobbles past me without looking, his hand still to his throat. For once he has nothing to say.

Then I'm alone with Andie. I look up at her, hardly seeing anything. She touches my shoulder.

"It's over, Evan."

BUT OF COURSE it's not over. When I finally come out, there's a crowd backstage. Nicky, still shaken, a light bandage over his throat, is talking to a TV reporter. I duck around them and take the back steps down onto the grass behind the stage, where Coop and Andie are talking.

The ambulance is pulling away, its lights flashing. "How is he?"

Coop and Andie turn toward me. "Not good," Coop says. "She hit an artery."

I sit down on the steps and light a cigarette, feel myself let go.

"What was going on in there?" Coop asks. "We heard the saxophone."

I nod. "Greg did it. She finally snapped, kept talking about how he could still play. He picked up his horn and started playing, then rushed her. Nicky got away, and she fell into Greg, and—"

"So Nicky Drew owes his life to Greg," Coop says.

"And you," Andie adds. "How did you know it was her?"

"I don't know. It didn't register at the time, but when Greg came on stage, I remember how shocked she looked."

"We got a call," Andie says. "Metro found the real cable girl tied up in her car in a parking lot."

We walk around to the front and stand by the edge of the stage. Before TV lights, Nicky steps up to the microphone and asks for quiet. There won't be any more concert, and the crowd still doesn't know what's happened.

"I'm sorry, everybody. We had something really bad happen here tonight, and we're not going to be able to do the second half." The crowd boos and yells as Nicky holds up his hand for quiet again. "Hey, I know, I know, you're disappointed, but when you see the news tonight, you'll understand why. Tell you what I'm going to do. I'm going to see to it that you get a refund out of my pocket, and Moontrane will be back for another concert as soon as we can book it. Okay, Las Vegas? Thanks for coming."

The audience cheers as Nicky waves and walks off.

"What a guy," I say.

Nicky hops off the stage and comes over. "I guess you were right, Evan. Thanks, man, thanks."

"Greg Sims is the one you want to thank."

"I know. Is he going to make it?" Nicky looks at Coop and Andie.

"Too early to tell," Andie says.

"Well, his hospital tab is on me, that's a promise." He turns back to me. "Evan, anytime you want to gig with me, you got it, okay?"

"Sure, Nicky, good luck."

We walk to Andie's car for the drive back to the hotel. Lost in my thoughts, I watch the Strip lights go by. I should call Ace, Cal, but right now I don't want to talk to anybody.

"What happens to Gillian now?"

Andie turns in the seat. "We'll be taking her back to L.A. She'll be charged with the four murders and the attempt on her brother, assault on Nicky Drew. There's plenty."

"Unless she gets a good lawyer and pleads insanity," Coop says.

"I don't even want to read about it. I just want to go home."

CODA

THE VOICE IN my headphones says, " 'Haiku Blues,' take one." Jeff and Gene look to me for the silent count-in, but there are two false starts—Gene and I coming in a beat too soon—before we're on track for the last tune of the day. After that, we're like three speed skaters leaning into the curves. I can imagine what it was like for Bill Evans and his trios. We haven't done more than two takes on any of the tunes, and this one is no different.

Jeff is nodding and smiling as I flip off the headphones and stand up at the piano. Through the glass I can see the engineer in the control room saying something to Cal and Paul Westbrook. Both are nodding their approval. The engineer leans forward and flips on the intercom microphone.

"Great, Evan. If you like it, we do."

I don't know if it's the atmosphere of the recording session, or the expectant looks of Jeff, Gene, and Paul Westbrook when I arrived. Maybe it was the sight of Milton, wagging his tail, letting me know Cal had come after all. I suspect, though, the euphoria I'm feeling is not from the music alone. I've survived Gillian and seen her brought to jail.

While we listen to the playback of the other tunes, I tell Cal what I'm planning to do. "Best idea I've heard in a long time," he says. He glances toward the studio monitor. "I won't be here tomorrow. You don't need me, Evan. You're playing good." He snaps on Milton's leash and walks toward the exit. "Send me a postcard," he calls over his shoulder.

I spent Sunday and Monday walking on the beach, coming closer and closer to deciding what I want to do next, ignoring phone messages, just clearing my mind. I'm sure the papers were full of the story of Gillian's capture, but I didn't look at even one or turn on the TV.

It took me until today, as I was driving to the studio, to finally come to a decision. Maybe I'd been waiting to see how the recording was going to go.

IN A COUPLE OF days, I pack up my books, CDs, and some other things and take the boxes to Coop's for storage. The furniture I donate. I'll leave my car with Coop as well.

Natalie and I meet once, and it's only slightly uncomfortable. She's read all the stories and now knows everything.

"I guess I let you down, didn't I?" she says. It's not really a question. She knows, but it may already be too late. We talk, and she halfway agrees with my decision. At the moment, things just aren't the same with us. Maybe they'll never be again, but I'll have a lot of time to think about that.

Two days before I'm scheduled to leave, I hear from Andie Lawrence, the first time since Las Vegas. "It was close, but Greg Sims is going to make it. I thought you'd want to know," she says.

"Thanks, that's good news."

"We flew Robert in from San Francisco, and we'll help them relocate once Greg's fully recovered."

"And?" I know there's more, I can feel it.

"Gillian. She wants to see you," Andie says.

I hold the phone tightly. "What do you mean?"

"Look, I know it's a lot to ask, Evan, but—"

"No way."

"The knife matches the entry wounds, and she's going

to give a full statement, but she insists on seeing you first.''
There's a long pause, then, ''It'll help our case if we have
her full cooperation.''

I think for a moment. Maybe I want to see her too. ''It'll
have to be before Saturday. That's when I leave.''

''Where are you going?''

''Little vacation.''

''All right, I'll make the arrangements.''

COOP PICKS ME UP. On the drive down to the jail, he says,
''You know you don't have to do this.''

''Yes, I do, Coop. I want this really over.''

''I know,'' Coop says. ''Just thought I'd throw that in.''

Andie is waiting inside. They take me to the visitor area.
Four guards ring Gillian as she's brought out in the jail
coveralls. I sit down opposite her and stare through the
glass. We both pick up the phone intercoms.

She glances once over her shoulder, then speaks into the
phone. ''I'm not going to say I'm sorry, Evan. I did what
I did, but I'm not sorry, except for Greg.''

After all those phone calls, the face that went with that
voice now stares at me. Her voice changes again, takes on
the quality it had on those calls. This is how she must have
looked when she talked to me.

''What do you want, Gillian?''

''I just wanted to see you once, under different condi-
tions, thank you for finding Greg, see that you understand.''

''I'll never understand what you did, Gillian. I don't
think you do either.''

''No, I guess you don't. But think about it, Evan—are
you so different from me?''

''I'm going, Gillian.'' I put down the phone, but she
motions me to pick it up again.

''What?''

She starts to speak, then stops. "Nothing," she says. Her smile is chilling as she puts down the phone. Accompanied by the guards, she gets up and walks out of my life for the last time.

COOP DRIVES ME to LAX. I get my bags out of the car and check them at the curb for the New York flight. We shake hands. "You have a direct connection to London?"

"No, might stop over for a couple of days, just kind of lose myself."

Coop nods. "Well, don't let me see you around here for a while."

"You won't. See you, Coop."

I make my way to the United gate and check in at the desk. No delays, but there's time to kill. I find a coffee cart in the corner and wait in line.

"Let me get that."

I turn and see Andie standing beside me. We get the coffee, sit down, and wait for my flight to be called.

She sips her coffee and stares straight ahead. "You know how much I'd like to get on this flight with you?"

"I know. It probably wouldn't work out though, would it?"

"Maybe not now," she says, "but I'd like to think it could have."

"I know." I see the disappointment in her face, hear the regret in her voice for what might have been

"What are you going to do in Europe?"

"Play some music, I hope. They like jazz over there. Then I'll see."

We both look toward the gate as the flight is announced. "Well, that's me."

We stand up. Andie hugs me, kisses me briefly. "Good-bye, Evan."

" 'Bye, Andie.''

"Oh, wait." She reaches in her purse, takes out an envelope. "You can read it on the plane."

"What is it?"

"You'll see."

I find my seat, stow my carry-on bag in the overhead compartment, and settle in the window seat, anxious to put L.A. behind me. I take out the envelope and open it.

Dear Evan,
You do have a lot of time to think. I hope some of your thoughts will be of me. One last thing from Gillian. She asked me to give it to you. Safe journey.
Love,
Andie

Another piece of paper, three lines on it.

Dizzy Atmosphere
Miles Smiles in a Silent Way
Bird Lives!

I look up and glance across at the flight attendant when she stops.

"Sir, could you fasten your—"

She's a mane of blond hair, a ready smile, and blue eyes that meet mine. "Evan?"

"Cindy?"

WINNING CAN BE MURDER

BILL CRIDER

A SHERIFF DAN RHODES MYSTERY

It's been a while since Sheriff Dan Rhodes's football days, but things haven't really changed. But the excitement of the upcoming state play-offs is short-lived when coach Brady Meredith is found shot to death.

His murder leads to rumors concerning illegal betting and black-market steroids. Then the sheriff's old nemesis, a biker named Rapper, reappears, causing too many coincidences for Rhodes's comfort.

Another corpse makes it a second down for a killer determined to lead Sheriff Rhodes into a game of sudden death.

Available July 2000 at your favorite retail outlet.

AILEEN SCHUMACHER

A TORY TRAVERS/ DAVID ALVAREZ MYSTERY

AFFIRMATIVE REACTION

Tory Travers planned to spend her afternoon crawling through a storm drain in an unfinished housing development project. She was looking for a leak. Instead she found a corpse.

When Detective David Alvarez arrives on the scene, romantic and political tensions heat up. The victim is Pamela Case, a county commissioner who has a tainted political history with the abandoned housing complex. Her murder exposes a life—and death—entangled in graft, corruption, suicide and blackmail.

Available July 2000 at your favorite retail outlet.

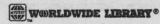

WORLDWIDE LIBRARY®

Visit us at www.worldwidemystery.com   WAS355